THE LIVES OF CHRISTOPHER CHANT

The childhood of Chrestomanci

Other titles by Diana Wynne Jones

Chrestomanci Series
Charmed Life*
The Magicians of Caprona*
Witch Week*
The Lives of Christopher Chant*
Mixed Magics*
Conrad's Fate*
The Pinhoe Egg

Howl Series
Howl's Moving Castle*
Castle in the Air*
House of Many Ways

Archer's Goon*
Black Maria*
Dogsbody
Eight Days of Luke
The Homeward Bounders
The Merlin Conspiracy*
The Ogre Downstairs
Power of Three
Stopping for a Spell
A Tale of Time City
Wilkins' Tooth

For older readers
Fire and Hemlock
Hexwood
The Time of the Ghost

For younger readers
Wild Robert

*Also available on audio

THE LIVES OF
CHRISTOPHER
CHANT

Illustrated by Tim Stevens

HarperCollins *Children's Books*

The official Diana Wynne Jones fansite
is at www.leemac.freeserve.co.uk

First published by Methuen Children's Books 1988
First published in hardback by HarperCollins *Children's Books* 2000
This edition published by HarperCollins *Children's Books* 2008
HarperCollins *Children's Books* is an imprint of
HarperCollins*Publishers* Ltd 77-85 Fulham Palace Road,
Hammersmith, London, W6 8JB

www.harpercollins.co.uk

1

Text copyright © Diana Wynne Jones 1988
Illustrations copyright © Tim Stevens 2000

ISBN 978 0 00 727820 6

The author and illustrator assert the moral right to be
identified as the author and illustrator of the work.

Printed and bound in Great Britain by
Clays Ltd, St Ives plc

This book is for Leo,
who got hit on the head
with a cricket bat

Author's Note

Everything in this book happens at least twenty-five years before the story told in *Charmed Life*.

CHAPTER ONE

✳

*I*t was years before Christopher told anyone about his dreams. This was because he mostly lived in the nurseries at the top of the big London house, and the nursery maids who looked after him changed every few months.

He scarcely saw his parents. When Christopher was small, he was terrified that he would meet Papa out walking in the park one day and not recognise him. He used to kneel down and look through the banisters on the rare days when Papa came home from the City before bedtime, hoping to fix Papa's face in his mind. All he got was a foreshortened view of a figure in a frock coat with a great deal of well-combed black whisker, handing a tall black hat to the footman, and then a view of a very neat white parting in black hair, as Papa marched rapidly under the stairway and out of sight. Beyond knowing that Papa was taller than most footmen, Christopher knew little else.

Some evenings, Mama was on the stairs to meet Papa, blocking Christopher's view with wide silk skirts and a multitude of frills and draperies. "Remind your master," she would say icily to the footman, "that there is a Reception in this house tonight and that he is required, for once in his life, to act as host."

Papa, hidden behind Mama's wide clothing, would reply in a deep gloomy voice, "Tell Madam I have a great deal of work brought home from the office tonight. Tell her she should have warned me in advance."

"Inform your master," Mama would reply to the footman, "that if I'd warned him, he would have found an excuse not to be here. Point out to him that it is my money that finances his business and that I shall remove it if he does not do this small thing for me."

Then Papa would sigh. "Tell Madam I am going up to dress," he would say. "Under protest. Ask her to stand aside from the stairs."

Mama never did stand aside, to Christopher's disappointment. She always gathered up her skirts and sailed upstairs ahead of Papa, to make sure Papa did as she wanted. Mama had huge lustrous eyes, a perfect figure and piles of glossy brown curls. The nursery maids told Christopher

Mama was a Beauty. At this stage in his life Christopher thought everyone's parents were like this; but he did wish Mama would give him a view of Papa just once.

He thought everyone had the kind of dreams he had, too. He did not think they were worth mentioning. The dreams always began the same way. Christopher got out of bed and walked round the corner of the night-nursery wall – the part with the fireplace, which jutted out – on to a rocky path high on the side of a valley. The valley was green and steep, with a stream rushing from waterfall to waterfall down the middle, but Christopher never felt there was much point in following the stream down the valley. Instead he went up the path, round a large rock, into the part he always thought of as The Place Between. Christopher thought it was probably a left-over piece of the world, from before somebody came along and made the world properly.

Formless slopes of rock towered and slanted in all directions. Some of it was hard and steep, some of it piled and rubbly, and none of it had much shape. Nor did it have much colour – most of it was the ugly brown you get from mixing every colour in a paintbox. There was always a formless wet mist hanging round this place, adding to the vagueness of everything. You could never see the sky. In fact, Christopher sometimes thought there might not *be* a sky: he had an idea the formless rock went on and on in a great arch overhead – but when he thought about it, that did not seem possible.

Christopher always knew in his dream that you could get

to Almost Anywhere from The Place Between. He called it Almost Anywhere, because there was one place that did not want you to go to it. It was quite near, but he always found himself avoiding it. He set off sliding, scrambling, edging across bulging wet rock, and climbing up or down, until he found another valley and another path. There were hundreds of them. He called them the Anywheres.

The Anywheres were mostly quite different from London. They were hotter or colder, with strange trees and stranger houses. Sometimes the people in them looked ordinary, sometimes their skin was bluish or reddish and their eyes were peculiar, but they were always very kind to Christopher. He had a new adventure every time he went on a dream. In the active adventures people helped him escape through cellars of odd buildings, or he helped them in wars, or in rounding up dangerous animals. In the calm adventures, he got new things to eat and people gave him toys. He lost most of the toys as he was scrambling back home over the rocks, but he did manage to bring back the shiny shell necklace the silly ladies gave him, because he could hang it round his neck.

He went to the Anywhere with the silly ladies several times. It had blue sea and white sand, perfect for digging and building in. There were ordinary people in it, but Christopher only saw them in the distance. The silly ladies came and sat on rocks out of the sea and giggled at him while he made sand-castles.

"Oh clistoffer!" they would coo, in lisping voices. "Tell

uth what make you a clistoffer." And they would all burst into screams of high laughter.

They were the only ladies he had seen without clothes on. Their skins were greenish and so was their hair. He was fascinated by the way the ends of them were big silvery tails that could curl and flip almost like a fish, and send powerful sprays of water over him from their big finned feet. He never could persuade them that he was not a strange animal called a clistoffer.

Every time he went to that Anywhere, the latest nursery maid complained about all the sand in his bed. He had learnt very early on that they complained even louder when they found his pyjamas muddy, wet and torn from climbing through The Place Between. He took a set of clothes out on to the rocky path and left them there to change into. He had to put new clothes there every year or so, when he grew out of the latest torn and muddy suit, but the nursery maids changed so often that none of them noticed. Nor did they notice the strange toys he brought back over the years. There was a clockwork dragon, a horse that was really a flute, and the necklace from the silly ladies which, when you looked closely, was a string of tiny pearl skulls.

Christopher thought about the silly ladies. He looked at his latest nursemaid's feet, and he thought that her shoes were about big enough to hide flippers. But you could never see any more of any lady because of her skirts. He kept wondering how Mama and the nursery maid walked about on nothing but a big limber tail instead of legs.

His chance to find out came one afternoon when the nursery maid put him into an unpleasant sailor-suit and led him downstairs to the drawing room. Mama and some other ladies were there with someone called Lady Badgett, who was a kind of cousin of Papa's. She had asked to see Christopher. Christopher stared at her long nose and her wrinkles. "Is she a witch, Mama?" he asked loudly.

Everyone except Lady Badgett – who went more wrinkled than ever – said, "Hush, dear!" After that, Christopher was glad to find they seemed to have forgotten him. He quietly lay down on his back on the carpet, and rolled from lady to lady. When they caught him, he was under the sofa gazing up Lady Badgett's petticoats. He was dragged out of the room in disgrace, very disappointed to discover that all the ladies had big thick legs, except Lady Badgett: her legs were thin and yellow like a chicken's.

Mama sent for him in her dressing-room later that day. "Oh, Christopher, how *could* you!" she said. "I'd just got Lady Badgett to the point of calling on me, and she'll never come again. You've undone the work of years!"

It was very hard work, Christopher realised, being a Beauty. Mama was very busy in front of her mirror with all sorts of little cut glass bottles and jars. Behind her, a maid was even busier, far busier than the nursery maids ever were, working on Mama's glossy curls. Christopher was so ashamed to have wasted all this work that he picked up a glass jar to hide his confusion.

Mama told him sharply to put it down. "Money isn't

everything, you see, Christopher," she explained. "A good place in Society is worth far more. Lady Badgett could have helped us both. Why do you think I married your papa?"

Since Christopher had simply no idea what could have brought Mama and Papa together, he put out his hand to pick up the jar again. But he remembered in time that he was not supposed to touch it, and picked up a big pad of false hair instead. He turned it round in his hands while Mama talked.

"You are going to grow up with Papa's good family and my money," she said. "I want you to promise me now that you will take your place in Society alongside the very best people. Mama intends you to be a great man – Christopher, are you listening?"

Christopher had given up trying to understand Mama. He held the false hair out instead. "What's this for?"

"Bulking out my hair," Mama said. "Please attend, Christopher. It's very important you begin *now* preparing yourself for the future. Put that hair *down*."

Christopher put the pad of hair back. "I thought it might be a dead rat," he said. And somehow Mama must have made a mistake because, to Christopher's great interest, the thing really *was* a dead rat. Mama and her maid both screamed. Christopher was hustled away while a footman came running with a shovel.

After that, Mama called Christopher to her dressing-room and talked to him quite often. He stood trying to remember not to fiddle with the jars, staring at his reflection in her mirror, wondering why his curls were black and Mama's rich brown, and why his eyes were so much more like coal than Mama's. Something seemed to stop there ever being another dead rat, but sometimes a spider could be encouraged to let itself down in front of the mirror, whenever Mama's talk became too alarming.

He understood that Mama cared very urgently about his future. He knew he was going to have to enter Society with the best people. But the only Society he had heard of was the Aid the Heathen Society that he had to give a penny to every Sunday in church, and he thought Mama meant that.

Christopher made careful enquiries from the nursery maid with the big feet. She told him Heathens were savages who ate people. Missionaries were the best people, and they were the ones Heathens ate. Christopher saw that he was going to be a missionary when he grew up. He found Mama's talk increasingly alarming. He wished she had chosen another career for him.

He also asked the nursery maid about the kind of ladies who had tails like fish. "Oh, you mean mermaids!" the girl said, laughing. "Those aren't real."

Christopher knew mermaids were not real, because he only met them in dreams. Now he was convinced that he would meet Heathens too, if he went to the wrong Almost Anywhere. For a time, he was so frightened of meeting Heathens that when he came to a new valley from The Place Between, he lay down and looked carefully at the Anywhere it led to, to see what the people were like there before he went on. But after a while, when nobody tried to eat him, he decided that the Heathens probably lived in the Anywhere which stopped you going to it, and gave up worrying until he was older.

When he was a little older, people in the Anywheres sometimes gave him money. Christopher learnt to refuse coins. As soon as he touched them, everything just stopped. He landed in bed with a jolt and woke up sweating. Once this happened when a pretty lady, who reminded him of Mama, tried laughingly to hang an earring in his ear. Christopher would have asked the nursery maid with big feet about it, but she had left long ago. Most of the ones who came after simply said, "Don't bother me now – I'm busy!" when he asked them things.

Until he learnt to read, Christopher thought this was what all nursery maids did: they stayed a month, too busy to talk, and then set their mouths in a nasty line and flounced out. He was amazed to read of Old Retainers, who stayed with families for a whole lifetime and could be persuaded to tell long (and sometimes very boring) stories about the family in the past. In his house, none of the servants stayed more than six months.

The reason seemed to be that Mama and Papa had given up speaking to one another even through the footman. They handed the servants notes to give to one another instead. Since it never occurred to either Mama or Papa to seal the notes, sooner or later someone would bring the note up to the nursery floor and read it aloud to the nursery maid. Christopher learnt that Mama was always short and to the point.

"Mr Chant is requested to smoke cigars only in his own room." Or, "Will Mr Chant please take note that the new laundry maid has complained of holes burnt in his shirts." Or, "Mr Chant caused me much embarrassment by leaving in the middle of my Breakfast Party."

Papa usually let the notes build up and then answered the lot in a kind of rambling rage.

My dear Miranda,

I shall smoke where I please and it is the job of that lazy laundry maid to deal with the results. But then your extravagance in employing foolish layabouts and rude louts is only for your own selfish comfort and never for mine. If you wish me to remain at your parties, try to employ a cook who knows bacon from old shoes and refrain from giving that idiotic tinkling laugh all the time.

Papa's replies usually caused the servants to leave overnight.

Christopher rather enjoyed the insight these notes gave him. Papa seemed more like a person, somehow, even if he was so critical. It was quite a blow to Christopher when he was cut off from them by the arrival of his first governess.

Mama sent for him. She was in tears. "Your papa has overreached himself this time," she said. "It's a mother's place to see to the education of her child. I want you to go to

16

a good school, Christopher. It's most important. But I don't want to *force* you into learning. I want your ambition to flower as well. But your papa comes crashing in with his *grim* notions and goes behind my back by appointing this governess who, knowing your papa, is bound to be *terrible*! Oh my poor child!"

Christopher realised that the governess was his first step towards becoming a missionary. He felt solemn and alarmed. But when the governess came, she was simply a drab lady with pink eyes, who was far too discreet to talk to servants. She only stayed a month, to Mama's jubilation.

"Now we can really start your education," Mama said. "I shall choose the next governess myself."

Mama said that quite often over the next two years, for governesses came and went just like nursery maids before them. They were all drab, discreet ladies, and Christopher got their names muddled up. He decided that the chief difference between a governess and a nursery maid was that a governess usually burst into tears before she left – and that was the only time a governess ever said anything interesting about Mama and Papa.

"I'm sorry to do this to you," the third – or maybe the fourth – governess wept, "because you're a nice little boy, even if you *are* a bit remote, but the *atmosphere* in this house! Every night *he's* home – which thank God is rarely! – I have to sit at the dining-table with them in utter silence. And *she* passes me a note to give to *him*, and *he* passes me one for *her*. Then they open the notes and look daggers at one another and then at me. I can't stand any more!"

The ninth – or maybe the tenth – governess was even more indiscreet. "I know they hate one another," she sobbed, "but *she's* no call to hate me too! She's one of those who can't abide other women. And she's a sorceress, I think – I can't be sure, because she only does little things – and *he's* at least as strong as *she* is. He may even be an enchanter. Between them they make such an atmosphere – it's no wonder they can't keep any servants! Oh, Christopher, forgive me for talking like this about your parents!"

All the governesses asked Christopher to forgive them and he forgave them very readily, for this was the only time now that he had news of Mama and Papa. It gave him a wistful sort of feeling that perhaps other people had parents who were not like his. He was also sure that there was some sort of crisis brewing. The hushed thunder of it reached as far as the schoolroom, even though the governesses would not let him gossip with the servants any more.

He remembered the night the crisis broke, because that was the night when he went to an Anywhere where a man under a yellow umbrella gave him a sort of candlestick of little bells. It was so beautiful that Christopher was determined to bring it home. He held it in his teeth as he scrambled across the rocks of The Place Between. To his joy, it was in his bed when he woke up. But there was quite a different feeling to the house. The twelfth governess packed and left straight after breakfast.

CHAPTER TWO

✷

Christopher was called to Mama's dressing-room that
afternoon. There was a new governess sitting on the
only hard chair, wearing the usual sort of ugly greyish
clothes and a hat that was uglier than usual. Her drab cotton
gloves were folded on her dull bag and her head hung down
as if she were timid or put-upon, or both. Christopher found
her of no interest. All the interest in the room was centred on
the man standing behind Mama's chair with his hand on
Mama's shoulder.

"Christopher, this is my brother," Mama said happily.
"Your Uncle Ralph."

Mama pronounced it Rafe. It was more than a year before

Christopher discovered it was the name he read as Ralph.

Uncle Ralph took his fancy completely. To begin with, he was smoking a cigar. The scents of the dressing-room were changed and mixed with the rich incense-like smoke, and Mama was not protesting by even so much as sniffing. That alone was enough to show that Uncle Ralph was in a class by himself. Then he was wearing tweeds, strong and tangy and almost fox-coloured, which were a little baggy here and there, but blended beautifully with the darker foxiness of Uncle Ralph's hair and the redder foxiness of his moustache. Christopher had seldom seen a man in tweeds or without whiskers. This did even more to assure him that Uncle Ralph was someone special. As a final touch, Uncle Ralph smiled at him like sunlight on an autumn forest. It was such an engaging smile that Christopher's face broke into a return smile almost of its own accord.

"Hallo, old chap," said Uncle Ralph, rolling out blue smoke above Mama's glossy hair. "I know this is not the best way for an uncle to recommend himself to a nephew, but I've been sorting the family affairs out, and I'm afraid I've had to do one or two quite shocking things, like bringing you a new governess and arranging for you to start school in autumn. Governess over there. Miss Bell. I hope you like one another. Enough to forgive me anyway."

He smiled at Christopher in a sunny, humorous way which had Christopher rapidly approaching adoration. All the same, Christopher glanced dubiously at Miss Bell. She looked back, and there was an instant when a sort of hidden prettiness in her almost came out into the open. Then she blinked pale eyelashes and murmured, "Pleased to meet you," in a voice as uninteresting as her clothes.

"She'll be your last governess, I hope," said Mama. Because of that, Christopher ever after thought of Miss Bell as the Last Governess. "She's going to prepare you for school. I wasn't meaning to send you away yet, but your uncle says— Anyway, a good education is important for your career and, to be blunt with you, Christopher, your papa has made a most *vexatious* hash of the money – which is mine, not his, as you know – and lost practically all of it. Luckily I had your uncle to turn to and—"

"And once turned to, I don't let people down," Uncle Ralph said, with a quick flick of a glance at the governess. Maybe he meant she should not be hearing this. "Fortunately, there's plenty left to send you to school, and then your mama is going to recoup a bit by living abroad. She'll like that – eh, Miranda? And Miss Bell is going to be found another post with glowing references. Everyone's going to be fine."

His smile went to all of them one by one, full of warmth and confidence. Mama laughed and dabbed scent behind her ears. The Last Governess almost smiled, so that the hidden prettiness half-emerged again. Christopher tried to grin a strong manly grin at Uncle Ralph, because that seemed to be the only way to express the huge, almost hopeless adoration that was growing in him. Uncle Ralph laughed, a golden brown laugh, and completed the conquest of Christopher by fishing in a tweed pocket and tipping his nephew a bright new sixpence.

Christopher would have died rather than spend that sixpence. Whenever he changed clothes, he transferred the sixpence to the new pockets. It was another way of expressing his adoration of Uncle Ralph. It was clear that Uncle Ralph had stepped in to save Mama from ruin, and this made him the first good man that Christopher had met. And on top of that, he was the only person outside the Anywheres who had bothered to speak to Christopher in that friendly man-to-man way.

Christopher tried to treasure the Last Governess too, for Uncle Ralph's sake, but that was not so easy. She was so very boring. She had a drab, calm way of speaking, and she never raised her voice or showed impatience, even when he was stupid about Mental Arithmetic or Levitation, both of which all the other governesses had somehow missed out on.

"If a herring and a half cost three-ha'pence, Christopher," she explained drearily, "that's a penny and a half for a fish and a half. How much for a whole fish?"

"I don't know," he said, trying not to yawn.

"Very well," the Last Governess said calmly. "We'll think again tomorrow. Now look in this mirror and see if you can't make it rise in the air just an inch."

But Christopher could not move the mirror any more than he could understand what a herring cost. The Last Governess put the mirror aside and quietly went on to puzzle him about French. After a few days of this,

Christopher tried to make her angry, hoping she would turn more interesting when she shouted. But she just said calmly, "Christopher, you're getting silly. You may play with your toys now. But remember you only take one out at a time, and you put that back before you get out another. That is our rule."

Christopher had become rapidly and dismally accustomed to this rule. It reduced the fun a lot. He had also become used to the Last Governess sitting beside him while he played. The other governesses had seized the chance to rest, but this one sat in a hard chair efficiently mending his clothes, which reduced the fun even more. Nevertheless, he got the candlestick of chiming bells out of the cupboard, because that was fascinating in its way. It was so arranged that it played different tunes, depending on which bell you touched first.

When he had finished with it, the Last Governess paused in her darning to say, "That goes in the middle of the top shelf. Put it back before you take that clockwork dragon." She waited to listen to the chiming that showed Christopher had done what she said. Then, as she drove the needle into the sock again, she asked in her dullest way, "Who gave you the bells, Christopher?"

No one had ever asked Christopher about anything he had brought back from the Anywheres before. He was rather at a loss. "A man under a yellow umbrella," he answered. "He said they bring luck on my house."

"What man where?" the Last Governess wanted to know

24

– except that she did not sound as if she cared if she knew or not.

"An Almost Anywhere," Christopher said. "The hot one with the smells and the snake charmers. The man didn't say his name."

"That's not an answer, Christopher," the Last Governess said calmly, but she did not say anything more until the next time, two days later, when Christopher got out the chiming bells again. "Remember where they go when you've finished with them," she said. "Have you thought yet where the man with the yellow umbrella was?"

"Outside a painted place where some gods live," Christopher said, setting the small silvery bellcups ringing. "He was nice. He said it didn't matter about money."

"Very generous," remarked the Last Governess. "Where was this painted house for gods, Christopher?"

"I told you. It was an Almost Anywhere," Christopher said.

"And I told you that that is not an answer," the Last Governess said. She folded up her darning. "Christopher, I insist that you tell me where those bells came from."

"Why do you want to know?" Christopher asked, wishing she would leave him in peace.

"Because," the Last Governess said with truly ominous calm, "you are not being frank and open like a nice boy should be. I suspect you stole those bells."

At this monstrous injustice, Christopher's face reddened and tears stood in his eyes. "*I haven't!*" he cried out. "He

25

gave them to me! People always give me things in the Anywheres, only I drop most of them. Look." And regardless of her one-toy-at-a-time rule, he rushed to the cupboard, fetched the horse flute, the mermaids' necklace and the clockwork dragon, and banged them down in her darning basket. "Look! These are from other Anywheres."

The Last Governess gazed at them with terrible impassiveness. "Am I to believe you have stolen these too?" she said. She put the basket and the toys on the floor and stood up. "Come with me. This must be reported to your mama at once."

She seized Christopher's arm and in spite of his yells of "I *didn't*, I *didn't*!" she marched him inexorably downstairs.

Christopher leant backwards and dragged his feet and implored her not to. He knew he would never be able to explain to Mama. All the notice the Last Governess took was to say, "Stop that disgraceful noise. You're a big boy now."

This was something all the governesses agreed on. But Christopher no longer cared about being big. Tears poured disgracefully down his cheeks and he screamed the name of the one person he knew who saved people. "Uncle Ralph! I'll explain to Uncle Ralph!"

The Last Governess glanced down at him at that. Just for a moment, the hidden prettiness flickered in her face. But to Christopher's despair, she dragged him to Mama's dressing-room and knocked on the door.

Mama turned from her mirror in surprise. She looked at Christopher, red-faced and gulping and wet with tears. She looked at the Last Governess. "Whatever is going on? Is he ill?"

"No, Madam," the Last Governess said in her dullest way. "Something has happened which I think your brother should be informed of at once."

"Ralph?" said Mama. "You mean I'm to write to Ralph? Or is it more urgent that that?"

"Urgent, Madam, I think," the Last Governess said drearily. "Christopher said that he is willing to confess to his uncle. I suggest, if I may make so bold, that you summon him now."

Mama yawned. This governess bored her terribly. "I'll do my best," she said, "but I don't answer for my brother's temper. He lives a very busy life, you know." Carelessly, she pulled one of her dark glossy hairs out of the silver backed brush she had been using. Then, much more carefully, she began teasing hairs out of her silver and crystal hair-tidy.

Most of the hairs were Mama's own dark ones, but Christopher, watching Mama's beautiful pearly nails delicately pinching and pulling at the hairs, while he sobbed and swallowed and sobbed again, saw that one of the hairs was a much redder colour. This was the one Mama pulled out. She laid it across her own hair from the brush. Then, picking up what seemed to be a hatpin with a glittery knob, she laid that across both hairs and tapped it with one sharp, impatient nail. "Ralph," she said, "Ralph Weatherby Argent. Miranda wants you."

One of the mirrors of the dressing-table turned out to be a window, with Uncle Ralph looking through it, rather irritably, while he knotted his tie. "What is it?" he said. "I'm busy today."

"When *aren't* you?" asked Mama. "Listen, that governess is here looking like a wet week as usual. She's brought Christopher. Something about a confession. *Could* you come and sort it out? It's beyond me."

"*Is* she?" said Uncle Ralph. He leaned sideways to look through the mirror – or window, or whatever – and when he saw Christopher, he winked and broke into his sunniest smile. "Dear, dear. This does look upsetting. I'll be along at once."

Christopher saw him leave the window and walk away to one side. Mama had only time to turn to the Last Governess and say, "There, I've done my best!" before the door of her dressing-room opened and Uncle Ralph strode in.

Christopher quite forgot his sobs in the interest of all this. He tried to think what was on the other side of the wall of Mama's dressing-room. The stairs, as far as he knew. He supposed Uncle Ralph *could* have a secret room in the wall about one foot wide, but he was much more inclined to think he had been seeing real magic. As he decided this, Uncle Ralph secretly passed him a large white handkerchief and walked cheerfully into the middle of the room to allow Christopher time to wipe his face.

"Now what's all this about?" he said.

"I've no idea," said Mama. "She'll explain, no doubt."

Uncle Ralph cocked a ginger eyebrow at the Last Governess.

"I found Christopher playing with an artefact," the Governess said tediously, "of a kind I have never seen before, made of metal that is totally unknown to me. He then revealed he had three more artefacts, each one different from the other, but he was unable to explain how he had come by them."

Uncle Ralph looked at Christopher, who hid the handkerchief behind him and looked nervously back. "Enough to get anyone into hot water, old chap," Uncle Ralph said. "Suppose you take me to look at these things and explain where they do come from?"

Christopher heaved a great happy sigh. He had known he could count on Uncle Ralph to save him. "Yes, please," he said.

They went back upstairs with the Last Governess processing ahead and Christopher hanging gratefully on to Uncle Ralph's large warm hand. When they got there, the Governess sat quietly down to her sewing again as if she felt she had done her bit. Uncle Ralph picked up the bells and jingled them. "By Jove!" he said. "These sound like nothing else in the universe!"

He took them to the window and carefully examined each bell. "Bullseye!" he said. "You clever woman! They *are* like nothing else in the universe. Some kind of strange alloy,

I think, different for each bell. Handmade by the look of them." He pointed genially to the tuffet by the fire. "Sit there, old chap, and oblige me by explaining what you did to get these bells here."

Christopher sat down, full of willing eagerness. "I had to hold them in my mouth while I climbed through The Place Between," he explained.

"No, no," said Uncle Ralph. "That sounds like near the end. Start with what you did in the beginning before you got the bells."

"I went down the valley to the snake-charming town," Christopher said.

"No, before that, old chap," said Uncle Ralph. "When you set off from here. What time of day was it, for instance? After breakfast? Before lunch?"

"No, in the night," Christopher explained. "It was one of the dreams."

In this way, by going carefully back every time Christopher missed out a step, Uncle Ralph got Christopher to tell him in detail about the dreams, and The Place Between, and the Almost Anywheres he came to down the valleys. Since Uncle Ralph, far from being angry, seemed steadily more delighted, Christopher told him everything he could think of.

"What did I tell you!" he said, possibly to the Governess. "I can always trust my hunches. Something *had* to come out of a heredity like this! By Jove, Christopher old chap, you must be the only person in the world who can bring back solid objects from a spirit trip! I doubt if even old de Witt can do that!"

Christopher glowed to find Uncle Ralph so pleased with him, but he could not help feeling resentful about the Last Governess. "*She* said I stole them."

"Take no notice of her. Women are always jumping to the wrong conclusions," Uncle Ralph said, lighting a cigar. At this, the Last Governess shrugged her shoulders up and smiled a little. The hidden prettiness came out stronger than Christopher had ever seen it, almost as if she was human and sharing a joke.

Uncle Ralph blew a roll of blue smoke over them both, beaming like the sun coming through the clouds. "Now the next thing, old chap," he said, "is to do a few experiments to test this gift of yours. Can you control these dreams of yours? Can you say *when* you're about to go off to your Almost Anywheres – or can't you?"

Christopher thought about it. "I go when I want to," he said.

"Then have you any objection to doing me a test run, say tomorrow night?" Uncle Ralph asked.

"I could go tonight," Christopher offered.

"No, tomorrow," said Uncle Ralph. "It'll take me a day to get things set up. And when you go, this is what I want you to do."

He leant forward and pointed his cigar at Christopher, to let him know he was serious. "You set out as usual when you're ready and try to do two experiments for me. First,

I'm going to arrange to have a man waiting for you in your Place Between. I want you to see if you can find him. You may have to shout to find him – I don't know: I'm not a spirit traveller myself – but anyway, you climb about and see if you can make contact with him. *If* you do, then you do the second experiment. The man will tell you what that is. And if they both work, then we can experiment some more. Do you think you can do that? You'd like to help, wouldn't you, old chap?"

"Yes!" said Christopher.

Uncle Ralph stood up and patted his shoulder. "Good lad. Don't let anyone deceive you, old chap. You have a very exciting and important gift here. It's so important that I advise you not to talk about it to anyone but me and Miss Bell over there. Don't tell anyone, not even your mama. Right?"

"Right," said Christopher. It was wonderful that Uncle Ralph thought him important. He was so glad and delighted that he would have done far more for Uncle Ralph than just not tell anyone. That was easy. There was no one to tell.

"So it's our secret," said Uncle Ralph, going to the door. "Just the three of us – and the man I'm going to send, of course. Don't forget you may have to look quite hard to find him, will you?"

"I won't forget," Christopher promised eagerly.

"Good lad," said Uncle Ralph, and went out of the door in a waft of cigar smoke.

CHAPTER THREE

✳

Christopher thought he would never live through the time until tomorrow night. He burned to show Uncle Ralph what he could do. If it had not been for the Last Governess, he would have made himself ill with excitement, but she managed to be so boring that she somehow made everything else boring too. By the time Christopher went to bed that next night, he was almost wondering if it was worth dreaming.

But he did dream, because Uncle Ralph had asked him to, and got out of bed as usual and walked round the fireplace to the valley, where his clothes were lying on the rocky path as usual. By now this lot of clothes were torn, covered with mud and assorted filth from a hundred Almost Anywheres, and at least two sizes too small. Christopher put them on quickly, without bothering to do up buttons that would not meet. He never wore shoes because they got in the way as he climbed the rocks. He pattered round the crag in his bare feet into The Place Between.

It was formless and unfinished as ever, all slides and jumbles of rocks rearing in every direction and high overhead. The mist billowed as formlessly as the rocks. It was one of the times when rain slanted in it, driven this way and that by the hither-thither winds that blew in The Place Between. Christopher hoped he would not have to spend too long here hunting for Uncle Ralph's man. It made him feel so small, besides being cold and wet. He dutifully braced himself on a slide of rubbly sand and shouted.

"Hallo!"

The Place Between made his voice sound no louder than a bird cheeping. The windy fog seemed to snatch the sound away and bury it in a flurry of rain. Christopher listened for a reply, but for minutes on end the only noise was the hissing hum of the wind.

He was wondering whether to shout again, when he heard a little cheeping thread of sound, wailing its thin way back to him across the rocks. "Hallooo!" It was his own shout. Christopher was sure of it. Right from the start of his dreams, he had known that The Place Between liked to have everything that did not belong back to the place it came from. That was why he always climbed back to bed faster than he did when he climbed out to a new valley. The Place pushed him back.

Christopher thought about this. It probably did no good to shout. If Uncle Ralph's man was out there in the mist, he would not be able to stand and wait for very long, without getting pushed back to the valley he came from. So the man would have to wait in the mouth of a valley and hope that Christopher found him.

Christopher sighed. There were such thousands and thousands of valleys, high up, low down, turning off at every angle you could think of, and some valleys turned off other valleys – and that was only if you crawled round the side of the Place that was nearest. If you went the other way, towards the Anywhere that did not want people, there were probably many thousands more. On the other hand, Uncle Ralph would not want to make it too difficult. The man must be quite near.

Determined to make Uncle Ralph's experiment a success if he could, Christopher set off, climbing, sliding, inching across wet rock with his face close to the cold hard smell of it. The first valley he came to was empty. "Hallo?" he called into it. But the river rushed down green empty space and he could see no one was there. He backed out and climbed up and sideways to the next. And there, before he reached the opening, he could see someone through the mist, dark and shiny with rain, crouching on a rock and scrabbling for a handhold overhead.

"Hallo?" Christopher asked.

"Well, I'll be – is that Christopher?" the person asked. It was a strong young man's voice. "Come on out where we can see one another."

With a certain amount of heaving and slipping, both of them scrambled round a bulge of rock and dropped down into another valley, where the air was calm and warm. The grass here was lit pink by a sunset in the distance.

"Well, well," said Uncle Ralph's man. "You're about half the size I expected. Pleased to meet you, Christopher. I'm Tacroy."

He grinned down at Christopher. Tacroy was as strong and young as his voice, rather squarely and sturdily built, with a roundish brown face and merry-looking hazel eyes.

Christopher liked him at once – partly because Tacroy was the first grown man he had met who had curly hair like his own. It was not quite like. Where Christopher's hair made loose black rounds, Tacroy's hair coiled tight, like a mass of little pale brown springs. Christopher thought Tacroy's hair must hurt when a governess or someone made him comb it. This made him notice that Tacroy's curls were quite dry. Nor was there any trace of the shiny wetness that had been on his clothes a moment before. Tacroy was wearing a greenish worsted suit, rather shabby, but it was not even damp.

"How did you get dry so quickly?" Christopher asked him.

Tacroy laughed. "I'm not here quite as bodily as you seem to be. And you're soaked through. How was that?"

"The rain in The Place Between," Christopher said. "You were wet there too."

"Was I?" said Tacroy. "I don't visualise at all on the Passage – it's more like night with a few stars to guide by. I find it quite hard to visualise even here on the World Edge – though I can see you quite well, of course, since we're both willing it."

He saw that Christopher was staring at him, not understanding more than a word of this, and screwed his eyes up thoughtfully. This made little laughing wrinkles all round Tacroy's eyes. Christopher liked him better than ever. "Tell me," Tacroy said, waving a brown hand towards the rest of the valley, "what do you see here?"

"A valley," Christopher said, wondering what Tacroy saw, "with green grass. The sun's setting and it's making the stream down the middle look pink."

"Is it now?" said Tacroy. "Then I expect it would surprise you very much to know that all I can see is a slightly pink fog."

"Why?" said Christopher.

"Because I'm only here in spirit, while you seem to be actually here in the flesh," Tacroy said. "Back in London, my valuable body is lying on a sofa in a deep trance, tucked up in blankets and warmed by stone hot-water bottles, while a beautiful and agreeable young lady plays tunes to me on her harp. I insisted on the young lady as part of my pay. Do you think you're tucked up in bed somewhere too?"

When Tacroy saw that this question made Christopher

both puzzled and impatient, his eyes screwed up again. "Let's get going," he said. "The next part of the experiment is to see if you can bring a prepared package back. I've made my mark. Make yours, and we'll get down into this world."

"Mark?" said Christopher.

"Mark," said Tacroy. "If you don't make a mark, how do you think you will find your way in and out of this world, or know which one it is when you come to it?"

"Valleys are quite easy to find," Christopher protested. "And I can tell that I've been to this Anywhere before. It's got the smallest stream of all of them."

Tacroy shrugged with his eyes screwed right up. "My boy, you're giving me the creeps. Be kind and please me and scratch the number nine on a rock or something. I don't want to be the one who loses you."

Christopher obligingly picked up a pointed flint and dug away at the mud of the path until he had made a large wobbly 9 there.

He looked up to find Tacroy staring as if he was a ghost. "What's the matter?"

Tacroy gave a short wild-sounding laugh. "Oh nothing much. I can *see* it, that's all. That's only unheard of, that's all. Can *you* see *my* mark?"

Christopher looked everywhere he could think of, including up at the sunset sky, and had to confess that he could see nothing like a mark.

"Thank Heaven!" said Tacroy. "At least *that's* normal! But I'm still seriously wondering what you are. I begin to understand why your uncle got so excited."

They sauntered together down the valley. Tacroy had his hands in his pockets and he seemed quite casual, but Christopher got the feeling, all the same, that Tacroy usually went into an Anywhere in some way that was quicker and quite different. He caught Tacroy glancing at him several times, as if Tacroy was not sure of the way to go and was waiting to see what Christopher did. He seemed very relieved when they came to the end of the valley and found themselves on the rutty road among huge jungle trees. The sun was almost down. There were lights at the windows of the tumbledown old inn in front of them.

This was one of the first Anywheres Christopher had been to. He remembered it hotter and wetter. The big trees had been bright green and dripping. Now they seemed brown and a bit wilted, as far as he could tell in the pink light. When he followed Tacroy on to the crazily-built wooden verandah of the inn, he saw that the blobs of coloured fungus that had fascinated him last time had all turned dry and white. He wondered if the landlord would remember him.

"Landlord!" Tacroy shouted. When nothing happened, he said to Christopher, "Can you bang on the table? I can't."

Christopher noticed that the bent boards of the verandah creaked under his own feet, but not under Tacroy's. It did seem as if Tacroy was not really there in some way. He picked up a wooden bowl and rapped hard on the twisted table with it. It was another thing that made Tacroy's eyes screw up.

When the landlord shuffled out, he was wrapped in at least three knitted shawls and too unhappy to notice Christopher, let alone remember him.

"Ralph's messenger," Tacroy said. "I believe you have a package for me."

"Ah yes," shivered the landlord. "Won't you come inside out of this exceptionally bitter weather, sir? This is the hardest winter anyone has known for years."

Tacroy's eyebrows went up and he looked at Christopher. "I'm quite warm," Christopher said.

"Then we'll stay outside," Tacroy said. "The package?"

"Directly, sir," shivered the landlord. "But won't you take something hot to warm you up? On the house, sir."

"Yes, please," Christopher said quickly. Last time he was here he had been given something chocolatish which was not cocoa but much nicer. The landlord nodded and smiled and shuffled shivering back indoors. Christopher sat at the table. Even though it was almost dark now, he felt deliciously warm. His clothes were drying nicely. Crowds of fleshy moth-things were flopping at the lighted windows, but enough light came between them for him to see Tacroy sit down in the air and then slide himself sideways on to the chair on the other side of the table.

"You'll have to drink whatever-it-is for me," Tacroy said.

"That won't worry me," Christopher said. "Why did you tell me to write the number nine?"

"Because this set of worlds is known as Series Nine," Tacroy explained. "Your uncle seems to have a lot of dealings here. That was why it was easy to set the experiment up. If it works, I think he's planning a whole set of trips, all along the Related Worlds. You'd find that a bit boring, wouldn't you?"

"Oh no. I'd like it," Christopher said. "How many are there after nine?"

"Ours is Twelve," said Tacroy. "Then they go down to One, along the other way. Don't ask me why they go back to front. It's traditional."

Christopher frowned over this. There were a great many more valleys than that in The Place Between, all arranged higgledy-piggledy, too, not in any neat way that made you need to count up to twelve. But he supposed there must be some way in which Tacroy knew best – or Uncle Ralph did.

The landlord shuffled hastily out again. He was carrying two cups that steamed out a dark chocolate smell, although this lovely aroma was rather spoilt by a much less pleasant smell coming from a round leather container on a long strap, which he dumped on the table beside the cups. "Here we are," he said. "That's the package and here's to take the chill off you and drink to further dealings, sir. I don't know how you two can stand it out here!"

"We come from a cold and misty climate," Tacroy said. "Thanks," he added to the landlord's back, as the landlord scampered indoors again. "I suppose it must be tropical here usually," he remarked as the door slammed. "I wouldn't

41

know. I can't feel heat or cold in the spirit. Is that stuff nice?"

Christopher nodded happily. He had already drained one tiny cup. It was dark, hot and delicious. He pulled Tacroy's cup over and drank that in sips, to make the taste last as long as possible. The round leather bottle smelt so offensive that it got in the way of the taste. Christopher put it on the floor out of the way.

"You can lift it, I see, *and* drink," Tacroy said, watching him. "Your uncle told me to make quite sure, but I haven't any doubt myself. He said you lose things on the Passage."

"That's because it's hard carrying things across the rocks," Christopher explained. "I need both hands for climbing."

Tacroy thought. "Hm. That explains the strap on the bottle. But there could be all sorts of other reasons. I'd love to find out. For instance, have you ever tried to bring back something alive?"

"Like a mouse?" Christopher suggested. "I could put it in my pocket."

A sudden gleeful look came into Tacroy's face. He looked, Christopher thought, like a person about to be thoroughly naughty. "Let's try it," he said. "Let's see if you can bring back a small animal next. I'll persuade your uncle that we need to know that. I think I'll die of curiosity if we don't try it, even if it's the last thing you do for us!"

After that Tacroy seemed to get more and more impatient. At last he stood up in such a hurry that he stood right through the chair as if it wasn't there. "Haven't you finished yet? Let's get going."

Christopher regretfully stood the tiny cup on his face to get at the last drops. He picked up the round bottle and hung it around his neck by the strap. Then he jumped off the verandah and set off down the rutty road, full of eagerness to show Tacroy the town. Fungus grew like corals on all the porches. Tacroy would like that.

Tacroy called after him. "Hey! Where are you off to?"

Christopher stopped and explained. "No way," said Tacroy. "It doesn't matter if the fungus is sky-blue-pink. I can't hold this trance much longer, and I want to make sure you get back too."

This was disappointing. But when Christopher came close and peered at him, Tacroy did seem to be developing a faint, fluttery look, as if he might dissolve into the dark, or turn into one of the moth-things beating at the windows of the inn. Rather alarmed by this, Christopher put a hand on Tacroy's sleeve to hold him in place. For a moment, the arm hardly felt as if it was there – like the feathery balls of dust that grew under Christopher's bed – but after that first moment it firmed up nicely. Tacroy's outline grew hard and black against the dark trees. And Tacroy himself stood very still.

"I do believe," he said, as if he did not believe it at all, "that you've done something to fix me. What did you do?"

"Hardened you up," Christopher said. "You needed it so that we could go and look at the town. Come on."

But Tacroy laughed and took a firm grip on Christopher's arm – so firm that Christopher was sorry he had hardened him. "No, we'll see the fungus another time. Now I know you can do this too, it's going to be much easier. But I only contracted for an hour this trip. Come on."

As they went back up the valley, Tacroy kept peering round. "If it wasn't so dark," he said, "I'm sure I'd be seeing this as a valley too. I can hear the stream. This is amazing!" But it was clear that he could not see The Place Between. When they got to it, Tacroy went on walking as if he thought it was still the valley. When the wind blew the mist aside, he was not there any more.

Christopher wondered whether to go back into Nine, or on into another valley. But it did not seem such fun without company, so he let The Place Between push him back home.

Chapter Four

✴

*B*y the next morning, Christopher was heartily sick of the smell – it was more of a reek really – from the leather bottle. He put it under his bed, but it was still so bad that he had to get up and cover it with a pillow before he could get to sleep.

When the Last Governess came in to tell him to get up, she found it at once by the smell. "Dear Heavens above!" she said, dragging it out by its strap. "Would you credit this! I didn't believe even your uncle could ask for a whole bottleful of this stuff! Didn't he think of the danger?"

Christopher blinked up at her. He had never seen her so emotional. All her hidden prettiness had come out and she was staring at the bottle as if she did not know whether to be angry or scared or pleased. "What's in it?" he said.

"Dragons' blood," said the Last Governess. "And it's not even dried! I'm going to get this straight off to your uncle while you get dressed, or your mama will throw fits." She hurried away with the bottle at arm's length, swinging on its strap. "I think your uncle's going to be very pleased," she called over her shoulder.

There was no doubt about that. A day later a big parcel arrived for Christopher. The Last Governess brought it up to the schoolroom with some scissors and let him cut the string for himself, which added much to the excitement. Inside was a huge box of chocolates, with a vast red bow and a picture of a boy blowing bubbles on the top. Chocolates were so rare in Christopher's life that he almost failed to notice the envelope tucked into the bow. It had a gold sovereign in it and a note from Uncle Ralph.

Well done!!!! it said. *Next experiment in a week. Miss Bell will tell you when. Congratulations from your loving uncle.*

This so delighted Christopher that he let the Last Governess have first pick from the chocolates. "I think," she said dryly, as she picked the nutty kind that Christopher never liked, "that your Mama would like to be offered one before too many are gone." Then she plucked the note out of Christopher's fingers and put it in the fire as a hint that he was not to explain to Mama what he had done to earn the chocolates.

Christopher prudently ate the first layer before he offered

the box to Mama. "Oh dear, these are so bad for your teeth!" Mama said, while her fingers hovered over the strawberry and then the truffle. "You do seem to have taken your uncle's fancy – and that's just as well, since I've had to put all my money in his hands. It'll be your money one day," she said as her fingers closed on the fudge. "Don't let my brother spoil him too much," she said to the Last Governess. "And I think you'd better take him to a dentist."

"Yes, Madam," said the Last Governess, all meek and drab.

It was clear that Mama did not have the least suspicion what the chocolates were really about. Christopher was pleased to have been so faithful to Uncle Ralph's wishes, though he did wish Mama had not chosen the fudge.

The rest of the chocolates did not last quite the whole week, but they did take Christopher's mind off the excitement of the next experiment. In fact, when the Last Governess said calmly, the next Friday before bedtime, "Your uncle wants you to go on another dream tonight," Christopher felt more business-like than excited. "You are to try to get to Series Ten," said the Last Governess, "and meet the same man as before. Do you think you can do that?"

"Easy!" Christopher said loftily. "I could do it standing on my head."

"Which is getting a little swelled," remarked the Last Governess. "Don't forget to brush your hair and clean your teeth and don't get too confident. This is not really a game."

Christopher did honestly try not to feel too confident, but it *was* easy. He went out on to the path, where he put on his muddy clothes, and then climbed through The Place Between looking for Tacroy. The only difficulty was that the valleys were not arranged in the right order. Number Ten was not next one on from Nine, but quite a way lower down and further on. Christopher almost thought he was not going to find it. But at length he slid down a long slope of yellowish scree and saw Tacroy shining wetly through the mist as he crouched uncomfortably on the valley's lip. He held out a dripping arm to Christopher.

"Lord!" he said. "I thought you were never coming. Firm me up, will you? I'm fading back already. The latest girl is nothing like so effective."

Christopher took hold of Tacroy's cold woolly-feeling hand. Tacroy began firming up at once. Soon he was hard and wet and as solid as Christopher, and very pleased about it too. "This was the part your uncle found hardest to believe," he said while they climbed into the valley. "But I swore to him that I'd be able to see – oh – um. What do you see, Christopher?"

"It's the Anywhere where I got my bells," Christopher said, smiling round the steep green slopes. He remembered it perfectly. This Anywhere had a particular twist to the stream half-way down. But there was something new here – a sort of mistiness just beside the path. "What's that?" he asked, forgetting that Tacroy could not see the valley.

But Tacroy evidently could see the valley now he was

firmed up. He stared at the mistiness with his eyes ruefully wrinkled.

"Part of your uncle's experiment that doesn't seem to have worked," he said. "It's supposed to be a horseless carriage. He was trying to send it through to meet us. Do you think you can firm that up too?"

Christopher went to the mistiness and tried to put his hand on it. But the thing did not seem to be there enough for him to touch. His hand just went through.

"Never mind," said Tacroy. "Your uncle will just have to think again. And the carriage was only one of three experiments tonight." He insisted that Christopher wrote a big 10 in the dirt of the path, and then they set off down the valley. "If the carriage had worked," Tacroy explained, "we'd have tried for something bulky. As it is, I get my way and we try for an animal. Lordy! I'm glad you came when you did. I was almost as bad as that carriage. It's all that girl's fault."

"The lovely young lady with the harp?" asked Christopher.

"Alas, no," Tacroy said regretfully. "She took a fit when you firmed me up last time. It seems my body there in London went down to a thread of mist and she thought I was a goner. Screamed and broke her harp strings. Left as soon as I came back. She said she wasn't paid to harbour ghosts, pointed out that her contract was only for one trance, and refused to come back for twice the money. Pity. I hoped she was made of sterner stuff. She reminded me very much of another young lady with a harp who was once the light of my life." For a short while, he looked as sad as someone with such a merry face could. Then he smiled. "But I couldn't ask either of them to share my garret," he said. "So it's probably just as well."

"Did you need to get another one?" Christopher asked.

"I can't do without, unfortunately, unlike you," Tacroy said. "A professional spirit traveller has to have another medium to keep him anchored – music's the best way – and to call him back in case of trouble, and keep him warm, and make sure he's not interrupted by tradesmen with bills and so forth. So your uncle found this new girl in a bit of a hurry. She's stern stuff all right. Voice like a hatchet. Plays the flute like someone using wet chalk on a blackboard." Tacroy shuddered slightly. "I can hear it faintly all the time if I listen."

Christopher could hear a squealing noise too, but he thought it was probably the pipes of the snake charmers who sat in rows against the city wall in this Anywhere. They could see the city now. It was very hot here, far hotter than Nine. The high muddy-looking walls and the strange-shaped domes above them quivered in the heat, like things under water. Sandy dust blew up in clouds, almost hiding the dirty-white row of old men squatting in front of baskets blowing into pipes. Christopher looked nervously at the fat snakes, each one swaying upright in its basket.

Tacroy laughed. "Don't worry. Your uncle doesn't want a snake any more than you do!"

The City had a towering but narrow gate. By the time they reached it both were covered in sandy dust and Christopher was sweating through it, in trickles. Tacroy seemed enviably cool. Inside the walls it was even hotter. This was the one drawback to a thoroughly nice Anywhere.

The shady edges of the streets were crowded with people and goats and makeshift stalls under coloured umbrellas, so that Christopher was forced to walk with Tacroy down the blinding stripe of sun in the middle. Everyone shouted and chattered cheerfully. The air was thick with strange smells, the bleating of goats, the squawks of chickens, and strange clinking music. All the colours were bright, and brightest of all were the small gilded dolls-house things at the corners of streets. These were always heaped with flowers and dishes of food. Christopher thought they must belong to very small gods.

A lady under an electric blue umbrella gave him some of the sweetmeat she was selling. It was like a crisp bird's-nest soaked in honey. Christopher gave some to Tacroy, but Tacroy said he could only taste it the way you tasted food in dreams, even when Christopher firmed him up again.

"Does Uncle Ralph want me to fetch a goat?" Christopher asked, licking honey from his fingers.

"We'd have tried if the carriage had worked," Tacroy said. "But what your uncle's really hoping for is a cat from one of the temples. We have to find the Temple of Asheth."

Christopher led the way to the big square where all the large houses for gods were. The man with the yellow umbrella was still there, on the steps of the largest temple. "Ah yes. That's it," Tacroy said. But when Christopher set off hopefully to talk to the man with the yellow umbrella again, Tacroy said, "No, I think our best bet is to get in round the side somewhere."

They found their way down narrow side alleys that ran all round the temple. There were no other doors to the temple at all, nor did it have any windows. The walls were high and muddy-looking and totally blank except for wicked spikes on the top. Tacroy stopped quite cheerfully in a baking alley where someone had thrown away a cartload of old cabbages and looked up at the spikes. The ends of flowering creepers were twined among the spikes from the other side of the wall.

"This looks promising," he said, and leant against the wall. His cheerful look vanished. For a moment he looked frustrated and rather annoyed. "Here's a turn-up," he said. "You've made me too solid to get through, darn it!" He thought about it, and shrugged. "This was supposed to be experiment three anyway. Your uncle thought that if you could broach a way between the worlds, you could probably pass through a wall too. Are you game to try? Do you think you can get in and pick up a cat without me?"

Tacroy seemed very nervous and worried about it. Christopher looked at the frowning wall and thought that it was probably impossible. "I can try," he said, and largely to console Tacroy, he stepped up against the hot stones of the wall and tried to push himself through them. At first it *was* impossible. But after a moment, he found that if he turned himself sort of sideways in a peculiar way, he began to sink into the stones. He turned and smiled encouragingly at Tacroy's worried face. "I'll be back in a minute."

"I don't like letting you go on your own," Tacroy was saying, when there came a noise like SHLUCK! and Christopher found himself on the other side of the wall all mixed up in creepers. For a second he was blinded in the sun there. He could see and hear and feel that things were moving all over the yard in front of him, rushing away from him in a stealthy, blurred way that had him almost paralysed with terror. Snakes! he thought, and blinked and squinted and blinked again, trying to see them properly.

They were only cats, running away from the noise he had made coming through the wall. Most of them were well out of reach by the time he could see. Some had climbed high up the creepers and the rest had bolted for the various dark archways round the yard. But one white cat was slower than the others and was left trotting uncertainly and heavily across the harsh shadow in one corner.

That was the one to get. Christopher set off after it.

By the time he had torn himself free of the creepers, the white cat had taken fright. It ran. Christopher ran after it, through an archway hung with more creepers, across another, shadier yard, and then through a doorway with a curtain instead of a door. The cat slipped round the curtain. Christopher flung the curtain aside and dived after it, only to find it was so dark beyond that he was once more blinded.

"Who are *you*?" said a voice from the darkness. It sounded surprised and haughty. "You're not supposed to be here."

"Who are *you*?" Christopher said cautiously, wishing he could see something besides blue and green dazzle.

"I'm the Goddess of course," said the voice. "The Living Asheth. What are you doing here? I'm not supposed to see *anyone* but priestesses until the Day of Festival."

"I only came to get a cat," said Christopher. "I'll go away when I have."

"You're not allowed to," said the Goddess. "Cats are sacred to Asheth. Besides, if it's Bethi you're after, she's mine, and she's going to have kittens again."

Christopher's eyes were adjusting. If he peered hard at the corner where the voice came from, he could see someone about the same size as he was, sitting on what seemed to be a pile of cushions, and pick out the white hump of the cat clutched in the person's arms. He took a step forward to see better.

"Stay where you are," said the Goddess, "or I'll call down fire to blast you!"

Christopher, much to his surprise, found he could not move from the spot. He shuffled his feet to make sure. It was as if his bare soles were fastened to the tiles with strong rubbery glue. While he shuffled, his eyes started working properly.

The Goddess was a girl with a round, ordinary face and

long mouse-coloured hair. She was wearing a sleeveless rust-brown robe and rather a lot of turquoise jewellery, including at least twenty bracelets and a little turquoise-studded coronet. She looked a bit younger than he was – much too young to be able to fasten someone's feet to the floor. Christopher was impressed. "How did you do it?" he said.

The Goddess shrugged. "The power of the Living Asheth," she said. "I was chosen from among all the other applicants because I'm the best vessel for her power. Asheth picked me out by giving me the mark of a cat on my foot. Look." She tipped herself sideways on her cushions and stretched one bare foot with an anklet round it towards Christopher. It had a big purple birthmark on the sole. Christopher did not think it looked much like a cat, even when he screwed his eyes up so much that he felt like Tacroy. "You don't believe me," the Goddess said, rather accusingly.

"I don't know," said Christopher. "I've never met a goddess before. What do you do?"

"I stay in the temple unseen, except for one day every year, when I ride through the city and bless it," said the Goddess. Christopher thought that this did not sound very interesting, but before he could say so, the Goddess added, "It's not much fun, actually, but that's the way things are when you're honoured like I am. The Living Asheth always has to be a young girl, you see,"

"Do you stop being Asheth when you grow up then?" Christopher asked.

The Goddess frowned. Clearly she was not sure. "Well,

the Living Asheth never *is* grown up, so I suppose so – they haven't said." Her round, solemn face brightened up. "That's something to look forward to, eh Bethi?" she said, stroking the white cat.

"If I can't have that cat, will you let me have another one?" Christopher asked.

"It depends," said the Goddess. "I don't think I'm allowed to give them away. What do you want it for?"

"My uncle wants one," Christopher explained. "We're doing an experiment to see if I can fetch a live animal from your Anywhere to ours. Yours is Ten and ours is Twelve. And it's quite difficult climbing across The Place Between, so if you do let me have a cat, could you lend me a basket too, please?"

The Goddess considered. "How many Anywheres are there?" she asked in a testing kind of way.

"Hundreds," said Christopher, "but Tacroy thinks there's only twelve."

"The priestesses say there are twelve known Otherwheres," the Goddess said, nodding. "But Mother Proudfoot is fairly sure there are many more than that. Yes, and how did you get into the Temple?"

"Through the wall," said Christopher. "Nobody saw me."

"Then you could get in and out again if you wanted to?" said the Goddess.

"Easy!" said Christopher.

"Good," said the Goddess. She dumped the white cat in

the cushions and sprang to her feet, with a smart jangle and clack from all her jewellery. "I'll swop you a cat," she said. "But first you must swear by the Goddess to come back and bring me what I want in exchange, or I'll keep your feet stuck to the floor and shout for the Arm of Asheth to come and kill you."

"What do you want in exchange?" asked Christopher.

"Swear first," said the Goddess.

"I swear," said Christopher. But that was not enough. The Goddess hooked her thumbs into her jewelled sash and stared stonily. She was actually a little shorter than Christopher, but that did not make the stare any less impressive. "I swear by the Goddess that I'll come back with what you want in exchange for the cat – will that do?" said Christopher. "Now what do you want?"

"Books to read," said the Goddess. "I'm bored," she explained. She did not say it in a whine, but in a brisk way that made Christopher see it was true.

"Aren't there any books here?" he said.

"Hundreds," the Goddess said gloomily. "But they're all educational or holy. And the Living Goddess isn't allowed to touch *anything* in this world outside the Temple. Anything in this *world*. Do you understand?"

Christopher nodded. He understood perfectly. "Which cat can I have?"

"Throgmorten," said the Goddess. Upon that word, Christopher's feet came loose from the tiles. He was able to walk beside the Goddess as she lifted the curtain from the doorway and went out into the shady yard. "I don't mind you taking Throgmorten," she said. "He smells and he scratches and he bullies all the other cats. I hate him. But we'll have to be quick about catching him. The priestesses will be waking up from siesta quite soon. Just a moment!"

She dashed aside into an archway in a clash of anklets that made Christopher jump. She whirled back almost at once, a whirl of rusty robe, flying girdle, and swirling mouse-coloured hair. She was carrying a basket with a lid. "This should do," she said. "The lid has a good strong fastening." She led the way through the creeper-hung archway into the courtyard with the blinding sunlight. "He's usually lording it over the other cats somewhere here," she said. "Yes, there he is – that's him in the corner."

Throgmorten was ginger. He was at that moment glaring at a black and white female cat, who had lowered herself into a miserable crouch while she tried to back humbly away. Throgmorten swaggered towards her, lashing a stripy snake-like tail, until the black and white cat's nerve broke and she bolted. Then he turned to see what Christopher and the Goddess wanted.

"Isn't he horrible?" said the Goddess. She thrust the basket at Christopher. "Hold it open and shut the lid down quick after I've got him into it."

Throgmorten was, Christopher had to admit, a truly unpleasant cat. His yellow eyes stared at them with a blank and insolent leer, and there was something about the set of his ears – one higher than the other – which told Christopher that Throgmorten would attack viciously anything that got in his way. This being so, he was puzzled that Throgmorten should remind him remarkably much of Uncle Ralph. He supposed it must be the gingerness.

At this moment, Throgmorten sensed they were after him. His back arched incredulously. Then, he fairly levitated up into the creepers on the wall, racing and scrambling higher and higher, until he was far above their heads.

"No, you *don't*!" said the Goddess.

And Throgmorten's arched ginger body came flying out of the creepers like a furry orange boomerang and landed slap in the basket. Christopher was deeply impressed – so impressed that he was a bit slow getting the lid down. Throgmorten came pouring over the edge of the basket again in an instant ginger stream. The Goddess seized him and crammed him back, whereupon a large number of flailing ginger legs – at least seven, to Christopher's bemused eyes – clawed hold of her bracelets and her robe and her legs under the robe, and tore pieces off them.

Christopher waited and aimed for an instant when one of Throgmorten's heads – he seemed to have at least three, each with more fangs than seemed possible – came into range. Then he banged the basket lid on it, hard. Throgmorten, for the blink of an eye, became an ordinary dazed cat instead of a fighting devil. The Goddess shook him off into the basket. Christopher slapped the lid on. A huge ginger paw loaded with long pink razors at once oozed itself out of the latch hole and tore several strips off Christopher while he fastened the basket.

"Thanks," he said, sucking his wounds.

"I'm glad to see the back of him," said the Goddess, licking a slash on her arm and mopping blood off her leg with her torn robe.

A melodious voice called from the creeper-hung archway. "Goddess, dear! Where are you?"

"I have to go," whispered the Goddess. "Don't forget the books. You swore to a swop. *Coming*!" she called, and went running back to the archway, clash-tink, clash-tink.

Christopher turned quickly to the wall and tried to go through it. And he could not. No matter how he tried turning that peculiar sideways way, it would not work. He knew it was Throgmorten. Holding a live cat snarling in a basket made him part of this Anywhere and he had to obey its usual rules. What was he to do? More melodious voices were calling to the Goddess in the distance, and he could see people moving inside at least two more of the archways round the yard. He never really considered putting the basket down. Uncle Ralph wanted this cat. Christopher ran for it instead, sprinting for the nearest archway that seemed to be empty.

Unfortunately the jigging of the basket assured Throgmorten that he was certainly being kidnapped. He protested about it at the top of his voice – and Christopher would never have believed that a mere cat could make such a powerful noise. Throgmorten's voice filled the dark passages beyond the archway, wailing, throbbing, rising to a shriek like a dying vampire's, and then falling to a strong curdled contralto howl. Then it went up to a shriek again.

Before Christopher had run twenty yards, there were shouts behind him, and the slap of sandals and the thumping of bare feet. He ran faster than ever, twisting into a new passage whenever he came to one, and sprinting down that, but all the time Throgmorten kept up his yells of protest from the basket, showing the pursuers exactly where to follow. Worse, he fetched more. There were twice the number of shouts and thumping feet behind by the time Christopher saw daylight. He burst out into it, followed by a jostling mob.

And it was not really daylight, but a huge confusing temple, full of worshippers and statues and fat painted pillars. The daylight was coming from great open doors a hundred yards away. Christopher could see the man with the yellow umbrella outlined beyond the doors and knew exactly where he was. He dashed for the doors, dodging pillars and sprinting round people praying. "Wong – *wong* – WONG-*WONG*!" howled Throgmorten from the basket in his hand.

"Stop thief!" screamed the people chasing him. "Arm of Asheth!"

Christopher saw a man in a silver mask, or maybe a woman – a silver-masked person anyway – standing on a flight of steps carefully aiming a spear at him. He tried to dodge, but there was no time, or the spear followed him somehow. It crashed into his chest with a jolting thud.

Things seemed to go very slowly then. Christopher stood still, clutching the howling basket, and stared disbelievingly at the shaft of the spear sticking out of his chest through his dirty shirt. He saw it in tremendous detail. It was made of beautifully polished brown wood, with words and pictures carved along it. About half-way up was a shiny silver hand-grip which had designs that were almost rubbed out with wear. A few drops of blood were coming out where the wood met his shirt. The spear-head must be buried deep inside him. He looked up to see the masked person advancing triumphantly towards him. Beyond, in the doorway, Tacroy must have been fetched by the noise. He was standing frozen there, staring in horror.

Falteringly, Christopher put out his free hand and took hold of the spear by the hand-grip to pull it out. And everything stopped with a bump.

CHAPTER FIVE

✳

*I*t was early morning. Christopher realised that what had
woken him were angry cat noises from the basket lying on
its side in the middle of the floor. Throgmorten wanted out.
Instantly. Christopher sat up beaming with triumph because
he had proved he could bring a live animal from an
Anywhere. Then he remembered he had a spear sticking out
of his chest. He looked down. There was no sign of a spear.
There was no blood. Nothing hurt. He felt his chest. Then he
undid his pyjamas and looked. Incredibly he saw only
smooth pale skin without a sign of a wound.

He was all right. The Anywheres were really only a kind
of dream after all. He laughed.

"Wong!" Throgmorten said angrily, making the basket roll about.

Christopher supposed he had better let the beast out. Remembering those spiked tearing claws, he stood up on his bed and unhitched the heavy bar that held the curtains. It was hard to manoeuvre with the curtains hanging from it and sliding about, but Christopher rather thought he might need the curtains to shield him from Throgmorten's rage, so he kept them in a bunch in front of him. After a bit of swaying and prodding, he managed to get the brass point at the end of the curtain bar under the latch of the lid and open the basket.

The cat sounds stopped. Throgmorten seemed to have decided that this was a trick. Christopher waited, gently bouncing on his bed and clutching the bar and the bundle of curtain, for Throgmorten to attack. But nothing happened. Christopher leant forward cautiously until he could see into the basket. It contained a round ginger bundle gently moving up and down. Throgmorten, disdaining freedom now he had it, had curled up and gone to sleep.

"All right then," said Christopher. "*Be* like that!" With a bit of a struggle, he hitched the curtain pole back on its supports again and went to sleep himself.

Next time he woke, Throgmorten was exploring the room. Christopher lay on his back and warily watched Throgmorten jump from one piece of furniture to another all round the room. As far as he could tell, Throgmorten was not angry any more. He seemed simply full of curiosity.

Or maybe, Christopher thought, as Throgmorten gathered himself and jumped from the top of the wardrobe to the curtain pole, Throgmorten had a bet on with himself that he could get all round the night-nursery without touching the floor. As Throgmorten began scrambling along the pole, hanging on to it and the curtains with those remarkable claws of his, Christopher was sure of it.

What happened then was definitely not Throgmorten's fault. Christopher knew it was his own fault for not putting the curtain pole back properly. The end furthest from Throgmorten and nearest Christopher came loose and plunged down like a harpoon, with the curtains rattling along it and Throgmorten hanging on frantically.

For an instant, Christopher had Throgmorten's terror-stricken eyes glaring into his own as Throgmorten rode the pole down. Then the brass end hit the middle of Christopher's chest. It went in like the spear. It was not sharp and it was not heavy, but it went right into him all the same. Throgmorten landed on his stomach an instant later, all claws and panic. Christopher thought he screamed. Anyway, either he or Throgmorten made enough noise to fetch the Last Governess running. The last thing Christopher saw for the time being was the Last Governess in her white night dress, grey with horror, moving her hands in quick peculiar gestures and gabbling very odd words...

He woke up a long time later, in the afternoon by the light, very sore in front and not too sure of very much, to hear Uncle Ralph's voice.

"This is a damned nuisance, Effie, just when things were looking so promising! Is he going to be all right?"

"I think so," the Last Governess replied. The two of them were standing by Christopher's bed. "I got there in time to say a staunching spell and it seems to be healing." While Christopher was thinking, Funny, I didn't know she was a witch! she went on, "I haven't dared breathe a word to your sister."

"Don't," said Uncle Ralph. "She has her plans for him cut and dried, and she'll put a stop to mine if she finds out. Drat that cat! I've got things set up all over the Related Worlds on the strength of that first run and I don't want to cancel them. You think he'll recover?"

"In time," said the Last Governess. "There's a strong spell in the dressing."

"Then I shall have to postpone everything," Uncle Ralph said, not sounding at all pleased. "At least we've got the cat. Where's the thing got to?"

"Under the bed. I tried to fetch it out but I just got scratched for my pains," said the Last Governess.

"Women!" said Uncle Ralph. "I'll get it." Christopher heard his knees thump on the floor. His voice came up from underneath. "Here. Nice pussy. Come here, pussy."

There was a very serious outbreak of cat noises.

Uncle Ralph's knees went thumping away backwards and

his voice said quite a string of bad words. "The creature's a perfect devil!" he added. "It's torn lumps off me!" Then his voice came from higher up and further away. "Don't let it get away. Put a holding spell on this room until I get back."

"Where are you going?" the Last Governess asked.

"To fetch some thick leather gloves and a vet," Uncle Ralph said from by the door. "That's an Asheth Temple cat. It's almost priceless. Wizards will pay five hundred pounds just for an inch of its guts or one of its claws. Its eyes will fetch several thousand pounds each – so make sure you set a good tight spell. It may take me an hour or so to find a vet."

There was silence after that. Christopher dozed. He woke up feeling so much better that he sat up and took a look at his wound. The Last Governess had efficiently covered it with smooth white bandage. Christopher peered down inside it with great interest. The wound was a round red hole, much smaller than he expected. It hardly hurt at all.

While he wondered how to find out how deep it was, there was a piercing wail from the windowsill behind him. He looked round. The window was open – the Last Governess had a passion for fresh air – and Throgmorten was crouched on the sill beside it, glaring appealingly. When he saw Christopher was looking, Throgmorten put out one of his razor-loaded paws and scraped it down the space between the window and the frame. The empty air made a sound like someone scratching a blackboard.

"Wong," Throgmorten commanded.

Christopher wondered why Throgmorten should think

he was on his side. One way or another, Throgmorten had half killed him.

"Wong?" Throgmorten asked piteously.

On the other hand, Christopher thought, none of the half-killing had been Throgmorten's fault. And though Throgmorten was probably the ugliest and most vicious cat in any Anywhere, it did not seem fair to kidnap him and drag him to a strange world and then let him be sold to wizards, parcel by parcel.

"All right," he said and climbed out of bed. Throgmorten stood up eagerly, with his thin ginger snake of a tail straight up behind. "Yes, but I'm not sure how to break spells," Christopher said, approaching very cautiously. Throgmorten backed away and made no attempt to scratch. Christopher put his hand out to the open part of the window. The empty space felt rubbery and gave when he pressed it, but he could not put his hand through even if he shoved it hard. So he did the only thing he could think of and opened the window wider. He felt the spell tear like a rather tough cobweb.

"Wong!" Throgmorten uttered appreciatively. Then he was off. Christopher watching him gallop down a slanting drain and levitate to a windowsill when the drain stopped. From there it was an easy jump to the top of a bay window and then to the ground. Throgmorten's ginger shape went trotting away into the bushes and squeezed under the next-door fence, already with the air of looking for birds to kill and other cats to bully. Christopher put the window carefully back the way it had been and got back to bed.

When he woke up next, Mama was outside the door saying anxiously, "How is he? I hope it's not infectious."

"Not in the least, Madam," said the Last Governess.

So Mama came in, filling the room with her scents – which was just as well, since Throgmorten had left his own penetrating odour under the bed – and looked at Christopher. "He seems a bit pale," she said. "Do we need a doctor?"

"I saw to all that, Madam," said the Last Governess.

"Thank you," said Mama. "Make sure it doesn't interrupt his education."

When Mama had gone, the Last Governess fetched her umbrella and poked it under the bed and behind the furniture, looking for Throgmorten. "Where has it *got* to?" she said, climbing up to jab at the space on top of the wardrobe.

"I don't know," Christopher said truthfully, since he knew Throgmorten would be many streets away by now. "He was here before I went to sleep."

"It's vanished!" said the Last Governess. "A cat can't just vanish!"

Christopher said experimentally, "He was an Asheth Temple cat."

"True," said the Last Governess. "They *are* wildly magic by all accounts. But your uncle's not going to be at all pleased to find it gone."

This made Christopher feel decidedly guilty. He could

not go back to sleep, and when, about an hour later, he heard brisk heavy feet approaching the door, he sat up at once, wondering what he was going to say to Uncle Ralph.

But the man who came in was not Uncle Ralph. He was a total stranger – no, it was Papa! Christopher recognised the black whiskers. Papa's face was fairly familiar too, because it was quite like his own, except for the whiskers and a solemn, anxious look. Christopher was astonished because he had somehow thought – without anyone ever having exactly said so – that Papa had left the house in disgrace after whatever went wrong with the money.

"Are you all right, son?" Papa said, and the hurried, worried way he spoke, and the way he looked round nervously at the door, told Christopher that Papa had indeed left the house and did not want to be found here. This made it plain that Papa had come specially to see Christopher, which astonished Christopher even more.

"I'm quite well, thank you," Christopher said politely. He had not the least idea how to talk to Papa, face to face. Politeness seemed safest.

"Are you sure?" Papa asked, staring attentively at him. "The life-spell I have for you showed— In fact it stopped, as if you were – um— Frankly I thought you might be dead."

Christopher was more astonished still. "Oh no, I'm feeling much better now," he said.

"Thank God for that!" said Papa. "I must have made an error setting the spell – it seems a habit with me just now. But I have drawn up your horoscope too, and checked it several times, and I must warn you that the next year and a half will be a time of acute danger for you, my son. You must be very careful."

"Yes," said Christopher. "I will." He meant it. He could still see the curtain rod coming down if he shut his eyes. And he had to keep trying not to think at all of the way the spear had stuck out of him.

Papa leant a little closer and looked furtively at the door again. "That brother of your mama's – Ralph Argent – I hear he's managing your mama's affairs," he said. "Try to have as little to do with him as you can, my son. He is not a nice person to know." And having said that, Papa patted Christopher's shoulder and hurried away. Christopher was quite relieved. One way and another, Papa had made him very uncomfortable. Now he was even more worried about what he would say to Uncle Ralph.

But to his great relief, the Last Governess told him that Uncle Ralph was not coming. He said that he was too annoyed about losing Throgmorten to make a good sick-visitor.

Christopher sighed thankfully and settled down to enjoy being an invalid. He drew pictures, he ate grapes, he read books, and he spun out his illness as long as he could. This was not easy. The next morning his wound was only a round itchy scab, and on the third day it was hardly there at all. On the fourth day, the Last Governess made him get up and have lessons as usual; but it had been lovely while it lasted.

On the day after that, the Last Governess said, "Your uncle wants to try another experiment tomorrow. He wants you to meet the man at Series Eight this time. Do you think you feel well enough?"

Christopher felt perfectly well, and provided nobody wanted him to go near Series Ten again, he was quite willing to go on another dream.

Series Eight turned out to be the bleak and stony Anywhere up above Nine. Christopher had not cared for it much when he had explored it on his own, but Tacroy was so glad to see him that it would have made up for a far worse place.

"Am I glad to see you!" Tacroy said, while Christopher was firming him up. "I'd resigned myself to being the cause of your death. I could *kick* myself for persuading your uncle to get you to fetch an animal! Everyone knows living creatures cause all sorts of problems, and I've told him we're never going to try that again. Are you really all right?"

"Fine," said Christopher. "My chest was smooth when I woke up." In fact the funny thing about both accidents was that Throgmorten's scratches had taken twice as long to heal as either wound. But Tacroy seemed to find this so hard to believe and to be so full of self-blame that Christopher got embarrassed and changed the subject. "Have you still got the young lady who's stern stuff?"

"Sterner than ever," Tacroy said, becoming much more cheerful at once. "The wretched girl's setting my teeth on edge with that flute at this moment. Take a look down the valley. Your uncle's been busy since you – since your accident."

Uncle Ralph had perfected the horseless carriage. It was sitting on the sparse stony grass beside the stream as firm as anything, though it looked more like a rough wooden sled than any kind of carriage. Something had been done so that Tacroy was able to take hold of the rope fastened to the front. When he pulled, the carriage came gliding down the valley after him without really touching the ground.

"It's supposed to return to London with me when I go back to my garret," he explained. "I know that doesn't seem likely, but your uncle swears he's got it right this time. The question is, will it go back with a load on it, or will the load stay behind? That's what tonight's experiment is to find out."

Christopher had to help Tacroy haul the sled up the long stony trail beyond the valley. Tacroy was never quite firm enough to give a good pull. At length they came to a bleak stone farm crouched half-way up the hill, where a group of thick-armed silent women were waiting in the yard beside a heap of packages carefully wrapped in oiled silk. The packages smelt odd, but that smell was drowned by the thick garlic breath from the women. As soon as the sled came to a stop, garlic rolled out in waves as the women picked up the packages and tried to load them on the sled. The parcels dropped straight through it and fell on the ground.

"No good," said Tacroy. "I thought you were warned. Let Christopher do it."

It was hard work. The women watched untrustingly while Christopher loaded the parcels and tied them in place with rope. Tacroy tried to help, but he was not firm enough and his hands went through the parcels. Christopher got tired and cold in the strong wind. When one of the women gave a stern, friendly smile and asked him if he would like to come indoors for a drink, he said yes gladly.

"Not today, thank you," Tacroy said. "This thing's still experimental and we're not sure how long the spells will hold. We'd better get back." He could see Christopher was disappointed. As they towed the sled away downhill, he said, "I don't blame you. Call this just a business trip. Your uncle aims to get this carriage corrected by the way it performs tonight. My devout hope is that he can make it firm enough to be loaded by the people who bring the load, and then we can count you out of it altogether."

"But I like helping," Christopher protested. "Besides, how would you pull it if I'm not there to firm you up?"

"There is that," Tacroy said. He thought about it while they got to the bottom of the hill and he started plodding up the valley with the rope straining over his shoulder. "There's something I must say to you," he panted. "Are you learning magic at all?"

"I don't think so," Christopher said.

"Well you should be," Tacroy panted. "You must have the strongest talent I've ever encountered. Ask your mother to let you have lessons."

"I think Mama wants me to be a missionary," Christopher said.

Tacroy screwed his eyes up over that. "Are you sure? Might you have misheard her? Wouldn't the word be *magician*?"

"No," said Christopher. "She says I'm to go into Society."

"Ah Society!" Tacroy panted wistfully. "I have dreams of myself in Society, looking handsome in a velvet suit and surrounded by young ladies playing harps."

"Do missionaries wear velvet suits?" asked Christopher. "Or do you mean Heaven?"

Tacroy looked up at the stormy grey sky. "I don't think this conversation is getting anywhere," he remarked to it. "Try again. Your uncle tells me you're going away to school soon. If it's any kind of a decent school, they should teach magic as an extra. Promise me that you'll ask to be allowed to take it."

"All right," said Christopher. The mention of school gave him a jab of nerves somewhere deep in his stomach. "What are schools like?"

"Full of children," said Tacroy. "I won't prejudice you." By this time he had laboured his way to the top of the valley, where the mists of The Place Between were swirling in front of them. "Now comes the tricky part," he said. "Your uncle thought this thing might have more chance of arriving with its load if you gave it a push as I leave. But before I go – next time you find yourself in a Heathen Temple and they start chasing you, drop everything and get out through the nearest wall. Understand? By the look of things, I'll be seeing you in a week or so."

Christopher put his shoulder against the back of the carriage and shoved as Tacroy stepped off into the mist holding the rope. The carriage tilted and slid downwards after him. As soon as it was in the mists it looked all light and papery like a kite, and like a kite it plunged and wallowed down out of sight.

Christopher climbed back home thoughtfully. It shook him to find he had been in the Anywhere where the Heathens lived without knowing it. He had been right to be nervous of Heathens. Nothing, he thought, would possess him to go back to Series Ten now. And he did wish that Mama had not decided that he should be a missionary.

CHAPTER SIX

✳

*F*rom then on, Uncle Ralph arranged a new experiment
every week. He had, Tacroy said, been very pleased
because the carriage and the packages had arrived in
Tacroy's garret with no hitch at all. Two wizards and a
sorcerer had refined the spell on it until it could stay in
another Anywhere for up to a day. The experiments
became much more fun. Tacroy and Christopher would
tow the carriage to the place where the load was waiting,
always carefully wrapped in packages the right size for
Christopher to handle. After Christopher had loaded
them, he and Tacroy would go exploring.

Tacroy insisted on the exploring. "It's his perks," he

explained to the people with the packages. "We'll be back in an hour or so."

In Series One they went and looked at the amazing ring-trains, where the rings were on pylons high above the ground and miles apart, and the trains went hurtling through them with a noise like the sky tearing, without even touching the rings. In Series Two they wandered a maze of bridges over a tangle of rivers and looked down at giant eels resting their chins on sandbars, while even stranger creatures grunted and stirred in the mud under the bridges. Christopher suspected that Tacroy enjoyed exploring as much as he did. He was always very cheerful during this part.

"It makes a change from sloping ceilings and peeling walls. I don't get out of London very much," Tacroy confessed while he was advising Christopher how to build a better sand-castle on the sea-shore in Series Five. Series Five turned out to be the Anywhere where Christopher had met the silly ladies. It was all islands. "This is better than a Bank Holiday at Brighton any day!" Tacroy said, looking out across the bright blue crashing waves. "Almost as good as an afternoon's cricket. I wish I could afford to get away more."

"Have you lost all your money then?" Christopher asked sympathetically.

"I never had any money to lose," Tacroy said. "I was a foundling child."

Christopher did not ask any more just then, because he was busy hoping that the mermaids would appear the way they used to. But though he looked and waited, not a single mermaid came.

He went back to the subject the following week in Series Seven. As they followed a gypsy-looking man who was guiding them to see the Great Glacier, he asked Tacroy what it meant to be a foundling child.

"It means someone found me," Tacroy said cheerfully. "The someone in my case was a very agreeable and very devout Sea Captain, who picked me up as a baby on an island somewhere. He said the Lord had sent me. I don't know who my parents were."

Christopher was impressed. "Is that why you're always so cheerful?"

Tacroy laughed. "I'm mostly cheerful," he said. "But today I feel particularly good because I've got rid of the flute-playing girl at last. Your uncle's found me a nice grandmotherly person who plays the violin quite well. And maybe it's that, or maybe it's your influence, but I feel firmer with every step."

Christopher looked at him, walking ahead along the mountain path. Tacroy looked as hard as the rocks towering on one side and as real as the gypsy-looking man striding ahead of them both. "I think you're getting better at it," he said.

"Could be," said Tacroy. "I think you've raised my standards. And yet, do you know, young Christopher, until you came along, I was considered the best spirit traveller in the country?"

Here the gypsy man shouted and waved to them to come and look at the glacier. It sat above them in the rocks in a huge dirty-white V. Christopher did not think much of it. He could see it was mostly just dirty old snow – though it was certainly very big. Its giant icy lip hung over them, almost transparent grey, and water dribbled and poured off it. Series Seven was a strange world, all mountains and snow, but surprisingly hot too. Where the water poured off the glacier, the heat had caused a great growth of strident green ferns and flowing tropical trees. Violent green moss grew scarlet cups as big as hats, all dewed with water. It was like looking at the North Pole and the Equator at once. The three of them seemed tiny beneath it.

"Impressive," said Tacroy. "I know two people who are like this thing. One of them is your uncle."

Christopher thought that was a silly thing to say. Uncle Ralph was nothing like the Giant Glacier. He was annoyed with Tacroy all the following week. But he relented when the Last Governess suddenly presented him with a heap of new clothes, all sturdy and practical things. "You're to wear these when you go on the next experiment," she said. "Your uncle's man has been making a fuss. He says you always wear rags and your teeth were chattering in the snow last time. We don't want you ill, do we?"

Christopher never noticed being cold, but he was grateful to Tacroy. His old clothes had got so much too small that they got in the way when he climbed through The Place Between. He decided he liked Tacroy after all.

"I say," he said, as he loaded packages in a huge metal shed in Series Four, "can I come and visit you in your garret? We live in London too."

"You live in quite a different part," Tacroy said hastily. "You wouldn't like the area my garret's in at all."

Christopher protested that this didn't matter. He wanted to see Tacroy in the flesh and he was very curious to see the garret. But Tacroy kept making excuses. Christopher kept on asking, at least twice every experiment, until they went to bleak and stony Series Eight again, where Christopher was exceedingly glad of his warm clothes. There, while Christopher stood over the farmhouse fire warming his fingers round a mug of bitter malty tea, gratitude to Tacroy made him say yet again, "Oh, *please* can't I visit you in your garret?"

"Oh, do stow it, Christopher," Tacroy said, sounding rather tired of it all. "I'd invite you like a shot, but your uncle made a condition that you only see me like this while we're on an experiment. If I told you where I live, I'd lose this job. It's as simple as that."

"I could go round all the garrets," Christopher suggested cunningly, "and shout Tacroy and ask people until I found you."

"You could *not*," said Tacroy. "You'd draw a complete blank if you tried. Tacroy is my spirit name. I have quite a different name in the flesh."

Christopher had to give in and accept it, though he did not understand in the least.

Meanwhile, the time when he was to go to school was suddenly almost there. Christopher tried carefully not to think of it, but it was hard to forget when he had to spend such a lot of time trying on new clothes. The Last Governess sewed name tapes – C. CHANT – on the clothes and packed them in a shiny black tin trunk – also labelled C. CHANT in bold white letters. This trunk was shortly taken away by a carrier whose thick arms reminded Christopher of the women in Series Eight, and the same carrier took away all Mama's trunks too, only hers were addressed to Baden Baden while Christopher's said, 'Penge School, Surrey'.

The day after that, Mama left for Baden Baden. She came to say goodbye to Christopher, dabbing her eyes with a blue lace handkerchief that matched her travelling suit. "Remember to be good and learn a lot," she said. "And don't forget your mama wants to be very proud of you when you grow up." She put her scented cheek down for Christopher to kiss and said to the Last Governess, "Mind you take him to the dentist now."

"I won't forget, Madam," the Last Governess said in her dreariest way. Somehow her hidden prettiness never seemed to come out in front of Mama.

Christopher did not enjoy the dentist. After banging and scraping round Christopher's teeth as if he were trying to make them fall out, the dentist made a long speech about how crooked and out of place they were, until Christopher began to think of himself with fangs like Throgmorten's. He made Christopher wear a big shiny toothbrace, which he was supposed never to take out, even at night. Christopher hated the brace. He hated it so much that it almost took his mind off his fears about school.

The servants covered the furniture with dust sheets and left one by one, until Christopher and the Last Governess were the only people in the house. The Last Governess took him to the station in a cab that afternoon and put him on the train to school.

On the platform, now the time had come, Christopher was suddenly scared stiff. This really was the first step on the road to becoming a missionary and being eaten by Heathens. Terror seemed to drain the life out of him, down from his face, which went stiff, and out through his legs, which went wobbly. It seemed to make his terror worse that he had not the slightest idea what school was like.

He hardly heard the Last Governess say, "Goodbye, Christopher. Your uncle says he'll give you a month at school to settle down. He'll expect you to meet his man as usual on October the eighth in Series Six. October the eighth. Have you got that?"

"Yes," Christopher said, not attending to a word, and got into the carriage like someone going to be executed.

There were two other new boys in the carriage. The small thin one called Fenning was so nervous that he had to keep leaning out of the window to be sick. The other one was called Oneir, and he was restfully ordinary. By the time the train drew into the school station, Christopher was firm friends with them both. They decided to call themselves the

Terrible Three, but in fact everyone in the school called them the Three Bears. "Someone's been sitting in *my* chair!" they shouted whenever the three came into a room together. This was because Christopher was tall, though he had not known he was before, and Fenning was small, while Oneir was comfortably in the middle.

Before the end of the first week, Christopher was wondering what he had been so frightened of. School had its drawbacks, of course, like its food, and some of the masters, and quite a few of the older boys, but those were nothing beside the sheer fun of being with a lot of boys your own age and having two real friends of your own. Christopher discovered that you dealt with obnoxious masters and most older boys the way you dealt with Governesses: you quite politely told them the truth in the way they wanted to hear it, so that they thought they had won and left you in peace.

Lessons were easy. In fact most of the new things Christopher learnt were from the other boys. After less than three days, he had learnt enough – without quite knowing how – to realise that Mama had never intended him to be a missionary at all. This made him feel a bit of a fool, but he did not let it bother him. When he thought of Mama, he thought much more kindly of her, and threw himself into school with complete enjoyment.

The one lesson he did not enjoy was magic. Christopher found, rather to his surprise, that someone had put him down for magic as an extra. He had a dim notion that Tacroy might have arranged it. If so, Christopher showed no sign of the strong gift for magic Tacroy thought he had. The elementary spells he had to learn bored him nearly to tears.

"Please control your enthusiasm, Chant," the magic master said acidly. "I'm heartily sick of looking at your tonsils." Two weeks into the term, he suggested Christopher gave up magic.

Christopher was tempted to agree. But he had discovered by then that he was good at other lessons, and he hated the thought of being a failure even in one thing. Besides, the Goddess had stuck his feet to the spot by magic, and he wanted very much to learn to do that too. "But my mother's paying for these lessons, sir," he said virtuously. "I will try in future." He went away and made an arrangement with Oneir, whereby Christopher did Oneir's algebra and Oneir made the boring spells work for Christopher. After that, he cultivated a vague look to disguise his boredom and stared out of the window.

"Wool-gathering again, Chant?" the magic teacher took to asking. "Can't you muster an honest yawn these days?"

Apart from this one weekly lesson, school was so entirely to Christopher's taste that he did not think of Uncle Ralph or anything to do with the past for well over a month. Looking back on it later, he often thought that if he had known what a short time he was going to be at that school, he would have taken care to enjoy it even more.

At the start of November, he got a letter from Uncle Ralph:

Old chap,

What exactly are you playing at? I thought we had an arrangement. The experiments have been waiting for you since October and a lot of people's plans have been thrown out. If something's wrong and you can't do it, write and tell me. Otherwise get off your hambones, there's a good chap, and contact my man as usual next Thursday.

Your affectionate but puzzled uncle,
Ralph

This caused Christopher quite a rush of guilt. Oddly enough, though he did think of Tacroy going uselessly into trances in his garret, most of his guilt was about the Goddess. School had taught him that you did not take swears and swops lightly. He had sworn to swop Throgmorten for books, and he had let the Goddess down, even though she was only a girl. School considered that far worse than not doing what your uncle wanted. In his guilt, Christopher realised that he was going to have to spend Uncle Ralph's sovereign at last, if he was to give the Goddess anything near as valuable as Throgmorten. A pity, because he now knew that a gold sovereign was big money. But at least he would still have Uncle Ralph's sixpence.

The trouble was, school had also taught him that girls were a Complete Mystery and quite different from boys. He had no idea what books girls liked. He was forced to consult Oneir, who had an older sister.

"All sorts of slush," Oneir said, shrugging. "I can't remember what."

"Then could you come down to the bookshop with me and see if you can see some of them?" Christopher asked.

"I might," Oneir agreed. "What's in it for me?"

"I'll do your geometry tonight as well as your algebra," Christopher said.

On this understanding, Oneir went down to the bookshop with Christopher in the space between lessons and tea. There he almost immediately picked out *The Arabian Nights (Unexpurgated)*. "This one's good," he said. He followed it with something called *Little Tanya and the Fairies*, which Christopher took one look at and put hastily back on the shelf. "I know my sister's read that one," Oneir said, rather injured. "Who's the girl you want it for?"

"She's about the same age as us," Christopher said and, since Oneir was looking at him for a further explanation and he was fairly sure Oneir was not going to believe in someone called the Goddess, he added, "I've got this cousin called Caroline." This was quite true. Mama had once shown him a studio photo of his cousin, all lace and curls. Oneir was not to know that this had nothing whatsoever to do with the sentence that had gone before.

"Wait a sec then," Oneir said, "and I'll see if I can spot some of the real slush." He wandered on along the shelf, leaving Christopher to flip through *The Arabian Nights*. It did look good, Christopher thought. Unfortunately he could see from the pictures that it was all about somewhere very like the Goddess's own Anywhere. He suspected the Goddess would call it educational. "Ah, here we are! This is sure-fire slush!" Oneir called, pointing to a whole row of books. "These Millie books. Our house is full of the things."

Millie Goes to School, Christopher read, *Millie of Lowood House*, *Millie Plays the Game*. He picked up one called *Millie's Finest Hour*. It had some very brightly-coloured schoolgirls on the front and in small print: "Another moral and uplifting story about your favourite schoolgirl. You will weep with Millie, rejoice with Millie, and meet all your friends from Lowood House School again …"

"Does your sister really like these?" he asked incredulously.

"Wallows in them," said Oneir. "She reads them over and over again and cries every time."

Though this seemed a funny way to enjoy a book, Christopher was sure Oneir knew best. The books were two and sixpence each. Christopher chose out the first five, up to *Millie in the Upper Fourth*, and bought *The Arabian Nights* for himself with the rest of the money. After all, it *was* his gold sovereign. "Could you wrap the Millie books in something waterproof?" he asked the assistant. "They have to go to a foreign country." The assistant obligingly produced some sheets of waxed paper and, without being asked, made a handle for the parcel out of string.

That night Christopher hid the parcel in his bed. Oneir pinched a candle from the kitchens and read aloud from *The Arabian Nights*, which turned out to have been a remarkably good buy. 'Unexpurgated' seemed to mean that all sorts of interesting dirty bits had been put in. Christopher was so absorbed that he almost forgot to work out how he might get to The Place Between from the dormitory. It was probably important to go round a corner. He decided the best corner was the one beyond the wash-stands, just beside Fenning's bed, and then settled down to listen to Oneir until the candle burnt out. After that, he would be on his way.

To his exasperation, nothing happened at all. Christopher lay and listened to the snores, the mutters and the heavy breathing of the other boys for hours. At length he got up with the parcel and tiptoed across the cold floor to the corner beyond Fenning's bed. But he knew this was not right, even before he bumped into the wash-stands. He went back to bed, where he lay for further hours, and nothing happened even when he went to sleep.

The next day was Thursday, the day he was supposed to meet Tacroy. Knowing he would be too busy to deliver the books that night, Christopher left them in his bedside locker and read aloud from *The Arabian Nights* himself, so that he could control the time when everyone went to sleep. And so he did. All the other boys duly began to snore and mutter and puff as they always did, and Christopher was left lying awake alone, unable to get to The Place Between or to fall asleep either.

By this time he was seriously worried. Perhaps the only way to get to the Anywheres was from the night nursery of the house in London. Or perhaps it was an ability he had simply grown out of. He thought of Tacroy in a useless trance and the Goddess vowing the vengeance of Asheth on him, and he heard the birds beginning to sing before he got to sleep that night.

CHAPTER SEVEN

✳

The next morning Matron noticed Christopher stumbling about aching-eyed and scarcely awake. She pounced on him. "Can't sleep, can you?" she said. "I always watch the ones with toothbraces. I don't think these dentists realise how uncomfortable they are. I'm going to come and take that away from you before lights out tonight and you can come and fetch it in the morning. I make Mainwright Major do that too – it works wonders, you'll see."

Christopher had absolutely no faith in this idea. Everyone knew this was one of the bees in Matron's bonnet. But, to his surprise, it worked. He found himself dropping asleep as soon as Fenning began reading *The Arabian Nights*.

He had just presence of mind to fumble the parcel of books from his locker, before he was dead to the world. And here an even more surprising thing happened. He got out of bed, carrying the parcel, and walked across the dormitory without anyone appearing to notice him at all. He walked right beside Fenning, and Fenning just went on reading with the stolen candle balanced on his pillow. Nobody seemed to realise when Christopher walked round the corner, out of the dormitory and on to the valley path.

His clothes were lying in the path and he put them on, hanging the parcel from his belt so that he would have both hands free for The Place Between. And there was The Place Between.

So much had happened since Christopher had last been here that he saw it as if this was the first time. His eyes tried to make sense of the shapeless way the rocks slanted, and couldn't. The formlessness stirred a formless kind of fear in him, which the wind and the mist and the rain beating in the mist made worse. The utter emptiness was more frightening still.

As Christopher set off climbing and sliding down to Series Ten, with the wind wailing round him and the fog drops making the rocks wet and slippery, he thought he had been right to think, when he was small, that this was the part left over when all the worlds were made. The Place Between was exactly that. There was no one here to help him if he slipped and broke a leg. When the parcel of books unbalanced him and he did slip, and skidded twenty feet before he could stop, his heart was in his mouth. If he had not known that he had climbed across here a hundred times, he would have known he was mad to try.

It was quite a relief to clamber into the hot valley and walk down to the muddy-walled city. The old men were still charming snakes outside it. Inside was the same hot clamour of smells and goats and people under umbrellas. And Christopher found he was still afraid, except that now he was afraid of someone pointing at him and shouting, "There's the thief that stole the Temple cat!" He kept feeling that spear thudding into his chest. He began to get annoyed with himself. It was as if school had taught him how to be frightened.

When he got to the alley beside the Temple wall – where turnips had been thrown away this time – he was almost too scared to go on. He had to make himself push into the spiked wall by counting to a hundred and then telling himself he had to go. And when he was most of the way through, he stopped again, staring through the creepers at the cats in the blazing sun, and did not seem to be able to go on. But the cats took no notice of him. No one was about. Christopher told himself that it was *silly* to come all this way just to stand in a wall. He pulled himself out of the creepers and tiptoed to the overgrown archway, with the parcel of books butting him heavily with every step.

The Goddess was sitting on the ground in the middle of the shady yard, playing with a large family of kittens. Two of them were ginger, with a strong look of Throgmorten. When she saw Christopher, the Goddess jumped to her feet with an energetic clash of jewellery, scattering kittens in all directions.

"You've brought the books!" she said. "I never thought you would."

"I always keep my word," Christopher said, showing off a little.

The Goddess watched him unhitch the parcel from his belt as if she could still scarcely believe it. Her hands trembled a little as she took the waxy parcel, and trembled even more as she knelt on the tiles and tore and ripped and pulled until the paper and string came off. The kittens seized on the string and the wrappings and did all sorts of acrobatics with them, but the Goddess had eyes only for the books. She knelt and gazed. "Ooh! Five of them!"

"Just like Christmas," Christopher remarked.

"What's Christmas?" the Goddess asked absently. She was absorbed in stroking the covers of the books. When she had done that, she opened each one, peeped inside, and then shut it hastily as if the sight was too much. "Oh, I remember," she said. "Christmas is a Heathen festival, isn't it?"

"The other way round," said Christopher. "You're the Heathens."

"No, we're not. Asheth's true," said the Goddess, not

really attending. "Five," she said. "That should last me a week if I read slowly on purpose. Which is the best one to start with?"

"I brought you the first five," Christopher said. "Start with *Millie Goes to School*."

"You mean there are *more*!" the Goddess exclaimed. "How many?"

"I didn't count – about five," Christopher said.

"*Five*! You don't want another cat, do you?" said the Goddess.

"No," Christopher said firmly. "One Throgmorten is quite enough, thanks."

"But I've nothing else to swop!" said the Goddess. "I *must* have those other five books!" She jumped up with an impetuous clash of jewellery and began wrestling to unwind a snake-like bracelet from the top of her arm. "Perhaps Mother Proudfoot won't notice if this is missing. There's a whole chest of bracelets in there."

Christopher wondered what she thought he would do with the bracelet. Wear it? He knew what school would think of that.

"Hadn't you better read these books first? You might not like them," he pointed out.

"I know they're perfect," said the Goddess, still wrestling.

"I'll bring you the other books as a present," Christopher said hastily.

"But that means I'll have to do something for you.

Asheth always pays her debts," the Goddess said. The bracelet came off with a twang. "Here. I'll *buy* the books from you with this. Take it." She pushed the bracelet into Christopher's hand.

The moment it touched him, Christopher found himself falling through everything that was there. The yard, the creepers, the kittens, all turned to mist – as did the Goddess's round face, frozen in the middle of changing from eagerness to astonishment – and Christopher fell out of it, down and down, and landed violently on his bed in the dark dormitory. CRASH!

"What was that?" said Fenning, quavering a little, and Oneir remarked, apparently in his sleep, "Help, someone's fallen off the ceiling."

"Shall I fetch Matron?" asked someone else.

"Don't be an ass. I just had a dream," Christopher said, rather irritably, because it had given him quite a shock. It was a further shock to find he was in pyjamas and not in the clothes he *knew* he had put on in the valley. When the other boys had settled down, he felt all over his bed for the parcel of books, and when they did not seem to be there, felt for the bracelet instead. He could not find that either.

He searched again in the morning, but there was no sign of it. He supposed that was not so surprising, when he thought how much Uncle Ralph had said Throgmorten was worth. Twelve-and-sixpenceworth of books was a pretty poor swop for several thousand poundsworth of cat. Something must have noticed he was cheating the Goddess.

He knew he was going to have to find the money for those other five books somehow and take them to the Goddess. Meanwhile, he had missed Tacroy, and he supposed he had better try to meet him next Thursday instead. He was not looking forward to it. Tacroy was bound to be pretty annoyed by now.

When Thursday came, Christopher nearly forgot Tacroy. It was only by accident that he happened to fall asleep during a particularly tedious story in *The Arabian Nights*. *The Arabian Nights* had become the dormitory's favourite reading. They took it in turns to steal a candle and read aloud to the others. It was Oneir's turn that night, and Oneir read all on one note like the school Chaplain reading the Bible. And that night he was deep into a confusing set of people who were called Calendars – Fenning made everyone groan by suggesting they got their name from living in the part of the world where dates grew – and Christopher dropped off to sleep. Next thing he knew, he was walking out into the valley.

Tacroy was sitting in the path beside the heap of Christopher's clothes. Christopher eyed those clothes and wondered how they got there. Tacroy was sitting with his arms wrapped around his knees as if he were resigned to a long wait, and he seemed quite surprised to see Christopher.

"I didn't expect to see you!" he said, and he grinned, though he looked tired.

Christopher felt ashamed and awkward. "I suppose you must be pretty angry—" he began.

"Stow it," said Tacroy. "I get paid for going into trances and you don't. It's just a job for me – though I must say I miss you being around to firm me up." He stretched his legs out across the path, and Christopher could see stones and grass through the green worsted trousers. Then he stretched his arms above his head and yawned. "You don't really want to go on with these experiments, do you?" he asked. "You've been busy with school, and that's much more fun than climbing into valleys of a night, isn't it?"

Because Tacroy was being so nice about it, Christopher felt more ashamed than ever. He had forgotten how nice Tacroy was. Now he thought about it, he had missed him quite badly. "Of course I want to go on," he said. "Where are we going tonight?"

"Nowhere," said Tacroy. "I'm nearly out of this trance as it is. This was just an effort to contact you. But if you really want to go on, your uncle is sending the carriage to Series Six next Thursday – you know, the place that's living in an Ice Age. You *do* want to go on – really?" Tacroy looked at Christopher with his eyes screwed into anxious lines. "You don't have to, you know."

"Yes, but I will," Christopher said. "See you next Thursday." And he dashed back to bed, where, to his delight, something seemed to be happening to the Calendars at last.

The rest of that term passed very swiftly, from lesson to lesson, from tale to tale in *The Arabian Nights*, from Thursday to Thursday. Climbing across The Place

Between to meet Tacroy the first Thursday, Christopher still felt quite frightened, but it made a difference knowing that Tacroy was waiting for him outside the fifth valley along. Soon he was used to it again, and the experiments went on as before.

Someone had arranged for Christopher to stay for the Christmas holidays with Uncle Charles and Aunt Alice, the parents of his cousin Caroline. They lived in a big house in the country quite near, in Surrey too, and Cousin Caroline, in spite of being three years younger and a girl, turned out to be good fun. Christopher enjoyed learning all the things people did in the country, including snowballing with the stable lads and Caroline, and trying to sit on Caroline's fat pony, but he was puzzled that no one mentioned Papa. Uncle Charles was Papa's brother. He realised that Papa must be in disgrace with his whole family. In spite of this, Aunt Alice made sure he had a good Christmas, which was kind of her. Christopher's most welcome Christmas present was another gold sovereign inside a card from Uncle Ralph. That meant he could afford more books for the Goddess.

As soon as school started again, he went down to the bookshop and bought the other five Millie books, and had them wrapped in waxed paper like the others. That was another twelve-and-sixpence towards the cost of Throgmorten. At this rate, he thought, he would be carrying parcels of books across The Place Between for the rest of his life.

In the Temple, the Goddess was in her dimly-lit room bent over *Millie's Finest Hour*. When Christopher came in, she jumped and stuffed the book guiltily under her cushions.

"Oh, it's only you!" she said. "Don't ever come in quietly like that again, or I shall be a Dead Asheth on the spot! Whatever happened last time? You turned into a ghost and went down through the floor."

"I've no idea," said Christopher, "except that I fell on my bed with a crash. I've brought you the other five books."

"*Wonderfu—*!" the Goddess began eagerly. Then she stopped and said soberly, "It's very kind of you, but I'm not sure Asheth wants me to have them, after what happened when I tried to give you the bracelet."

"No," said Christopher. "I think Asheth must know that Throgmorten's worth thousands of pounds. I could bring you the whole school library and it still wouldn't pay for him."

"Oh," said the Goddess. "In that case— How *is* Throgmorten, by the way?"

Since Christopher had no idea, he said airily, "Trotting around bullying other cats and scratching people," and changed the subject before the Goddess realised he was only guessing. "Were the first five books all right?"

The Goddess's round face became all smile, so much smile that her face could hardly hold it and she spread her arms out as well. "They're the most marvellous books in this world! It's like really *being* at Lowood House School. I cry every time I read them."

Oneir had got it right, Christopher thought, watching the Goddess unwrap the new parcel with little cries of pleasure and much chinking of bracelets.

"Oh Millie *does* get to be Head Girl!" she cried out, picking up *Head Girl Millie*. "I've been wondering and wondering whether she would. She must have got the better of that awful prig Delphinia after all."

She stroked the book lovingly, and then took Christopher by surprise by asking, "What happened when you took Throgmorten? Mother Proudfoot told me that the Arm of Asheth killed the thief."

"They tried," Christopher said awkwardly, trying to sound casual.

"In that case," said the Goddess, "you were very brave to honour the swop and you deserve to be rewarded. Would you like a reward – not a swop or a payment, a reward?"

"If you can think of one," Christopher said cautiously.

"Then come with me," said the Goddess. She got up briskly, clash-tink. She collected the new books and the old one from among the cushions, and gathered up the paper and the string. Then she threw the whole bundle at the wall. All of it, all six books and the wrapping, turned over on itself and shut itself out of sight, as if a lid had come down on an invisible box. There was nothing to tell that any of it had been there. Once again Christopher was impressed. "That's so Mother Proudfoot won't know," the Goddess explained as she led the way into the shady yard. "I like her a lot, but she's very stern and she's into everything."

"How do you get the books back?" asked Christopher.

"I beckon the one I want," said the Goddess, pushing through the creeper in the archway. "It's a by-product of being the Living Asheth."

She led him across the blazing yard, among the cats, to an archway he remembered rather too well for comfort. It was the one he had fled into with Throgmorten yowling in the basket. Christopher began to be nervously and gloomily certain that the Goddess's idea of a reward was nothing like his own.

"Won't there be a lot of people?" he asked, hanging back rather.

"Not for a while. They snore for hours in the hot season," the Goddess said confidently.

Christopher followed her reluctantly along a set of dark passages, not quite the way he had run before, he thought, though it was hard to be sure. At length they came to a wide archway hung with nearly-transparent yellow curtains. There was a rich gleam of daylight beyond. The Goddess parted the curtains and waved Christopher through, tink-clash. There seemed to be an old, dark tree in front of them, so old that it was thoroughly worm-eaten and had lost most of its branches. And something was making a suffocating smell, a little like church incense, but much thicker and stronger. The Goddess marched round the tree, down some shallow

102

steps, and into the space full of rich daylight, which was blocked off by more yellow curtains a few yards away, like a tall golden room. Here she turned round to face the tree.

"This is the Shrine of Asheth," she said. "Only initiates are allowed here. This is your reward. Look. Here I am."

Christopher turned round and felt decidedly cheated. From this side, the tree turned out to be a monstrous statue of a woman with four arms. From the front it looked solid gold. Clearly the Temple had not bothered to coat the back of the wooden statue with gold, but they had made up for it on the front. Every visible inch of the woman shone buttery yellow gold, and she was hung with golden chains, bracelets, anklets and ear-rings. Her skirt was cloth-of-gold and she had a big ruby embedded in each of her four golden palms. More precious stones blazed from her high crown. The Shrine was made so that daylight slanted dramatically down from the roof, touching each precious stone with splendour, but veiled by the thick smoke climbing from golden burners beside the woman's huge golden feet. The effect was decidedly Heathen.

After waiting a moment for Christopher to say something, the Goddess said, "This is Asheth. She's me and I'm her, and this is her Divine Aspect. I thought you'd like to meet me as I really am."

Christopher turned to the Goddess, meaning to say, No you're not: you haven't got four arms. But the Goddess was standing in the smoky yellow space with her arms stretched out to the side in the same position as the statue's top pair of arms, and she did indeed have four arms. The lower pair were misty and he could see the yellow curtain through them, but they had the same sort of bracelets and they were arranged just like the statue's lower pair of arms. They were obviously as real as Tacroy before he was firmed up. So he looked up at the statue's smooth golden face. He thought it looked hard and a little cruel behind its blank golden stare.

"She doesn't look as clever as you," he said. It was the only thing he could think of that was not rude.

"She's got her Very Stupid expression on," the Goddess said. "Don't be fooled by that. She doesn't want people to know how clever she really is. It's a very useful expression. I use it a lot in lessons when Mother Proudfoot or Mother Dowson go boring on."

It *was* a useful expression, Christopher thought, a good deal better than his vague look which he used in magic lessons. "How do you make it?" he asked with great interest.

Before the Goddess could reply, footsteps padded behind the statue. A strong voice, musical but sharp, called out, "Goddess? What are you doing in the Shrine at this hour?"

Christopher and the Goddess went into two separate states of panic. Christopher turned to plunge out through the other set of yellow curtains, heard sandals slapping about out there too, and turned back in despair. The Goddess whispered, "Oh *blast* Mother Proudfoot! She seems to know where I am by *instinct* somehow!" and she spun round in circles trying to wrestle a bracelet off her upper arm.

A long bare foot and most of a leg in a rust-coloured robe appeared round the golden statue. Christopher gave himself up for lost. But the Goddess, seeing she was never going to get the bracelet off in time, snatched his hand and held it against the whole heap of jingling jewellery on her arm.

Just as before, everything turned misty and Christopher fell through it, into his bed in the dormitory. Crash!

"I wish you wouldn't *do* that!" Fenning said, waking up with a jump. "Can't you control those dreams of yours?"

"Yes," Christopher said, sweating at his narrow escape. "I'm never going to have a dream like that again." It was a silly set-up anyway – a live girl pretending to be a goddess, who was only a worm-eaten wooden statue. He had nothing against the Goddess herself. He admired her quick thinking, and he would have liked to learn both the Very Stupid expression and how you did that vanishing trick with the books. But it was not worth the danger.

CHAPTER EIGHT

✴

*F*or the rest of the spring term, Christopher went regularly to the Anywheres with Tacroy, but he did not try to go to one on his own. By now Uncle Ralph seemed to have a whole round of experiments set up. Christopher met Tacroy in Series One, Three, Five, Seven and Nine, and then in Eight, Six, Four and Two, always in that order, but not always in the same place or outside the same valley.

In each Anywhere people would be waiting with a pile of packages which, by the weight and feel, had different things inside each time. The parcels in Series One were always knobby and heavy, and in Four they were smooth boxes. In Series Two and Five, they were squashy and smelt of fish, which made sense since both those Anywheres had so much water in them. In Series Eight, the women always breathed garlic and those parcels had the same strong odour every time. Beyond that, there seemed no rule.

Christopher got to know most of the people who supplied the packages, and he laughed and joked with them as he loaded the horseless carriage. And as the experiments went on, Uncle Ralph's wizards gradually perfected the carriage. By the end of term, it moved under its own power and Tacroy and Christopher no longer had to drag it up the valleys to The Place Between.

In fact, the experiments had become so routine that they were not much of a change from school. Christopher thought of other things while he worked, just as he did in magic lessons and English and Chapel at school.

"Why don't we ever go to Series Eleven?" he asked as they walked up one of the valleys from Series One with another heavy knobby load gliding behind on the carriage.

"Nobody goes to Eleven," Tacroy said shortly. Christopher could see he wanted to change the subject. He asked why. "Because," said Tacroy, "because they're peculiar, unfriendly people there, I suppose – if you can call them people. Nobody knows much about them because they make damn sure nobody sees them. And that's all I know, except that Eleven's not a Series. There's only one world." Tacroy refused to say more than that, which was annoying, because Christopher had a strong feeling that Tacroy did know more. But Tacroy was in a bad mood that week. His grandmotherly lady had gone down with flu and Tacroy was making do with the stern flute-playing young lady.

"Somewhere in our world," he said, sighing, "there is a young lady who plays the harp and doesn't mind if I turn transparent, but there are too many difficulties in the way between us."

Probably because Tacroy kept saying things like this, Christopher now had a very romantic image of him starving in his garret and crossed in love. "*Why* won't Uncle Ralph let me come and see you in London?" he asked.

"I told you to stow it, Christopher," Tacroy said, and he stopped further talk by stepping out into the mists of The Place Between with the carriage billowing behind him.

Tacroy's romantic background nagged at Christopher all that term, particularly when a casual word he dropped in the dormitory made it clear that none of the other boys had ever met a foundling child. "I wish I was one," Oneir said. "I wouldn't have to go into my father's business then." After that, Christopher felt he would not even mind meeting the flute-playing young lady.

But this was driven out of his mind when there proved to be a muddle over the arrangements for the Easter holidays. Mama wrote and said he was to come to her in Genoa, but at the last moment she turned out to be going to Weimar instead, where there was no room for Christopher. He had to spend nearly a week at school on his own after everyone had gone home, while the school wrote to Uncle Charles, and Uncle Charles arranged for Papa's other brother, Uncle Conrad, to have him in four days' time. Meanwhile, since the school was closing, Christopher was sent to stay with Uncle Ralph in London.

Uncle Ralph was away, to Christopher's disappointment. Most of his house was shut up, with locked doors everywhere, and the only person there was the housekeeper. Christopher spent the few days wandering round London by himself.

It was almost as good as exploring an Anywhere. There were parks and monuments and street musicians, and every road, however narrow, was choked with high-wheeled carts and carriages. On the second day Christopher found himself at Covent Garden market, among piles of fruit and vegetables, and he stayed there till the evening, fascinated by the porters. Each of them could carry at least six loaded baskets in a tall pile on his head, without even wobbling. At last, he turned to come away and saw a familiar sturdy figure in a green worsted suit walking down the narrow street ahead of him.

"Tacroy!" Christopher screamed and went racing after him.

Tacroy did not appear to hear. He went walking on, with his curly head bent in a rather dejected way, and turned the corner into the next narrow street before Christopher had caught up. When Christopher skidded round the corner, there was no sign of him. But he knew it had been, unmistakably, Tacroy. The garret must be somewhere quite near. He spent the rest of his stay in London hanging round Covent Garden, hoping for another glimpse of Tacroy, but it did no good. Tacroy did not appear again.

After that, Christopher went to stay at Uncle Conrad's house in Wiltshire, where the sole drawback proved to be his cousin Francis. Cousin Francis was the same age as Christopher, and he was the kind of boy Fenning called "a stuck up pratterel". Christopher despised Francis on this account, and Francis despised Christopher for having been brought up in town and never having ridden to hounds. In fact, there was another reason too, which emerged when Christopher fell heavily off the quietest pony in the stables for the seventh time.

"Can't do magic, can you?" Francis said, looking smugly down at Christopher from the great height of his trim bay gelding. "I'm not surprised. It's your father's fault for marrying that awful Argent woman. No one in my family has anything to do with your father now."

Since Christopher was fairly sure that Francis had used magic to bring him off the pony, there was not much he could do but clench his teeth and feel that Papa was well shot of this particular branch of the Chants. It was a relief to go back to school again.

It was more than a relief. It was the cricket season. Christopher became obsessed with cricket almost overnight. So did Oneir. "It's the King of Games," Oneir said devoutly,

110

and went and bought every book on the subject that he could afford. He and Christopher decided they were going to be professional cricketers when they grew up. "And my father's business can just go hang!" Oneir said.

Christopher quite agreed, only in his case it was Mama's plans for Society. I've made up my mind for myself! he thought. It was like being released from a vow. He was quite surprised to find how determined and ambitious he was. He and Oneir practised all day, and Fenning, who was no good really, was persuaded to run after the balls. In between they talked cricket, and at night Christopher had normal ordinary dreams, all about cricket.

It seemed quite an interruption on the first Thursday, when he had to give up dreams of cricket and meet Tacroy in Series Five.

"I saw you in London," Christopher said to him. "Your garret's near Covent Garden, isn't it?"

"Covent Garden?" Tacroy said blankly. "It's nowhere near there. You must have seen someone else." And he stuck to that, even when Christopher described in great detail which street it was and what Tacroy had looked like. "No," he said. "You must have been running after a complete stranger."

Christopher *knew* it had been Tacroy. He was puzzled. But there seemed no point in going on arguing. He began loading the carriage with fishy smelling bundles and went back to thinking about cricket. Naturally, not thinking what he was doing, he let go of a bundle in the wrong place. It fell half through Tacroy and slapped to the ground, where it lay leaking an even fishier smell than before. "Pooh!" said Christopher. "What is this stuff?"

"No idea," said Tacroy. "I'm only your uncle's errand boy. What's the matter? Is your mind somewhere else tonight?"

"Sorry," Christopher said, collecting the bundle. "I was thinking of cricket."

Tacroy's face lit up. "Are you bowler or batsman?"

"Batsman," said Christopher. "I want to be a professional."

"I'm a bowler myself," said Tacroy. "Slow leg-spin and though I say it myself, I'm not half bad. I play quite a lot for – well, it's a village team really, but we usually win. I usually end up taking seven wickets – and I can bat a bit too. What are you, an opener?"

"No, I fancy myself as a stroke player," Christopher said.

They talked cricket all the time Christopher was loading the carriage. After that they walked on the beach with the blue surf crashing beside them and went on talking cricket. Tacroy several times tried to demonstrate his skill by picking up a pebble, but he could not get firm enough to hold it. So Christopher found a piece of driftwood to act as a bat and Tacroy gave him advice on how to hit.

After that, Tacroy gave Christopher a coaching session in whatever Anywhere they happened to be, and both of them talked cricket non-stop. Tacroy was a good coach. Christopher learnt far more from him than he did from the sports master at school. He had more and more splendid ambitions of playing professionally for Surrey or somewhere, cracking the ball firmly to the boundary all round the ground. In fact, Tacroy taught him so well that he began to have quite real, everyday ambitions of getting into the school team.

They were reading Oneir's cricket books aloud in the dormitory now. Matron had discovered *The Arabian Nights* and taken it away, but nobody minded. Every boy in the dormitory, even Fenning, was cricket mad. And Christopher was most obsessed of all.

Then disaster struck. It began with Tacroy saying, "By the way, there's a change of plan. Can you meet me in Series Ten next Thursday? Someone seems to be trying to spoil your uncle's experiments, so we have to change the routine."

Christopher was distracted from cricket by slight guilt at that. He knew he ought to make a further payment for Throgmorten, and he was afraid that the Goddess might have supernatural means of knowing he had been to Series Ten without bringing her any more books. He went rather warily to the valley.

Tacroy was not there. It took Christopher a good hour of climbing and scrambling to locate him at the mouth of quite a different valley. By this time Tacroy had become distinctly misty and unfirm.

"Dunderhead," Tacroy said while Christopher hastily firmed him up. "I was going to lose this trance any second.

113

You *know* there's more than one place in a series. What got into you?"

"I was probably thinking of cricket," Christopher said.

The place beyond the new valley was nothing like as primitive and Heathen-seeming as the place where the Goddess lived. It was a vast dockside with tremendous cranes towering overhead. Some of the biggest ships Christopher had ever seen, enormous rusty iron ships, very strangely shaped, were tied up to cables so big that he had to step over them as if they were logs. But he knew it was still Series Ten when the man waiting with an iron cart full of little kegs said, "Praise Asheth! I thought you were never coming!"

"Yes, make haste," Tacroy said. "This place is safer than that Heathen city, but there may be enemies around all the same. Besides, the sooner you finish, the sooner we can get to work on your forward defensive play."

Christopher hurried to roll the little kegs from the iron cart to the carriage. When all the kegs were in, he hurried to fasten the straps that held the loads on it. And, of course, because he was hurrying, one of the straps slithered out of his hand and fell back on the other side of the carriage. He had to lean right over the load to get it. He could hear iron clanking in the distance and a few shouts, but he thought nothing of it, until Tacroy suddenly sprang into sight beside him.

"Off there! Get off!" Tacroy shouted, tugging uselessly at Christopher with misty hands.

Christopher, still lying across the kegs, looked up to see a giant hook on the end of a chain travelling towards him faster than he could run.

That was really all he knew about it. The next thing he knew – rather dimly – was that he was lying in the path in his own valley beside his pyjamas. He realised that the iron hook must have knocked him out and it was lucky that he had been more or less lying across the carriage or Tacroy would never have got him home. A little shakily, he got back into his pyjamas. His head ached, so he shambled straight back to bed in the dormitory.

In the morning he did not even have a headache. He forgot about it and went straight out after breakfast to play cricket with Oneir and six other boys.

"Bags I bat first!" he shouted.

Everyone shouted it at the same time. But Oneir had been carrying the bat and he was not going to let go. Everyone, including Christopher, grabbed at him. There was a silly laughing tussle, which ended when Oneir swung the bat round in a playful, threatening circle.

The bat met Christopher's head with a heavy THUK. It hurt. He remembered hearing several other distinct cracks, just over his left ear, as if the bones of his skull were breaking up like an ice puddle. Then, in a way that was remarkably like the night before, he knew nothing at all for quite a long time.

When he came round, he knew it was much later in the day. Though the sheet had somehow got over his face, he could see late evening light coming in through a window high up in one corner. He was very cold, particularly his feet. Someone had obviously taken his shoes and socks off to put him to bed. But where had they put him? The window was in the wrong place for the dormitory – or for any other room he had slept in for that matter. He pushed the sheet off and sat up.

He was on a marble slab in a cold, dim room. It was no wonder he felt cold. He was only wearing underclothes. All round him were other marble slabs, most of them empty. But some slabs had people lying on them, very still and covered all over with white sheets.

Christopher began to suspect where he might be. Wrapping the sheet round him for what little warmth it gave, he slid down from the marble slab and went over to the nearest white slab with a person on it. Carefully he pulled back the sheet. This person had been an old tramp and he was dead as a doornail – Christopher poked his cold, bristly face to make sure. Then he told himself to keep quite calm, which was a sensible thing to tell himself, but much too late. He was already in the biggest panic of his life.

There was a big metal door down at the other end of the cold room. Christopher seized its handle and tugged. When the door turned out to be locked, he kicked it and beat at it with both hands and rattled the handle. He was still telling himself to be sensible, but he was shaking all over, and the panic was rapidly getting out of control.

After a minute or so, the door was wrenched open by

a fat, jolly-looking man in a white overall, who stared into the room irritably. He did not see Christopher at first. He was looking over Christopher's head, expecting someone taller.

Christopher wrapped the sheet round himself accusingly. "What do you mean by locking this door?" he demanded. "Everybody's dead in here. They're not going to run away."

The man's eyes turned down to Christopher. He gave a slight moan. His eyes rolled up to the ceiling. His plump body slid down the door and landed at Christopher's feet in a dead faint.

Christopher thought *he* was dead too. It put the last touch to his panic. He jumped over the man's body and rushed down the corridor beyond, where he found himself in a hospital. There a nurse tried to stop him, but Christopher was beyond reason by then. "Where's school?" he shrieked at her. "I'm missing cricket practice!" For half an hour after that the hospital was in total confusion, while everyone tried to catch a five foot corpse clothed mostly in a flying sheet, which raced up and down the corridors shrieking that it was missing cricket practice.

They caught him at last outside the maternity ward, where a doctor hastily gave him something to make him sleep. "Calm down, son," he said. "It's a shock to us too, you know. When I last saw you, your head was like a run-over pumpkin."

117

"I'm missing cricket practice, I tell you!" Christopher said.

He woke up next day in a hospital bed. Mama and Papa were both there, facing one another across it, dark clothes and whiskers on one side, scents and pretty colours on the other. As if to make it clear to Christopher that this was a bad crisis, the two of them were actually speaking to one another.

"Nonsense, Cosimo," Mama was saying. "The doctors just made a mistake. It was only a bad concussion after all and we've both had a fright for nothing."

"The school Matron said he was dead too," Papa said sombrely.

"And she's a flighty sort of type," Mama said. "I don't believe a word of it."

"Well I do," said Papa. "He had more than one life, Miranda. It explains things about his horoscope that have always puzzled —"

"Oh *fudge* to your wretched horoscopes!" Mama cried. "Be quiet!"

"I shall not be quiet where I know the truth!" Papa more or less shouted. "I have done what needs to be done and sent a telegram to de Witt about him."

This obviously horrified Mama. "What a wicked thing to do!" she raged. "And without consulting me! I tell you I shall *not* lose Christopher to your gloomy connivings, Cosimo!"

At this point both Mama and Papa became so angry

that Christopher closed his eyes. Since the stuff the doctor had given him was still making him feel sleepy, he dropped off almost at once, but he could still hear the quarrel, even asleep. In the end he climbed out of bed, slipping past Mama and Papa without either of them noticing, and went to The Place Between. He found a new valley there, leading to somewhere where there was some kind of circus going on. Nobody in that world spoke English, but Christopher got by quite well, as he had often done before, by pretending to be deaf and dumb.

When he came slipping back, the room was full of soberly-dressed people who were obviously just leaving. Christopher slipped past a stout, solemn young man in a tight collar, and a lady in a grey dress who was carrying a black leather instrument case. Neither of them knew he was there. By the look of things, the part of him left lying in the bed had just been examined by a specialist. As Christopher slipped round Mama and got back into bed, he realised that the specialist was just outside the door, with Papa and another man in a beard.

"I agree that you were right in the circumstances to call me in," Christopher heard an old, dry voice saying, "but there is only one life present, Mr Chant. I admit freakish things can happen, of course, but we have the report of the school magic teacher to back up our findings in this case. I am afraid I am not convinced at all…" The old, dry voice went away up the corridor, still talking, and the other people followed, all except Mama.

"What a relief!" Mama said. "Christopher, are you awake? I thought for a moment that that dreadful old man was going to get hold of you, and I would never have forgiven your papa! Never! I don't want you to grow up into a boring, law-abiding *policeman* sort of person, Christopher. Mama wants to be proud of you."

CHAPTER NINE

✳

Christopher went back to school the next day. He was rather afraid that Mama was going to be disappointed in him when he turned out to be a professional cricketer, but that did not alter his ambition in the least.

Everyone at school treated him as if he were a miracle. Oneir apologised, almost in tears. That was the only thing which made Christopher uncomfortable. Otherwise he basked in the attention he got. He insisted on playing cricket just as before, and he could hardly wait for next Thursday to come so that he could tell Tacroy all his adventures.

On Wednesday morning the Headmaster sent for

Christopher. To his surprise, Papa was there with the Head, both of them standing uneasily beside the Head's mahogany desk. "Well, Chant," the Head said, "we shall be sorry to lose our nine days' wonder so quickly. Your father has come to fetch you away. It seems you are to go to a private tutor instead."

"What? Leave school, sir?" Christopher said. "But it's cricket practice this afternoon, sir!"

"I have suggested to your father that you might remain at least until the end of term," the Head said, "but it seems that the great Dr Pawson will not agree to it."

Papa cleared his throat. "These Cambridge Dons," he said. "We both know what they are, Headmaster." He and the Head smiled at one another, rather falsely.

"Matron is packing you a bag now," said the Head. "In due course, your box and your school report will be sent after you. Now we must say goodbye, as I gather your train leaves in half an hour." He shook hands with Christopher, a brisk, hard, headmasterly shake, and Christopher was whisked away, there and then, in a cab with Papa, without even a chance to say goodbye to Oneir and Fenning.

He sat in the train seething about it, staring resentfully at Papa's whiskered profile.

"I was hoping to get into the school cricket team," he said pointedly, when Papa did not seem to be going to explain.

"Shame about that," Papa said, "but there will be other cricket teams no doubt. Your future is more important than cricket, my son."

"My future *is* cricket," Christopher said boldly. It was the first time he had come right out with his ambition to an adult. He went hot and cold at his daring in speaking like this to Papa. But he was glad too, because this was an important step on the road to his career.

Papa gave a melancholy smile. "There was a time when I myself wanted to be an engine driver," he said. "These whims pass. It was more important to get you to Dr Pawson before the end of term. Your mama was planning to take you abroad with her then."

Christopher's teeth clenched so tightly with anger that his toothbrace cut his lip. Cricket a whim indeed! "Why is it so important?"

"Dr Pawson is the most eminent Diviner in the country," said Papa. "I had to pull a few strings to get him to take you on at such short notice, but when I put the case to him, he himself said that it was urgent not to give de Witt time to forget about you. De Witt will revise his opinion of you when he finds you have a gift for magic after all."

"But I can't *do* magic," Christopher pointed out.

"And there must be some reason why not," said Papa. "On the face of it, your gifts should be enormous, since I am an enchanter, and so are both my brothers, while your mama – this I will grant her – is a highly gifted sorceress. And *her* brother, that wretched Argent fellow, is an enchanter too."

Christopher watched houses rushing past behind Papa's profile as the train streamed into the outskirts of London, while he tried to digest this. No one had told him about his heredity before. Still, he supposed there were duds born into the most wizardly families. He thought he must be a dud. So Papa was truly an enchanter? Christopher resentfully searched Papa for the signs of power and riches that went with an enchanter, and the signs did not seem to be there. Papa struck him as threadbare and mournful. The cuffs of his frock coat were worn and his hat looked dull and unprosperous. Even the black whiskers were thinner than Christopher remembered, with streaks of grey in them.

But the fact was, enchanter or not, Papa had snatched him out of school in the height of the cricket season, and from the way the Head had talked, he was not expected to go back. Why not? Why had Papa taken it into his head to do this to him?

Christopher brooded about this while the train drew into the Great Southern terminus and Papa towed him through the bustle to a cab. Galloping and rattling towards St Pancras Cross, he realised that it was going to be difficult even to see Tacroy and get some cricket coaching that way. Papa had told him to have nothing to do with Uncle Ralph, and Papa was an enchanter.

In the small sooty carriage of the train to Cambridge, Christopher asked resentfully, "Papa, what made you decide to take me to Dr Pawson?"

"I thought I had explained," Papa said. That, for a while seemed all he was going to say. Then he turned towards Christopher, sighing rather, and Christopher saw that he had just been gathering himself for a serious talk. "Last Friday," he said, "you were certified dead, my son, by two doctors and a number of other people. Yet when I arrived to identify your body on Saturday, you were alive and recovering and showing no signs of injury. This made me certain that you had more than one life – the more so as I suspect that this has happened once before. Tell me, Christopher, that time last year when they told me a curtain pole had fallen on you – you were mortally injured then, weren't you? You may confess to me. I shan't be angry."

"Yes," Christopher said reluctantly. "I suppose I was."

"I thought so!" Papa said with dismal satisfaction. "Now, my son, those people who are lucky enough to have several lives are always, invariably, highly gifted enchanters. It was clear to me last Saturday that you are one. This was why I sent for Gabriel de Witt. Now Monsignor de Witt—" Here Papa lowered his voice and looked nervously round the sooty carriage as if he thought Monsignor de Witt could hear "—is the strongest enchanter in the world. He has nine lives. Nine, Christopher. This makes him strong enough to control the practice of magic throughout this world and several others. The Government has given him that task. For this reason you will hear some people call him the Chrestomanci. The post bears that title."

"But," said Christopher, "what has all this and the kress toe mancy got to do with pulling me out of school?"

"Because I wish de Witt to take an interest in your case," said Papa. "I am a poor man now. I can do nothing for you. I have made considerable sacrifices to afford Dr Pawson's fee, because I think de Witt was wrong when he said you were a normal boy with only one life. My hope is that Dr Pawson can prove he was wrong and that de Witt can then be persuaded to take you on to his staff. If he does, your future is assured."

Take me on to his staff, Christopher thought. Like Oneir in his father's business having to start as an office boy. "I don't think," he said, "that I want my future assured like that."

His father looked at him sorrowfully. "There speaks your mama in you," he said. "Proper tuition should cure that sort of levity."

This did nothing to reconcile Christopher to Papa's plans. But I said that for *myself*! he thought angrily. It had nothing to *do* with Mama! He was still in a state of seething resentment when the train steamed into Cambridge, and he walked with Papa through streets full of young men in gowns like the coats people wore in Series Seven, past tall turreted buildings that reminded him of the Temple of Asheth, except that the Cambridge buildings had more windows. Papa had rented rooms in a lodging house, a dark, mingy place that smelt of old dinners.

"We shall be staying here together while Dr Pawson sorts you out," he told Christopher. "I have brought ample work with me, so that I can keep a personal eye on your wellbeing."

This about put the lid on Christopher's angry misery. He wondered if he dared go to The Place Between to meet

Tacroy on Thursday with a full grown enchanter keeping a careful eye on him. To crown it all, the lodging house bed was even worse than the beds at school and twanged every time he moved. He went to sleep thinking he was about as miserable as he could be. But that was before he saw Dr Pawson and realised his miseries had only just begun.

Papa delivered him to Dr Pawson's house in the Trumpington Road at ten the next morning. "Dr Pawson's learning gives him a disconcerting manner at times," Papa said, "but I know I can trust my son to bear himself with proper politeness notwithstanding."

This sounded ominous. Christopher's knees wobbled while the housemaid showed him into Dr Pawson's room. It was a bright, bright room stuffed full of clutter. A harsh voice shouted out of the clutter.

"Stop!"

Christopher stood where he was, bewildered.

"Not a step further. And keep your *knees* still, boy! Lord, how the young do fidget!" the harsh voice bellowed. "How am I to assess you if you won't stay still? Now, what do you say?"

The largest thing among the clutter was a fat armchair. Dr Pawson was sitting in it, not moving a muscle except for a quiver from his vast purple jowls. He was probably too fat to move. He was vastly, hugely, grossly fat. His belly was like a small mountain with a checked waistcoat stretched over it. His hands reminded Christopher of some purple bananas he had seen in Series Five. His face was stretched, and purple too, and out of it glared two merciless watery eyes.

"How do you do, sir?" Christopher said, since Papa trusted him to be polite.

"No, *no*!" shouted Dr Pawson. "This is an examination, not a social call. What's your problem – Chant your name is, isn't it? State your problem, Chant."

"I can't do magic, sir," Christopher said.

"So can't a lot of people. Some are born that way," Dr Pawson bawled. "Do better than that, Chant. Show me. Don't do some magic and let me see."

Christopher hesitated, out of bewilderment mostly.

"Go on, boy!" howled Dr Pawson. "Don't do it!"

"I can't not do something I can't do," Christopher said, thoroughly harassed.

"Of course you can!" yelled Dr Pawson. "That's the essence of magic. Get on with it. Mirror on the table beside you. Levitate it and be quick about it!"

If Dr Pawson hoped to startle Christopher into succeeding, he failed. Christopher stumbled to the table, looked into the elegant silver-framed mirror that was lying there, and went through the words and gestures he had learnt at school. Nothing at all happened.

"Hm," said Dr Pawson. "Don't do it again."

Christopher realised he was supposed to try once more. He tried, with shaking hands and voice, and exasperated misery growing inside him. This was hopeless! He hated Papa for dragging him off to be terrorised by this appalling fat man. He wanted to cry, and he had to remind himself, just as if he were his own Governess, that he was far too big for that. And, as before, the mirror simply lay where it was.

"Um," said Dr Pawson. "Turn round, Chant. No, *right* round boy, slowly, so that I can see all of you. Stop!"

Christopher stopped and stood and waited. Dr Pawson shut his watery eyes and lowered his purple chins. Christopher suspected he had gone to sleep. There was utter silence in the room except for clocks ticking among the clutter. Two clocks were the kind with all the works showing, one was a grandfather, and one was a mighty marble timepiece that looked as if it had come off someone's grave. Christopher nearly jumped out of his skin when Dr Pawson suddenly barked at him like the clap of doom.

"EMPTY YOUR POCKETS, CHANT!"

Eh? thought Christopher. But he did not dare disobey. He began hurriedly unloading the pockets of his Norfolk jacket: Uncle Ralph's sixpence which he always kept, a shilling of his own, a greyish handkerchief, a note from Oneir about algebra, and then he was down to shaming things like string and rubber bands and furry toffees. He hesitated.

"All of it!" yelled Dr Pawson. "Out of every single pocket. Put it all down on the table."

Christopher went on unloading: a chewed rubber, a bit of pencil, peas for Fenning's pea-shooter, a silver threepenny bit he had not known about, a cough drop, fluff, more fluff, string, a marble, an old pen nib, more rubber bands, more fluff, more string. And that was it.

Dr Pawson's eyes glared over him. "No, that's *not* all! What else have you got on you? Tie-pin. Get rid of that too."

Reluctantly Christopher unpinned the nice silver tie-pin Aunt Alice had given him for Christmas. And Dr Pawson's eyes continued to glare at him.

"Ah!" Dr Pawson said. "And that stupid thing you have on your teeth. That's got to go too. Get it out of your mouth and put it on the table. What the devil's it *for* anyway?"

"To stop my teeth growing crooked," Christopher said rather huffily. Much as he hated the toothbrace, he hated even more being criticised about it.

"What's wrong with crooked teeth?" howled Dr Pawson, and he bared his own teeth. Christopher rather started back from the sight. Dr Pawson's teeth were brown, and they lay higgledy-piggledy in all directions, like a fence trampled by cows. While Christopher was blinking at them, Dr Pawson bellowed, "Now do that levitation spell again!"

Christopher ground his teeth – which felt quite straight by contrast and very smooth without the brace – and turned to the mirror again. Once more he looked into it, once more said the words, and once more raised his arms aloft. And as his arms went up, he felt something come loose with them – come loose with a vengeance.

Everything in the room went upwards except Christopher, the mirror, the tie-pin, the toothbrace and the money. These slid to the floor as the table surged upwards, but were collected by the carpet which came billowing up after it. Christopher hastily stepped off the carpet and stood watching everything soar around him – all the clocks, several tables, chairs, rugs, pictures, vases, ornaments, and Dr Pawson too. He and his armchair both went up, majestically, like a balloon, and bumped against the ceiling. The ceiling bellied upwards and the chandelier plastered itself sideways against it. From above came crashing, shrieks, and an immense airy grinding. Christopher could feel that the roof of the house had come off and was on its way to the sky, pursued by the attics. It was an incredible feeling.

"STOP THAT!" Dr Pawson roared.

Christopher guiltily took his arms down.

Instantly everything began raining back to the ground again. The tables plunged, the carpets sank, vases, pictures and clocks crashed to the floor all round. Dr Pawson's armchair plummeted with the rest, followed by pieces of the chandelier, but Dr Pawson himself floated down smoothly, having clearly done some prudent magic of his own.

Up above, the roof came down thunderously. Christopher could hear tiles falling and chimneys crashing, as well as smashings and howls from upstairs. The upper floors seemed now to be trying to get through to the ground. The walls of the room buckled and oozed plaster, while the windows bent and fell to pieces. It was about five minutes before the slidings and smashings died away, and the dust settled even more slowly. Dr Pawson sat among the wreckage and the blowing dust and stared at Christopher.

Christopher stared back, very much wanting to laugh.

A little old lady suddenly materialised in the armchair opposite Dr Pawson's. She was wearing a white nightgown and a lacy cap over her white hair. She smiled at Christopher in a steely way. "So it was you, child," she said to Christopher. "Mary-Ellen is in hysterics. Don't *ever* do that again, or I'll put a Visitation on you. I'm still famed for my Visitations, you know." Having said this, she was gone as suddenly as she had come.

"My old mother," said Dr Pawson. "She's normally bedridden, but as you can see, she's very strongly moved. As is almost everything else." He sat and stared at Christopher a while longer, and Christopher went on struggling not to laugh. "Silver," Dr Pawson said at last.

"Silver?" asked Christopher.

"Silver," said Dr Pawson. "Silver's the thing that's stopping you, Chant. Don't ask me why at the moment. Maybe we'll never get to the bottom of it, but there's no question about the facts. If you want to work magic, you'll have to give up money except for coppers and sovereigns, throw away that tie-pin, and get rid of that stupid brace."

Christopher thought about Papa, about school, about cricket, in a flood of anger and frustration which gave him courage to say, "But I don't think I do want to work magic, sir."

"Yes you do, Chant," said Dr Pawson. "For at least the next month." And while Christopher was wondering how to contradict him without being too rude, Dr Pawson gave out another vast bellow. "YOU HAVE TO PUT EVERYTHING BACK, CHANT!"

And this is just what Christopher had to do. For the rest of the morning he went round the house, up to every floor and then outside into the garden, while Dr Pawson trundled beside him in his armchair and showed him how to cast holding-spells to stop the house falling down. Dr Pawson never seemed to leave that armchair. In all the time Christopher spent with him, he never saw Dr Pawson walk. Around midday, Dr Pawson sent his chair gliding into the kitchen, where a cook-maid was sitting dolefully in the midst of smashed butter crocks, spilt milk, bits of basin and dented saucepans, and dabbing at her eyes with her apron.

"Not hurt in here are you?" Dr Pawson barked. "I put a holder on first thing to make sure the range didn't burst and set the house on fire – that sort of thing. That held, didn't it? Water pipes secure?"

"Yes, sir," gulped the cook-maid. "But lunch is ruined, sir."

"We'll have to have a scratch lunch for once," said Dr Pawson. His chair swung round to face Christopher. "By this evening," he said, "this kitchen is going to be mended. Not holding-spells. Everything as new. I'll show you how. Can't have the kitchen out of action. It's the most important place in the house."

"I'm sure it is, sir," Christopher said, eyeing Dr Pawson's mountain of a stomach.

Dr Pawson glared at him. "I can dine in college," he said,

"but my mother needs her nourishment."

For the rest of that day Christopher mended the kitchen, putting crockery back together, recapturing spilt milk and cooking sherry, taking dents out of pans, and sealing a dangerous split at the back of the range. While he did, Dr Pawson sat in his armchair warming himself by the range fire and barking things like, "Now put the eggs together, Chant. You'll need the spell to raise them first, then the dirt-dispeller you used on the milk. *Then* you can start the mending-spell."

While Christopher laboured, the cook-maid, who was obviously even more frightened of Dr Pawson than Christopher was, edged round him trying to bake a cake and prepare the roast for supper.

One way and another, Christopher probably learnt more practical magic that day than he had in two and a half terms at school. By the evening he was exhausted. Dr Pawson barked, "You can go back to your father for now. Be here at nine tomorrow prompt. There's still the rest of the house to see to."

"Oh Lord!" Christopher groaned, too weary to be polite. "Can't someone help me at all? I've learnt my lesson."

"What gave you the idea there was only one lesson to learn?" bawled Dr Pawson.

Christopher tottered back to the lodging house carrying the toothbrace, the money and the tie-pin wrapped in the grey handkerchief. Papa looked up from a table spread with horoscope sheets. "Well?" he asked with gloomy eagerness.

Christopher fell into a lumpy chair. "Silver," he said. "Silver stops me working magic. And I hope I *have* got more than one life because Dr Pawson's going to kill me at this rate."

"Silver?" said Papa. "Oh dear! Oh dear, dear!" He was very sad and silent all through the cabbage soup and sausages the lodging house provided for supper. After supper he said, "My son, I have a confession to make. It is my fault that silver stops you working magic. Not only did I cast your horoscope when you were born, but I also cast every other spell I knew to divine your future. And you can imagine my horror when each kind of forecast foretold that silver would mean danger or death to you."

Papa paused, drumming his fingers on the horoscope sheets and staring absently at the wall. "Argent," he said musingly. "Argent means silver. Could I have got it wrong?" He pulled himself sadly back together. "Well it is too late to do anything about that, except to warn you again to have nothing to do with your Uncle Ralph."

"But why is it your fault?" Christopher asked, very uncomfortable at the way Papa's thoughts were going.

"There is no getting round Fate," Papa said, "as I should have known. I cast my strongest spells and put forth all my power to make silver neutral to you. Silver – any contact with silver – seems to transform you at once into an ordinary person without a magic gift at all – and I see now that this could have its dangers. I take it you *can* work magic when you are not touching silver?"

Christopher gave a weary laugh. "Oh yes. Like anything."

Papa brightened a little. "That's a relief. Then my sacrifice here was not in vain. As you may know, Christopher, I very foolishly lost your mama's money and my own by investing it where I thought my horoscopes told me to." He shook his head sadly. "Horoscopes are tricky, particularly with money. Be that as it may, I am finished. I regard myself as a failure. You are all I have left to live for, my son. Any success I am to know, I shall know through you."

If Christopher had not been so tired, he would have found this decidedly embarrassing. Even through his weariness, he found he was annoyed that he was expected to live for Papa and not on his own account. Would it be fair, he wondered, to use magic to make yourself a famous cricketer? You could make the ball go anywhere you wanted. Would Papa regard this as success? He knew perfectly well that Papa would not.

By this time, his eyes were closing themselves and his head was nodding. When Papa sent him off to bed, Christopher fell on to the twanging mattress and slept like a log. He had meant, honestly meant, to go to The Place Between and tell Tacroy all that had happened, but either he was just too tired or too scared that Papa would guess. Whatever the reason was, he did not have dreams of any kind that night.

CHAPTER TEN

✳

*F*or the next three weeks, Dr Pawson kept Christopher so hard at work mending the house that he fell into bed each night too weary to dream. Each morning when Christopher arrived, Dr Pawson was sitting in his armchair in the hall, waiting for him.

"To work, Chant!" he would bark.

Christopher took to replying, "Really, sir? I thought we were going to have a lazy day like yesterday."

The strange thing about Dr Pawson was that he did not mind this kind of remark in the least. Once Christopher got used to him, he discovered that Dr Pawson rather liked people to stand up to him, and once he had discovered that,

Christopher found that he did not really hate Dr Pawson – or only in the way you hate a violent thunderstorm you happen to be caught in. He found he quite liked rebuilding the house, though perhaps the thing which he really liked was working magic that actually did something.

Every spell he did had a real use. That made it far more interesting than the silly things he had tried to learn at school. And the hard work was much easier to bear when he was able to say things to Dr Pawson that would have caused masters at school to twist his ears and threaten to cane him for insolence.

"Chant!" Dr Pawson howled from his armchair in the middle of the lawn. "Chant! The chimney pots on the right are crooked."

Christopher was balanced on the tiles of the roof, shivering in the wind. It was raining that day, so he was having to maintain a shelter-spell for the roof and for the lawn while he worked. And he had put the chimneys straight four times already. "Yes, sir, of course, sir!" he screamed back. "Would you like them turned to gold too, sir?"

"None of that or I'll make you *do* it!" Dr Pawson yelled.

When Christopher came to mend Dr Pawson's mother's room, he made the mistake of trying to treat old Mrs Pawson the same way. She was sitting up in a bed heaped with plaster from the ceiling, looking quite comfortable and composed, knitting something striped and long. "I saved the looking-glass, child," she remarked with a pleasant smile, "but that is as far as my powers stretch. Be good enough to mend the chamber-pot first, and count yourself fortunate, child, that it had not been used. You will find it under the bed."

Christopher fished it out in three broken white pieces and got to work.

"Mend it quite straight," old Mrs Pawson said, her knitting needles clattering away. "Make sure the handle is not crooked and the gold rim round the top is quite regular. Please do not leave any uncomfortable lumps or unsightly bulges, child."

Her voice was gentle and pleasant and it kept interrupting the spell. At length Christopher asked in exasperation, "Would you like it studded with diamonds, too? Or shall I just give it a posy of roses in the bottom?"

"Thank you, child," said Mrs Pawson. "The posy of roses, please. I think that's a charming idea."

Dr Pawson, sitting by in his armchair, was full of glee at Christopher's discomfiture. "Sarcasm never pays, Chant," he bawled. "Roses require a creation-spell. Listen carefully."

After that, Christopher had to tackle the maids' rooms. Then he had to mend all the plumbing. Dr Pawson gave him a day off on Sundays so that Papa could take him to church. Christopher, now he knew what he could do, toyed with the idea of making the church spire melt like a candle, but he never quite dared to do it, with Papa pacing soberly beside him. Instead, he experimented in other ways.

Every morning, while he was walking up the Trumpington Road, he tried to coax the trees that lined it into a different pattern. He got so good at it that before long he could shunt them up the road in a long line and crowd them into a wood at the end.

In the evenings, tired though he was, he could not resist trying to make the lodging-house supper taste better. But food magic was not easy.

"What *do* they put in sausages these days?" Papa remarked. "These taste of strawberry."

Then came a morning when Dr Pawson shouted from his chair in the hall, "Right, Chant, from now on you finish the mending in the afternoons. In the mornings we teach you some control."

"Control?" Christopher said blankly. By this time the house was nearly finished and he was hoping that Dr Pawson would soon have finished with him too.

"That's right," Dr Pawson bawled. "You didn't think I'd let you loose on the world without teaching you to control your power, did you? As you are now, you're a menace to everyone. And don't tell me you haven't been trying to see what you can do, because I won't believe you."

Christopher looked at his feet and thought of what he had just been doing with the trees in the Trumpington Road. "I've hardly done anything, sir."

"Hardly anything! What do boys know of restraint?" said Dr Pawson. "Into the garden. We're going to raise a wind, and you're going to learn to do it without moving so much as a blade of grass."

They went into the garden, where Christopher raised a whirlwind. He thought it rather expressed his feelings.

Luckily it was quite small and only destroyed the rose bed. Dr Pawson cancelled it with one flap of his purple banana hand. "Do it again, Chant."

Learning control was boring, but it was a good deal more restful. Dr Pawson obviously knew this. He began setting Christopher homework to do in the evenings. All the same, even after disentangling the interlacing spells in the problems he had been set, Christopher began to feel for the first time that he had some brain left over to think with. He thought about silver first. Keeping Uncle Ralph's silver sixpence in his pocket had stopped him doing such a lot. And that beastly toothbrace had stopped him doing even more. What a waste! No wonder he had not been able to take the books to the Goddess until Matron made him take the brace out.

He must have been using magic to get to the Anywheres all these years without knowing it – except that he *had* known it, in an underneath sort of way. Tacroy had known, and he had been impressed. And the Goddess must have realised too, when her silver bracelet turned Christopher into a ghost. Here Christopher tried to go on thinking about the Goddess, but he found he kept thinking of Tacroy instead. Tacroy would now have gone into a trance uselessly for three weeks running. Tacroy made light of it, but Christopher suspected that going into a trance took a lot out of a person. He really would have to let Uncle Ralph know what had happened.

Glancing over at Papa, who was hard at work with a special pen marking special symbols on horoscopes under the big oil lamp, Christopher started writing a letter to Uncle Ralph, pretending it was part of his homework. The oil lamp cast shadows on Papa's face, removing the threadbare look and making him look unusually kind and stern. Christopher told himself uneasily that Papa and Uncle Ralph just did not like one another. Besides, Papa had not actually forbidden him to write to Uncle Ralph.

All the same, it took several nights to write the letter. Christopher did not want to seem disloyal to Papa. In the end, he simply wrote that Papa had taken him away from school to be taught by Dr Pawson. It was a lot of effort for such a short letter. He posted it next day on his way up the Trumpington Road with a sense of relief and virtue.

Three days later, Papa had a letter from Mama. Christopher could tell at once from Papa's face that Uncle Ralph had told Mama where they were. Papa threw the letter on the fire and fetched his hat. "Christopher," he said, "I shall be coming with you to Dr Pawson's today."

This made Christopher certain that Mama was in Cambridge too. As he walked up the Trumpington Road beside Papa, he tried to work out what his feelings were about that.

But he did not have much time to think. A strong wind, scented with roses, swept round the pair of them, hurling Christopher sideways and snatching Papa's hat from his head. Papa made a movement to chase his hat – which was just rolling under a brewer's dray – and then dived round and seized Christopher's arm instead.

"Hats are expendable," he said. "Keep walking, son."

They kept walking, with the wind hurling and buffeting round them. Christopher could actually feel it trying to curl around him in order to pull him away. But for Papa's grip on his arm, he would have been carried across the road. He was impressed. He had not known Mama's magic was this strong.

"I can control it if you want," he called to Papa above the noise. "Dr Pawson taught me wind control."

"No, Christopher," Papa panted sternly, looking strange and most undignified, with his coat flapping and his hair blowing in all directions. "A gentleman *never* works magic against a woman, particularly his own mama."

Gentlemen, it seemed to Christopher, made things unreasonably difficult for themselves in that case. The wind blew stronger and stronger, the nearer they got to the gate of Dr Pawson's house. Christopher thought they would never cover the last yard or so. Papa was forced to seize the gatepost to hold them both in place while he tried to undo the latch. Whereupon the wind made a last, savage snatch. Christopher felt his feet leave the ground, and knew he was about to soar away.

He made himself very heavy just in time. He did it because it was a contest, really, because he did not like being on the losing side. He would not at all have minded seeing Mama. But he very much hoped Papa would not notice the rather large dents his feet had made in the ground just outside the gate.

Inside the gate there was no more wind. Papa smoothed his hair and rang the doorbell.

"Aha!" shouted Dr Pawson from his armchair while Mary-Ellen was opening the door. "The expected trouble has come to pass, I see. Chant, oblige me by going upstairs and reading aloud to my mother while I talk to your father."

Christopher went up the stairs as slowly as he dared, hoping to hear what was being said. All he caught was Dr Pawson's voice, hardly shouting at all. "I've been in touch almost daily for a week, but they still can't—" After that the door shut.

Christopher went on up the stairs and knocked at the door of old Mrs Pawson's room.

She was sitting up in bed, still knitting. "Come and sit on that chair so that I can hear you," she said in her gentle voice, and gave him a gentle but piercing smile. "The Bible is here on the bedside table. You may start from the beginning of Genesis, child, and see how far you can get. I expect the negotiations will take time. Such things always do."

Christopher sat down and began to read. He was stumbling among the people who begat other people when Mary-Ellen came in with coffee and biscuits and gave him a welcome break. Ten minutes later, old Mrs Pawson took up her knitting and said, "Continue, child." Christopher had got well into Sodom and Gomorrah and was beginning to run out of voice, when old Mrs Pawson cocked her white head on one side and said, "Stop now, child. They want you downstairs in the study."

Much relieved and very curious, Christopher put the Bible down and shot to the ground floor. Papa and Dr Pawson were sitting facing one another in Dr Pawson's crowded room. It had become more cluttered than ever over the last weeks, since it was stacked with pieces of clocks and ornaments from all over the house, waiting for Christopher to mend. Now it looked more disorganised still. Tables and carpets had been pushed to the walls to leave a large stretch of bare floorboards, and a design had been chalked on the boards. Christopher looked at it with interest, wondering what it had to do with Mama. It was a five-pointed star inside a circle. He looked at Papa, who was obviously delighted about something, and then at Dr Pawson, who was just as usual.

"News for you, Chant," said Dr Pawson. "I've run a lot of tests on you these last weeks – don't stare, boy, you didn't know I was doing it – and every one of those tests gives you nine lives. Nine lives and some of the strongest magic I've met. Naturally I got in touch with Gabriel de Witt. I happen to know he's been looking for a successor for years. Naturally all I got was a lot of guff about the way they'd already tested you and drawn a blank. That's Civil Servants for you. They need a bomb under them before they'll change their minds. So today, after the bother with your mama had given me the excuse we needed, I had a good old shout at them. They caved in, Chant. They're sending a man to fetch you to Chrestomanci Castle now."

Here Papa broke in as if he could not stop himself. "It's just what I've been hoping for, my son! Gabriel de Witt is to become your legal guardian, and in due course you will be the next Chrestomanci."

"Next Chrestomanci?" Christopher echoed. He stared at Papa, knowing there was no chance of deciding on a career for himself now. It was all settled. His visions of himself as a famous cricketer faded and fell and turned to ashes. "But I don't want—"

Papa thought Christopher did not understand. "You will become a very important man," he said. "You will watch over all the magic in this world and prevent any harm being done with it."

"But—" Christopher began angrily.

It was too late. The misty shape of a person was forming inside the five-pointed star. It solidified into a pale plump young man with a long face, very soberly dressed in a grey suit and a wide starched collar that looked much too tight for him. He was carrying a thing like a telescope. Christopher remembered him. The young man was one of the people who had been in the hospital room after everyone had thought Christopher was dead.

"Good morning," the young man said, stepping out of the star. "My name is Flavian Temple. Monsignor de Witt has sent me to examine your candidate."

"EXAMINE HIM!" shouted Dr Pawson. "I've already *done* that! What do you people take me for?" He rolled his angry eyes at Papa. "Civil Servants!"

Flavian Temple obviously found Dr Pawson quite as alarming as Christopher did. He flinched a bit. "Yes, doctor, we know you have. But my instructions are to verify your findings before proceeding. If this lad could just step into the pentagram."

"Go on, son," said Papa. "Stand inside the star."

With a furious, helpless feeling, Christopher stepped into the chalked pattern and stood there while Flavian Temple sighted down the telescope-thing at him. There must be a way of making yourself look as if you only had one life, he thought. There *had* to be! But he had no idea what it was you did.

Flavian Temple frowned. "I can only make it seven lives."

"He's already lost TWO, you fat young fool!" Dr Pawson bellowed. "Didn't they tell you anything? Tell him, Chant."

"I've lost two lives already," Christopher found himself saying. There was some kind of spell on the pattern. Otherwise he would have denied everything.

"SEE?" howled Dr Pawson.

Flavian Temple managed to turn a wince into a polite bow. "I do see, doctor. That being the case, I will of course take the boy to be interviewed by Monsignor de Witt."

Christopher perked up at this. Perhaps it was not settled after all. But Papa seemed to think it was. He came and laid an arm round Christopher's shoulders. "Goodbye, my son. This makes me a very proud and happy man. Say goodbye to Dr Pawson."

Dr Pawson behaved as if it was settled too. His chair trundled forward and he held out a big purple banana finger to Christopher. "Bye, Chant. Take no notice of the official way they go on. This Flavian's a fool Civil Servant like the rest of them."

As Christopher shook the purple finger, old Mrs Pawson materialised, sitting on the arm of Dr Pawson's chair in her crisp white nightdress, holding her knitting wrapped into a stripy bundle. "Goodbye, child," she said. "You read very nicely. Here is a present I've knitted for you. It's full of protection spells." She leaned forwards and draped the knitting round Christopher's neck. It was a scarf about ten feet long, striped in the colours of the rainbow.

"Thank you," Christopher said politely.

"Just move up – er, Christopher – but don't leave the pentagram," said Flavian. He stepped back inside the chalk marks, taking up more than half the space, and took hold of Christopher's arm to keep him inside it. Old Mrs Pawson waved a withered hand. And without anything more being said, Christopher found himself somewhere quite different. It was even more disconcerting than being carried off from school by Papa.

He and Flavian were standing in a much bigger pentagram that was made of white bricks, or tiles, built into the floor of a lofty space with a glass dome high overhead. Under the glass dome, a majestic pink marble staircase curled up to the next floor. Stately panelled doors with statues over them opened off the space all round – the most stately had a clock above it as well as a statue – and an enormous crystal chandelier hung from the glass dome on a long chain. Behind Christopher, when he twisted round to look, was a very grand front door. He could see he was in the front hall of a very big mansion, but nobody thought to tell him where he was.

There were people standing round the tiled pentagram, waiting for them. And a stately, dismal lot they looked too! Christopher thought. All of them, men and women alike, were dressed in black or grey. The men wore shiny white collars and cuffs and the women all wore neat black lace mittens. Christopher felt their eyes on him, sizing up, disapproving, coldly staring. He shrank into a very small grubby boy under those eyes and realised that he had been wearing the same set of clothes ever since he had left school.

Before he had a chance to do more than look around, a man with a little pointed grey beard stepped up to him and took the striped scarf away. "He won't be needing this," he said, rather shocked about it.

Christopher thought the man was Gabriel de Witt and was all prepared to hate him, until Flavian said, "No, of course, Dr Simonson," apologising for Christopher. "The old lady gave it to him, you know. Shall I—?"

Christopher decided to hate the bearded man anyway.

One of the ladies, a small plump one, stepped forward then. "Thank you, Flavian," she said in a final, bossy sort of way. "I'll take Christopher to Gabriel now. Follow me, young man." She turned and went swishing off towards the pink marble stairs. Flavian gave Christopher a nudge, and Christopher stepped out of the tiled pattern and followed her, feeling about a foot high and dirty all over. He knew his collar was sticking up at one side, and that his shoes were dusty, and he could feel the hole in his left sock sliding out of its shoe and showing itself to everyone in the hall as he went upstairs after the lady.

At the top of the stairs was a very tall solid-looking door, the only one in a row of doors that was painted black. The lady swished up to the black door and knocked. She opened it and pushed Christopher firmly inside. "Here he is, Gabriel," she said. Then she shut the door behind him and went away, leaving Christopher alone in an oval-shaped room where it seemed to be twilight or sunset.

The room was panelled in dark brown wood, with a dark brown carpet on the floor. The only furniture seemed to be a huge dark desk. As Christopher came in, a long thin figure reared up from behind the desk – about six foot six of skinny old man, Christopher realised, when his heart stopped thumping. The old man had a lot of white hair and the whitest face and hands Christopher had ever seen. His eyebrows jutted and his cheeks stood out in wide peaks, making the eyes between them look sunken and staring. Below that was a hooked beak of nose. The rest of the old man's face went into a small, sharp point, containing a long, grim mouth.

The mouth opened to say, "I am Gabriel de Witt. So we meet again, Master Chant."

Christopher knew he would have remembered if he had ever seen this old man before. Gabriel de Witt was even more memorable than Dr Pawson. "I've never seen you in my life before," he said.

"I have met you. You were unconscious at the time," Gabriel de Witt said. "I suppose this accounts for our being so strangely mistaken in you. I can see now at a glance that you do indeed have seven lives and should have nine."

There were quite a lot of windows in the twilight room, Christopher saw, at least six, in a high curving row near the ceiling. The ceiling was a sort of orange, which seemed to keep all the light from the windows to itself. All the same, it was a mystery to Christopher how a room with quite so many windows could end up being so very dark.

"In spite of this," Gabriel de Witt said, "I am very dubious about taking you on. Your heredity frankly appals me. The Chants give themselves out as a race of respectable enchanters, but they produce a black sheep every generation, while the Argents, though admittedly gifted, are the kind of people I would not nod to in the street. These traits have come out in both your parents. I gather your father is bankrupt and your mother a contemptible social climber."

Even Cousin Francis had not said anything quite as bald as this. Anger flared through Christopher. "Oh thank you, sir," he said. "There's nothing I like more than a polite warm welcome like that."

The old man's eagle eyes stared. He seemed puzzled. "I felt it only fair to be frank with you," he said. "I wished you to understand that I have agreed to become your legal guardian because we do not consider either of your parents a fit person to have charge of the future Chrestomanci."

"Yes, sir," said Christopher, angrier than ever. "But you needn't bother. I don't want to be the next Chrestomanci. I'd rather lose all my lives first."

Gabriel de Witt simply looked impatient. "Yes, yes, this is often the way, until we realise the job needs doing," he said. "I refused the post myself when it was first offered to me, but I was in my twenties and you are a mere child, even less capable of deciding than I was. Besides, we have no choice in the matter. You and I are the only nine-lifed enchanters in all the Related Worlds."

He made a gesture with one white hand. A small bell chimed somewhere and the plump young lady swished into the room. "Miss Rosalie here is my chief assistant," Gabriel de Witt said. "She will show you to your room and get you settled in. I have allotted Flavian Temple to you as a tutor, though I can ill spare him, and I will of course be teaching you myself twice a week as well."

Christopher followed Miss Rosalie's swishing skirt past the line of doors and down a long corridor. Nobody seemed to care what he felt. He wondered whether to show them by raising another whirlwind. But there was a spell on this place, a strong, thick spell. After Dr Pawson's teaching Christopher was sensitive to all spells, and though he was not sure what this one did, he was fairly sure it would make things like whirlwinds pretty useless. "Is this Chrestomanci Castle?" he asked angrily.

"That's right," Miss Rosalie said. "The Government took it over two hundred years ago after the last really wicked enchanter was beheaded." She turned to smile at him over her shoulder. "Gabriel de Witt's a dear, isn't he? I know he seems a bit dry at first, but he's adorable when you get to know him."

Christopher stared. *Dear* and *adorable* seemed to him the last words he would ever use to describe Gabriel de Witt.

Miss Rosalie did not see him stare. She was throwing open a door at the end of the corridor. "There," she said, rather proudly. "I hope you like it. We're not used to having children here, so we've all been racking our brains over how to make you feel at home."

There was not much sign of it, Christopher thought, staring round a large brown room with one high white bed looking rather lonely in one corner. "Thanks," he said glumly.

When Miss Rosalie left him, he found there was a brown spartan washroom at the other end of the room and a shelf by the window. There was a teddy bear on the shelf, a game of Snakes and Ladders and a copy of *The Arabian Nights* with all the dirty bits taken out. He put them in a heap on the floor and jumped on them. He knew he was going to hate Chrestomanci Castle.

CHAPTER ELEVEN

✻

*F*or the first week, Christopher could think of nothing else but how much he hated Chrestomanci Castle and the people in it. It seemed to combine the worst things about school and home, with a few special awfulnesses of its own. It was very grand and very big, and except when he was doing lessons, Christopher was forced to wander about entirely on his own, missing Oneir and Fenning and the other boys and cricket acutely, while the Castle people got on with their grown-up affairs as if Christopher was not there at all. He had nearly all his meals alone in the schoolroom, just like home, except that the schoolroom looked out on to the empty, shaven Castle lawns.

"We thought you'd be happier not having to listen to our grown-up talk," Miss Rosalie told him as they walked up the long drive from church on Sunday. "But of course you'll have Sunday lunch with us."

So Christopher sat at the long table with everyone else in their sober Sunday clothes and thought it would have made no difference if he hadn't been there. Voices hummed among the chinking cutlery, and not one of them spoke to him.

"And you have to add copper to sublimate, whatever the manuals say," the bearded Dr Simonson was telling Flavian Temple, "but after that you can, I find, put it straight to the pentacle with a modicum of fire."

"The Wraith's illegal dragon's blood is simply flooding the market now," said a young lady across the table. "Even the honest suppliers are not reporting it. They know they can evade taxes."

"But the correct words present problems," Dr Simonson told Flavian.

"I know statistics are misleading," said a younger man beside Christopher, "but my latest sample had twice the legal limit of poison balm. You only have to extrapolate to see how much the gang is bringing in."

"The flaming tincture *must* then be passed through gold," Dr Simonson proclaimed, and another voice cut across his saying, "That magic mushroom essence certainly came from Ten, but I think the trap we set there stopped that outlet." While Dr Simonson added, "If you wish to proceed without copper, you'll find it far more complicated."

Miss Rosalie's voice rang through his explanation from the other end of the table. "But Gabriel, they had actually butchered a whole tribe of mermaids! I know it's partly our wizards' fault for being willing to pay the earth for mermaid parts, but the Wraith really has to be stopped!"

Gabriel's dry voice answered in the distance, "That part of the operation has been closed down. It's the weapons coming in from One that present the biggest problem."

"My advice is that you then start with pentacle and fire," Dr Simonson droned on, "using the simpler form of words to start the process, but…"

Christopher sat silent, thinking that if he did get to be the next Chrestomanci he would forbid people to talk about their work at meal-times. Ever. He was glad when he was allowed to get up from the table and go. But when he did, the only thing to do was to wander about, feeling all the spells on the place itching at him like gnat bites. There were spells in the formal gardens to keep weeds down and encourage worms, spells to keep the giant cedars on the lawns healthy, and spells all round the grounds to keep intruders out. Christopher thought he could have broken that set quite easily and simply run away, except that the sensitivity he had learnt from Dr Pawson showed him that breaking that boundary spell would set alarms ringing in the lodge at the gate and probably all over the Castle too.

The Castle itself had an old crusty part with turrets, and a newer part, which were fused together into a rambling whole. But there was an extra piece of castle that stood out in the gardens and looked even older, so old that there were trees growing on top of its broken walls.

Christopher naturally wanted to explore this part, but there was a strong misdirection spell on it, which caused it to appear behind him, or to one side, whenever he tried to get to it.

So he gave up and wandered indoors, where the spells, instead of itching, pressed down on him like a weight. He hated the Castle spells most of all. They would not allow him to be as angry as he felt. They made everything blunt and muffled. In order to express his hatred, Christopher fell back more and more on silent scorn. When people did speak to him, and he had to answer, he was as sarcastic as he knew how to be.

This did not help him get on with Flavian Temple. Flavian was a kind and earnest tutor. In the ordinary way, Christopher would have quite liked him, even though Flavian wore his collars too tight and tried far too hard to be hushed and dignified like the rest of Gabriel de Witt's people. But he hated Flavian for being one of those people – and he very soon discovered that Flavian had no sense of humour at all.

"You wouldn't see a joke if it jumped up and hit you, would you?" Christopher said, the second afternoon. Afternoons were always devoted to magic theory or magic practical.

"Oh, I don't know," Flavian said. "Something in *Punch*

157

made me smile last week. Now, to get back to what we were saying – how many worlds do you think make up the Related Worlds?"

"Twelve," said Christopher, because he remembered that Tacroy sometimes called the Anywheres the Related Worlds.

"Very good!" said Flavian. "Though, actually, there are more than that, because each world is really a set of worlds, which we call a Series. The only one which is just a single world is Eleven, but we needn't bother with that. All the worlds were probably one world to begin with – and then something happened back in prehistory which could have ended in two contradictory ways. Let's say a continent blew up. Or it didn't blow up. The two things couldn't both be true at once in the same world, so that world became two worlds, side by side but quite separate, one with that continent and one without. And so on, until there were twelve."

Christopher listened to this with some interest, because he had always wondered how the Anywheres had come about. "And did the Series happen the same way?" he asked.

"Yes indeed," said Flavian, obviously thinking Christopher was a very good pupil. "Take Series Seven, which is a mountain Series. In prehistory, the earth's crust must have buckled many more times than it did here. Or Series Five, where all the land became islands, none of them larger than France. Now these are the same right across the Series, but the course of history in each world is different. It's history that makes the differences. The easiest example is our own

158

Series, Twelve, where our world, which we call World A, is orientated on magic – which is normal for most worlds. But the next world, World B, split off in the Fourteenth Century and turned to science and machinery. The world beyond that, World C, split off in Roman times and became divided into large empires. And it went on like that up to nine. There are usually nine to a Series."

"Why are they numbered back to front?" Christopher asked.

"Because we *think* One was the original world of the twelve," Flavian said. "Anyway it was the great Mages of One who first discovered the other worlds, and they did the numbering."

This was a much better explanation than the one Tacroy had given. Christopher felt obliged to Flavian for it. So that when Flavian asked, "Now what do you think makes us call these twelve the Related Worlds?" Christopher felt he owed him an answer.

"They all speak the same languages," he said.

"*Very* good!" said Flavian. His pale face went pink with surprise and pleasure. "You *are* a good pupil!"

"Oh, I'm absolutely brilliant," Christopher said bitterly.

Unfortunately, when Flavian turned to practical magic on alternate afternoons, Christopher was anything but brilliant. With Dr Pawson he had become used to spells that really did something. But with Flavian he went back to small elementary magics of the kind he had been doing at school. They bored Christopher stiff. He yawned and he spilt things and usually, keeping a special vague look on his face so that Flavian would not notice what he was doing, he made the spells work without going through more than half the steps.

"Oh, no," Flavian said anxiously, when he did notice. "That's enchanter's magic. We'll be starting on that in a couple of weeks. But you have to know basic witchcraft first. It's most important for you to know whether a witch or wizard is misusing the craft when you come to be the next Chrestomanci."

That was the trouble with Flavian. He was always saying, "When you come to be the next Chrestomanci." Christopher felt bitterly angry.

"Is Gabriel de Witt going to die soon?" he said.

"I don't imagine so. He still has eight lives left," said Flavian. "Why do you ask?"

"It was a whim," Christopher said, thinking angrily of Papa.

"Oh dear," Flavian said, worrying because he was failing to keep his pupil interested. "I know – we'll go out into the gardens and study the properties of herbs. You may like that part of witchcraft better."

Down into the gardens they went, into a raw grey day. It was one of those summers that was more like winter than many winters are. Flavian stopped under a huge cedar and invited Christopher to consider the ancient lore about cedarwood. Christopher was in fact quite interested to hear that cedar was part of the funeral pyre from which the Phoenix was reborn, but he was not going to let Flavian see he was.

As Flavian talked, his eye fell on the separate ruined piece of castle, and he knew that if he asked about that Flavian would only tell him that they would be doing misdirection spells next month – which put another thing he wanted to know into his mind. "When am I going to learn how to fasten a person's feet to the spot?" he asked.

Flavian gave him a sideways look. "We won't be doing magic that affects other people until next year," he said. "Come over to the laurel bushes now and let's consider those."

Christopher sighed as he followed Flavian over to the big laurels by the drive. He might have known Flavian was not going to teach him anything useful! As they approached the nearest bush, a ginger cat emerged from among the shiny leaves, stretching and glaring irritably. When it saw Flavian and Christopher, it advanced on them at a trot, purpose all over its savage, lop-eared face.

"Look out!" Flavian said urgently.

Christopher did not need telling. He knew what this particular cat could do. But he was so astonished at seeing Throgmorten here at Chrestomanci Castle that he forgot to move. "Who – whose cat is that?" he said.

Throgmorten recognised Christopher too. His tail went up, thinner and more snaky than ever, and he stopped and stared. "Wong?" he said incredulously. And he advanced again, but in a much more stately way, like a Prime Minister greeting a foreign President. "Wong," he said.

"Careful!" said Flavian, prudently backing behind Christopher. "It's an Asheth Temple cat. It's safest not to go near it."

Christopher of course knew that, but Throgmorten was so evidently meaning to be polite that he risked squatting down and cautiously holding out his hand. "Yes, wong to you too," he said. Throgmorten put forward his moth-eaten-looking orange nose and dabbed at Christopher's hand with it.

"Great heavens! The thing actually likes you!" said Flavian. "Nobody else dares get within yards of it. Gabriel's had to give all the outdoor staff special shielding spells or they said they'd leave. It tears strips off people through ordinary spells."

"How did it get here?" Christopher said, letting Throgmorten politely investigate his hand.

"Nobody knows – at least how it wandered in here from Series Ten," Flavian said. "Mordecai found it in London, brave man, and brought it here in a basket. He recognised it by its aura, and he said if *he* could, then most wizards would too and they'd kill it for its magical properties. Most of us think that wouldn't be much loss, but Gabriel agreed with Mordecai."

Christopher had still not learnt the names of all the sober-suited men round the Sunday lunch-table. "Which one is Mr Mordecai?" he said.

"Mordecai Roberts – he's a particular friend of mine, but

you won't have met him yet," said Flavian. "He works for us in London these days. Perhaps we could get on with herb lore now."

At that moment, a strange noise broke from Throgmorten's throat, a sound like wooden cogwheels not connecting very well. Throgmorten was purring. Christopher was unexpectedly touched. "Does he have a name?" he asked.

"Most people just call him That Thing," said Flavian.

"I shall call him Throgmorten," said Christopher, at which Throgmorten's cogwheels went round more noisily than ever.

"It suits him," said Flavian. "Now, please – consider this laurel."

With Throgmorten sauntering amiably beside him, Christopher heard all about laurels and found it all much easier to take. It amused him the way Flavian took care to keep well out of reach of Throgmorten.

From then on, in a stand-offish way, Throgmorten became Christopher's only friend in the Castle. They both seemed to have the same opinion of the people in it. Christopher once saw Throgmorten encounter Gabriel de Witt coming down the pink marble stairs. Throgmorten spat and flew at Gabriel's long thin legs, and Christopher was charmed and delighted at the speed with which those long thin legs raced up the stairs again to get away.

Christopher hated Gabriel more every time he had a lesson with him. He decided that the reason Gabriel's room always seemed so dark in spite of all its windows was because it reflected Gabriel's personality.

Gabriel never laughed. He had no patience with slowness, or mistakes, and he seemed to think Christopher ought to know everything he taught him at once, by instinct.

The trouble was that, the first week, when Flavian and Gabriel were teaching him about the Related Worlds, Christopher *had* known all about them, from the Anywheres, and this seemed to have given Gabriel the idea that Christopher was a good learner. But after that, they went on to the different kinds of magics, and Christopher just could not seem to get it through his head why witchcraft and enchanters' magic were not the same, or how wizardry differed from sorcery and both from magicians' magic.

It was always a great relief to Christopher when his lesson with Gabriel was over. Afterwards, Christopher usually sneaked Throgmorten indoors and the two of them explored the Castle together. Throgmorten was not allowed inside the Castle, which was why Christopher liked to have him there.

Once or twice, with luck and cunning from both of them, Throgmorten spent the night on the end of Christopher's bed, purring like a football rattle. But Miss Rosalie had a way of knowing where Throgmorten was. She nearly always arrived wearing gardening gloves and chased Throgmorten out with a besom. Luckily Miss Rosalie was often busy straight after lessons, so Throgmorten galloped beside

Christopher down the long corridors and through the rambling attics, thrusting his face into odd corners and remarking "Wong!" from time to time.

The Castle was huge. The weighty, baffling spells hung heavily over most of it, but there were parts that nobody used, where the spells seemed to have worn thin. Christopher and Throgmorten were both happiest in those parts. The third week, they discovered a big round room in a tower, which looked to have been a wizard's workshop at one time. It had shelves round the walls, three long work-benches, and a pentagram painted on the stone floor. But it was deserted and dusty and stuffy with the smell of old, old magic.

"Wong," Throgmorten said happily.

"Yes," Christopher agreed. It seemed a waste of a good room. When I'm the next Chrestomanci, he thought, I shall make sure this room is used. Then he was angry with himself, because he was not going to *be* the next Chrestomanci. He had caught the habit from Flavian.

But I could make this a secret workshop of my own, he thought. I could sneak stuff up here bit by bit.

The next day, he and Throgmorten went exploring for a new attic where there might be things Christopher could use to furnish the tower room. And they discovered a second tower up a second, smaller winding stair. The spells were worn away almost entirely here, because this tower was ruinous. It was smaller than the other tower room and half its roof was missing. Half the floor was wet with that afternoon's rain. Beyond that there was what had once been a mullioned window. It was now a slope of wet rubbly wall with one stone pillar standing out of it.

"Wong, wong!" Throgmorten uttered approvingly. He went trotting over the wet floor and jumped up on to the broken wall.

Christopher followed him eagerly. They both climbed out on to the slope of rubble beyond what was left of the window and looked down at the smooth lawn and the tops of the cedar trees. Christopher caught a glimpse of the separate piece of castle with the misdirection spell on it. It was almost out of sight beyond the knobbly stonework of the tower, but he thought he should be high enough to see into it over the trees growing on top of it. Holding on to the pillar that had been part of the window, he stepped further out on the broken slope and leaned right out to see.

The pillar snapped in half.

Christopher's feet shot forward on the slippery stones. He felt himself plunge through the air and saw the cedars rushing past upside down. Bother! he thought. Another life! He remembered that the ground stopped him with a terrible jolt. And he had a vague notion that Throgmorten somehow followed him down and then proceeded to make an appalling noise.

CHAPTER TWELVE

✳

*T*hey said he had broken his neck this time. Miss Rosalie told him that the spells on the Castle should have stopped his falling, or at least alerted people when he did fall. But as the spells were worn out there, it had been Throgmorten's howls that had fetched a horrified gardener. Because of this, Throgmorten was respectfully allowed to spend that night on the end of Christopher's bed, until the maids complained of the smell in the morning. Then Miss Rosalie appeared with her gardening gloves and her broom and chased Throgmorten out.

Christopher thought resentfully that there was very little difference between the way the Castle people treated

Throgmorten and the way they treated him. The bearded Dr Simonson, when he was not instructing everyone how to put tinctures to fire, turned out to be a medical magician. He came the following morning and, in an off-handed disapproving way, examined Christopher's neck.

"As I thought," he said. "Now the new life has taken over there is no sign of the break. Better stay in bed today because of the shock. Gabriel is going to want to talk to you about this escapade."

Then he went away and nobody else came near Christopher apart from maids with trays, except Flavian, who came and stood in the doorway sniffing cautiously at the strong odour Throgmorten had left in the room.

"It's all right," Christopher said. "Miss Rosalie's just chased him out."

"Good," said Flavian and he came over to Christopher's bed carrying a big armful of books.

"Oh wonderful!" Christopher said, eyeing the armful. "Lots of lovely work. I've been lying here itching to get on with some algebra!"

Flavian looked a little injured. "Well, no," he said. "These are things from the Castle library that I thought you might like." And he went away.

Christopher looked through the books and found they were stories from different parts of the world. Some were from different worlds. All of them looked pretty good. Christopher had not realised there was anything worth reading in the Castle library before and, as he settled down to read, he decided he would go and have a look for himself tomorrow.

But the smell of Throgmorten interrupted him. The combination of the smell and the books kept reminding him of the Goddess, and he kept remembering that he still had not paid for the hundredth part of Throgmorten. It took him quite an effort to forget about Series Ten and concentrate on his book, and as soon as he did, Miss Rosalie came in, flushed and breathless from a long pursuit of Throgmorten, and interrupted him again.

"Gabriel wants to see you about that fall," she said. "You're to go to his office at nine o'clock tomorrow." As she turned to go, she said, "I see you've got some books. Is there anything else I can get you? Games? You've got Snakes and Ladders, haven't you?"

"It takes two to play that," Christopher told her pointedly.

"Oh dear," Miss Rosalie said. "I'm afraid I don't know much about games." Then she went away again.

Christopher laid his book down and stared round his brown empty room, hating the Castle and all the people in it quite passionately. The room now had his school trunk in one corner, which made it seem emptier than ever by reminding him of all the company he was missing at school. There was an ideal corner for getting to the Anywheres between the trunk and the bare fireplace. He wished he could run away to somewhere where even magic could not find him, and never come back.

Then he realised that he *could* get away, after a fashion, by going to an Anywhere. He wondered why he had not tried all the time he had been at the Castle. He put it down to the Castle spells. They muffled your mind so. But now, either the shock of breaking his neck, or the new life he could feel sturdily and healthily inside him, or both, had started him thinking again. Perhaps he could go to an Anywhere and stay there for good.

The trouble was, when he went to the Anywheres, he seemed to have to leave a piece of himself behind in bed. But it *must* be possible to take the whole of yourself. From the things Flavian and Gabriel had said when they talked about the Related Worlds, Christopher was sure that some people did go to worlds in the other Series. He would just have to wait and learn how it was done. Meanwhile, there was nothing to stop him looking round for a suitable Anywhere to escape to.

Christopher read his books innocently until the maid came and turned out his gaslight for the night. Then he lay staring into the dark, trying to detach the part of himself that could go to the Anywheres. For quite a while, he could not do it. The Castle spells lay heavy on him, squashing all the parts of him into a whole. Then, as he got sleepier, he realised the way, and slipped out sideways from himself and went padding round the corner between the trunk and the fireplace.

There, it was like walking into a sheet of thick rubber that bounced him back into the room. The Castle spells again.

Christopher set his teeth, turned his shoulder into the rubberiness, and pushed. And pushed, and pushed, and walked forward a little with each push, but quietly and gently, not to alert anyone in the Castle – until, after about half an hour, he had the spell stretched as thin as it would go. Then he took a pinch of it in each hand and tore it gently apart.

It was wonderful to walk out through the split he had made, into the valley, and find his clothes still lying there, a little damp and too small again, but *there*. He put them on. Then, instead of going into The Place Between, he set off the other way, down the valley. It stood to reason that the valley led to one of the other worlds in Series Twelve. Christopher hoped it would be World B. One of his cunning ideas had been to hide quite near in the non-magical world, where he was sure no one, even Gabriel de Witt, would think of looking.

Probably it was World B, but he only stayed there half a minute. When he got to the end of the valley it was raining, pouring – souping down steadily sideways. Christopher found himself in a city full of rushing machines, speeding all round him on wheels that hissed on the wet black road. A loud noise made him look round just in time to see a huge red machine charging down on him out of the white curtain of rain. He saw a number on it and the words TUFNELL PARK, and sheets of water flew over him as he got frantically out of its way.

Christopher escaped up the valley again, soaking wet.

World B was the worst Anywhere he had ever been in. But he still had his other cunning idea, and that was to go to World Eleven, the world nobody ever went to. He went up the valley and round the jutting rock into The Place Between.

The Place was so desolate, so shapeless and so empty, that if he had not just been somewhere even more terrible he might have turned back. As it was, Christopher felt the same lonely horror he had felt the first time he had gone to The Place Between from school. But he ignored it and set off resolutely in the direction of the Anywhere that did not want you to get to it. He was sure now that this must be Eleven.

The way was across the mouth of his own valley, down, and then up a cliff of sheer slippery rock. Christopher had to cling with fingers and toes that were already cold and wet from World B. The Anywhere above kept pushing him away and the wind sweeping across reminded him of Mama's attack in Cambridge. Up, cling. Feel for a foothold. Then a handhold. Cling. Up.

Half-way up his foot slipped. A new gust of wind made his cold fingers too weak to hang on, and he fell.

He pitched down further than he had climbed up, upside down on to the back of his head. When he got to his knees, things in his neck grated and his head wobbled about. He felt very queer.

Somehow he made it back to the jutting crag, helped by the way The Place Between always pushed him back where he came from. Somehow he put his pyjamas on again and got through the slit in the Castle spells, back into bed. He fell asleep with a strong suspicion that he had broken his neck again. Good, he thought. Now I won't have to go and see Gabriel de Witt in the morning.

But there was nothing at all wrong with him when he woke up. Christopher would have been very puzzled had he not been dreading seeing Gabriel. He crawled along to breakfast and found there was a pretty, scented letter from Mama on his tray. Christopher picked it up eagerly, hoping it would take his mind off Gabriel. And it did not, or not straight away. He could tell it had been opened and then stuck down again. He could feel the spell still hanging about it. Hating the people in the Castle more than ever, he unfolded the letter.

Dear Christopher,

The laws are so unjust. Only your Papa's signature was required to sell you into slavery with that dreadful old man, and I have still not forgiven your Papa. Your uncle sends his sympathies and hopes to hear from you by next Thursday. Be polite to him, dear.

Your affectionate
Mama

Christopher was very pleased to think that Gabriel had read himself being called 'that dreadful old man' and he was impressed at the cunning way Uncle Ralph had sent his message through Mama. As he ate his breakfast, he rejoiced at the thought of seeing Tacroy again next Thursday. What a lucky thing he had made that split in the Castle spells! And 'slavery' was the right word for it, he thought, as he got up to go to Gabriel's office.

But on the way, he found himself thinking of the Goddess again, very guiltily this time. He really would have to take her some more books. Throgmorten was a cat worth paying for.

In his twilight room, Gabriel stood up behind his great black desk. That was a bad sign, but Christopher now had so many other things to think of that he was not as scared as he might have been. "Really, Christopher," Gabriel said in his driest voice, "a boy your age should know better than to climb about in a ruined tower. The result is that you have foolishly and carelessly wasted a life and now have only six left. You will need those lives when you are the next Chrestomanci. What have you to say for yourself?"

Christopher's anger rose. He felt it being pushed down again by the Castle spells, and that made him angrier than ever. "Why don't you make Throgmorten the next Chrestomanci?" he said. "He's got nine lives too."

Gabriel stared at him a second. "This is not a matter for jokes," he said. "Do you not realise the trouble you have caused? Some of my staff will have to go to the towers, and to the attics and cellars, in case you take it into your head to climb about there too, and it will take them days to make it all safe." At this, Christopher thought ruefully that they would certainly find and mend the split he had made and he would have to make another. "Please attend," said Gabriel. "I can ill spare any of my staff at this time. You are too young to be aware of this, but I wish to explain that we are all working full stretch just now in an effort to catch a gang of interworld villains." He looked at Christopher fiercely. "You have probably never heard of the Wraith."

After three boring Sunday lunches, Christopher felt he knew all about the Wraith. It was what everyone talked of all the time. But he sensed that Gabriel was quite likely to get side-tracked from telling him off if he went on explaining about the gang, so he said, "No, I haven't, sir."

"The Wraith is a gang of smugglers," Gabriel said. "We know they operate through London, but that is about all we know, for they are slippery as eels. In some way, despite all our traps and watchfulness, they smuggle in illicit magical produce by the hundredweight from all over the Related Worlds. They have brought in cartloads of dragons' blood, narcotic dew, magic mushrooms, eel livers from Series Two, poison balm from Six, dream juice from Nine and eternal fire from Ten. We set a trap in Ten, which took out at least one of their operatives, but that did not stop them. The only success we have had is in Series Five, where the Wraith was butchering mermaids and selling the parts in London. There we were helped by the local police and were able to put a stop to it. But — " By this time, Gabriel had his eyes fixed on the sunset light of his ceiling and seemed lost in his worries. "But this year," he said, "we have had reports of the most appalling weapons that the Wraith is bringing in from Series One, each one capable of destroying the strongest enchanter, and we still cannot lay hands on the gang." Here, to Christopher's dismay, Gabriel turned his eyes down to him. "You see what mischief your careless climbing could do? While we rush round the Castle on your account, we could miss our one chance of catching this gang. You should learn to think of others, Christopher."

"I do," Christopher said bitterly, "but none of you think of me. When most people die, they don't get told off for it."

"Go down to the library," said Gabriel, "and write one hundred times 'I must look before I leap'. And kindly shut the door when you leave."

Christopher went to the door and opened it, but he did not shut it. He left it swinging so that Gabriel would hear what he said as he went towards the pink marble staircase. "I must be the only person in the *world*," he called out, "*ever* to be punished for breaking my neck!"

"Wong," agreed Throgmorten, who was waiting for him on the landing.

Christopher did not see Throgmorten in time. He tripped over him and went crashing and sliding the whole way down the staircase. As he went, he could hear Throgmorten wailing again. Oh *no*! he thought.

When his next life took over, he was lying on his back near the pentacle in the hall, looking up into the glass dome. Almost the first thing he saw was the clock over the library, which said half past nine. It seemed as if every time he lost a

176

life, the new one took over more quickly and easily than the last. The next thing he saw was everyone in the Castle, standing round him staring solemnly. Just like a funeral! he thought.

"Did I break my neck again?" he asked.

"You did," said Gabriel de Witt, stepping up to lean over him. "Really, after what I had just said to you, it is too bad! Can you get up?"

Christopher turned over and got to his knees. He felt slightly bruised but otherwise all right. Dr Simonson strode over and felt his neck. "The fracture has vanished already," he said. Christopher could tell from his manner that he was not going to be allowed to stay in bed this time.

"Very well," said Gabriel. "Go to the library now, Christopher, and write the lines I gave you. In addition write one hundred times 'I have only five lives remaining'. That might teach you prudence."

Christopher limped to the library and wrote the lines at one of the red leather tables on paper headed *Government Property*. As he wrote, his mind was elsewhere, thinking how odd it was that Throgmorten always seemed to be there when he lost a life. And there was that time in Series Ten. Just before the hook hit him, a man had mentioned Asheth. Christopher began to be afraid he might be under a curse from Asheth. It made another very good reason for taking the Goddess some more books.

When the lines were done, Christopher got up and inspected the bookshelves. The library was large and lofty and seemed to contain thousands of books. But Christopher discovered that there were really ten times as many as the ones you saw. There was a spell-plate at the end of each shelf. When Christopher put his hand on one, the books at the right of the shelf moved up and vanished and new books appeared on the left. Christopher found the storybook section and stood with his hand on the plate, keeping the line of books slowly moving until he found the kind he wanted.

It was a long row of fat books by someone called Angela Brazil. Most of them had *School* in the title. Christopher knew at a glance they were just right for the Goddess. He took three and spread the others out. Each of them was labelled *Rare Book: Imported from World XIIB*, which made Christopher hope that they might just be valuable enough to pay for Throgmorten at last.

He carried the books up to his room in a pile of others he thought he might like to read himself, and it seemed just his luck that he had to meet Flavian in the corridor. "Lessons as usual this afternoon," Flavian said cheerfully. "Dr Simonson doesn't seem to think they'll harm you."

"Slavery as usual!" Christopher muttered as he went into his room.

But in fact that afternoon was not so bad. In the middle of practical magic, Flavian said suddenly, "Are you interested in cricket at all?"

What a question! Christopher felt his face light up even while he was answering coolly, "No, I'm only passionate about it. Why?"

"Good," said Flavian. "The Castle plays the village on Saturday, down on the village green. We thought you might like to work the scoreboard for us."

"Only if someone takes me out through the gate," Christopher said acidly. "The spell stops me going through on my own. Otherwise, yes – like a shot."

"Oh Lord! I should have got you a pass!" Flavian said. "I didn't realise you liked to go out. I go on long hikes all the time. I'll take you with me next time I go – there are all sorts of outdoor practicals we can do – only I think you'd better master witch-sight first."

Christopher saw that Flavian was trying to bribe him. They were on enchanter's magic now. Christopher had had no trouble learning how to conjure things from one place to another – it was a little like the levitation he had worked so spectacularly for Dr Pawson, and not unlike raising a wind too – and he had learnt with only a little more difficulty how to make things invisible. He thought he would not have too much trouble conjuring fire, either, as soon as Flavian allowed him to try. But he could not get the hang of witch-sight.

It was quite simple, Flavian kept telling him. It was only making yourself see through a magical disguise to what was really there. But when Flavian put an illusion spell on his right hand and held that hand out as a lion's paw, a lion's paw was all Christopher could see.

Flavian did it over and over again. Christopher yawned and looked vague and kept seeing a lion's paw. The only good thing was that while his mind wandered he hit on the perfect way to keep those books for the Goddess dry in The Place Between.

CHAPTER THIRTEEN

✳

*T*hat night Christopher went round the corner between
his trunk and the fireplace all prepared to tear a new
split in the Castle spells. To his surprise, the split was still
there. It looked as though the Castle people had no idea
he had made it. Very gently, not to disturb it, he tore two
long strips off it, one wide and one narrow. Then, with a
vague shimmering piece of spell in each hand, he went
back to the books and wrapped them in the wide piece.
The narrow piece he used like string to tie the parcel up,
leaving a loose length to tie to his belt. When he spat on
the parcel, the spit rolled off it in little round balls. Good.

Then it was like old times, climbing across the rocks

the well-known way, in clothes that had got even shorter and tighter since yesterday night. It did not worry Christopher at all that he had fallen last time. He knew this way too well. And again like old times, the old men were still charming snakes in front of the city walls. They must do it for religion or something, Christopher supposed, because they did not seem to want money for it. Inside the gates, the city was still the same loud smelly place, full of goats and umbrellas, and the small shrines at the street corners were still surrounded with offerings. The only difference was that it did not seem quite so hot here as last time, though it was still plenty hot enough for someone who had just come from an English summer.

Yet, oddly enough, Christopher was not comfortable here. He was not frightened of people throwing spears. It was because, after the hushed dignity and dark clothes at the Castle, this city made every nerve he had jangle. He had a headache long before he got to the Temple of Asheth. It made him need to rest a bit among the latest pile of old cabbages in the alley, before he could muster the inclination to push his way through the wall and the creepers. The cats were still sunning themselves in the yard. No one was about.

The Goddess was in a room further along from her usual one. She was on a big white cushion that was probably a bed, with more white cushions to prop her up and a shawl over her in spite of the heat. She had grown too, though not as much as Christopher. But he thought she might be ill. She was lying there, staring into nothing, and her face was not as round as he remembered, and a good deal paler.

"Oh, thanks," she said, as if she was thinking of something else, when Christopher dumped the parcel of books on her shawl. "I've nothing to swop."

"I'm still paying for Throgmorten," Christopher said.

"Was he that valuable?" the Goddess said listlessly. In a slow, lacklustre way she began stripping the spell off the books. Christopher was interested to see that she had no more trouble tearing it than he had. Being the Living Asheth obviously meant you were given strong magic. "These look good books," the Goddess said politely. "I'll read them – when I can concentrate."

"You're ill, aren't you?" said Christopher. "What have you got?"

"Not germs," the Goddess said weakly. "It's the Festival. It was three days ago. You know it's the one day in the year when I go out, don't you? After months and months all quiet and dark here in the Temple, there I am suddenly out in the sun, riding in a cart, dressed in huge heavy clothes and hung with jewels, with my face covered with paint. Everyone shouts. And they all jump up on the cart and try to touch me – for luck, you know, and not as if I was a person." Tears began slowly rolling down her face. "I don't think they notice I'm alive. And it goes on all day, the shouting and the sun and hands banging at me until I'm bruised all over." The tears rolled faster. "It used

183

to be exciting when I was small," she said. "But now it's too much."

The Goddess's white cat came galloping into the room and jumped possessively on to her lap. The Goddess stroked it weakly. Like Throgmorten sitting on my bed, Christopher thought. Temple cats know when their people are upset. He thought he could understand a little, after his own feelings in the city just now, the way the Festival had felt to the Goddess.

"I think it's being inside all year and then suddenly going out," the Goddess explained as she stroked Bethi.

Christopher had meant to ask if it was the curse of Asheth that kept killing him all the time, but he could see this was not the moment. The Goddess needed her mind taken off Asheth. He sat down on the tiles beside her cushions. "It was clever of you to see that silver stopped me doing magic," he said. "I didn't know myself – not until Papa took me to Dr Pawson." Then he told her about the levitation spell.

The Goddess smiled. When he told her about old Mrs Pawson and the chamberpot, she turned her face to him and almost laughed. It was obviously doing her so much good that he went on and told her about the Castle and Gabriel de Witt, and even managed to make that funny too. When he told her about the way he kept seeing a lion's paw, he had her in fits of laughter.

"But that's stupid of you!" she chuckled. "When there are things I can't do for Mother Proudfoot, I just pretend

184

I can. Just say you can see his hand. He'll believe you."

"I never thought of that," Christopher confessed.

"No, you're too honest," she said, and looked at him closely. "Silver forces you to tell the truth," she said. "The Gift of Asheth tells me. So you got into the habit of never lying." Mentioning Asheth sobered her up. "Thank you for telling me about yourself," she said seriously. "I think you've had a *rotten* life, even worse than mine!" Quite suddenly she was crying again. "People only want either of us for what *use* we are to them!" she sobbed. "You for your nine lives and me for my Goddess attributes. And both of us are caught and stuck and *trapped* in a life with a future all planned out by someone else – like a long, long tunnel with no way *out*!"

Christopher was a little astonished at this way of putting things, even though his anger at being forced to be the next Chrestomanci certainly made him feel trapped most of the time. But he saw the Goddess was mostly talking about herself. "You stop being the Living Asheth when you grow up," he pointed out.

"*Oh*, I do so want to stop!" the Goddess wept. "I want to stop being her *now*! I want to go to school, like Millie in the *Millie* books. I want to do Prep and eat stodge and learn French and play hockey and write lines—"

"You wouldn't want to write lines," Christopher said, quite anxious at how emotional she was getting. "Honestly, you wouldn't."

"Yes, I *do*!" screamed the Goddess. "I want to cheek

185

the Prefects and cheat in Geography tests and sneak on my friends! I want to be *bad* as well as good! I want to go to school and be *bad*, do you hear!"

By this time she was kneeling up on her cushion, with tears pouring off her face into the white cat's fur, making more noise than Throgmorten had when Christopher ran through the Temple with him in the basket. It was not surprising that somebody in sandals came hurrying and stumbling through the rooms beyond, calling breathlessly, "Goddess, *dear*! Goddess! What's wrong, love?"

Christopher spun himself round and dived through the nearest wall without bothering to get up first. He came out face down in the hot yard full of cats. There he picked himself up and sprinted for the outside wall. After that, he did not stop running until he reached the city gate. Girls! he thought. They really were a Complete Mystery. Fancy *wanting* to write lines!

Nevertheless, as he went up the valley and climbed through The Place Between, Christopher found himself thinking seriously about some of the things the Goddess had said. His life did indeed seem to be a long tunnel planned out by somebody else. And the reason he hated everyone so at the Castle was that he was just a Thing to them, a useful Thing with nine lives that was going to be moulded into the next Chrestomanci some day. He thought he would tell Tacroy that. Tacroy would understand. Tomorrow was Thursday, and he could see

Tacroy. He thought he had never looked forward to a Thursday more.

And he knew how to pretend he had witch-sight now. The next afternoon, when Flavian held out a lion's paw to him, Christopher said, "It's your hand. I can see it now."

Flavian was delighted. "Then we'll go on a nice long hike tomorrow," he said.

Christopher was not altogether sure he was looking forward to that. But he could hardly wait to see Tacroy again. Tacroy was the only person he knew who did not treat him as a useful Thing. He scrambled out of bed almost as soon as he was in it and shot through the slit in the spells, hoping Tacroy would realise and be early.

Tacroy was there, leaning against the crag at the end of the valley with his arms folded, looking as if he was resigned to a long wait. "Hallo!" he said, and sounded quite surprised to see Christopher at all.

Christopher realised that it was not going to be as easy as he had thought to pour out his troubles to Tacroy, but he beamed at Tacroy as he started scrambling into his clothes. "It's good to see you again," he said. "There's no end of things to tell you. Where are we going tonight?"

Tacroy said in a careful sort of way, "The horseless carriage is waiting in Eight. Are you sure you want to go?"

"Of course," Christopher said, doing up his belt.

"You can tell me your news just as well here," Tacroy said.

This was off-putting. Christopher looked up and saw

that Tacroy was unusually serious. His eyes were crinkled up unsmilingly. This made it too awkward to start telling Tacroy anything. "What's the matter?" he asked.

Tacroy shrugged. "Well," he said, "for a start, the last time I saw you, your head was bashed in — "

Christopher had forgotten that. "Oh, I never thanked you for getting me back here!" he said.

"Think nothing of it," said Tacroy. "Though I must say it was the hardest thing I've ever done in any line of work, keeping myself firm enough to bring the carriage through the interworld and heave you off here. I kept wondering why I was doing it too. You looked pretty thoroughly dead to me."

"I've got nine lives," Christopher explained.

"You've obviously got more than one," Tacroy agreed, grinning as if he did not really believe it. "Look, didn't that accident make you think? Your uncle's done hundreds of these experiments by now. We've fetched him a mass of results. It's all right for me – I get paid. But there's nothing in it for you that I can see, except the danger of getting hurt again."

Tacroy truly meant this, Christopher could see. "I don't mind," he protested. "Honestly. And Uncle Ralph did give me two sovereigns."

At this Tacroy threw back his curly head and laughed. "Two sovereigns! Some of the things we got him were worth hundreds of pounds – like that Asheth Temple cat, for instance."

"I know," Christopher said, "but I want to keep on with the experiments. The way things are now, it's the only pleasure I have in life." There, he thought. Now Tacroy will have to ask about my troubles.

But Tacroy only sighed. "Let's get going then."

It was not possible to talk to Tacroy in The Place Between. While Christopher climbed and slithered and panted, Tacroy was a floating nebulous ghost nearby, drifting in the wind, with rain beating through him. He did not firm up until the opening of the valley where Christopher had long ago written a large 8 in the mud of the path. The 8 was still there, as if it had been written yesterday. Beyond it the carriage floated. It had been improved again and was now painted a smart duck-egg blue.

"All set, I see," Tacroy said. They climbed down and picked up the guide ropes of the carriage. It immediately started to follow them smoothly down the valley. "How's the cricket?" Tacroy asked in a social sort of way.

Now was Christopher's chance to tell him things. "I haven't played," he said gloomily, "since Papa took me away from school. Up till yesterday, I didn't think they'd even heard of cricket at the Castle – you know I'm living at the Castle now?"

"No," said Tacroy. "Your uncle never has told me much about you. Which castle is this?"

"Chrestomanci Castle," said Christopher. "But yesterday my tutor said there was a match against the village this Saturday. Nobody dreams of asking me to play of course, but I get to work the scoreboard for it."

"Do you indeed?" said Tacroy. His eyes screwed into wrinkles.

"They don't know I'm here, of course," Christopher said.

"I should just think they don't!" Tacroy said, and the way he said it seemed to stop the conversation dead. They walked on in front of the carriage without speaking, until they came to the long hillside with the farmhouse squatting in a dip half-way up it. The place looked bleaker and more lonely than ever, under a heavy grey sky that made the rolls of moor and hill seem yellowish. Before they reached the farm, Tacroy stopped and kicked the carriage out of the way when it nudged the back of his legs, trying to go on. His face was as bleak and yellowish and wrinkled as the moors. "Listen, Christopher," he said, "those folk at Chrestomanci Castle are not going to be pleased to find you've been here doing this."

Christopher laughed. "They aren't! But they're not going to find out!"

"Don't be too sure about that," Tacroy said. "They're experts in every kind of magic there."

"That's what makes it such a good revenge on them," Christopher explained. "Here I am slipping out from under their stupid stuffy boring noses, when they think they've got me. I'm just a Thing to them. They're using me."

The people at the farmhouse had seen them coming. A

little group of women ran out into the yard and stood beside a heap of bundles. One waved. Christopher waved back and, since Tacroy did not seem to be as interested in his feelings as he had hoped, he set off up the hill. That started the carriage moving again.

Tacroy hurried to catch up. "Doesn't it occur to you," he said, "that your uncle may be using you too?"

"Not like the Castle people are," said Christopher. "I do these experiments of my own free will."

At this, Tacroy looked up at the low cloudy sky. "Don't say I didn't try!" he said to it.

The women breathed garlic over Christopher when they greeted him in the farmyard, just as they always did. As usual, that smell mixed with the smell from the bundles as he loaded them. The bundles always had this smell in Eight – a sharp, heady, coppery smell. Now, after the practical lessons he had had from Flavian, Christopher paused and sniffed it. He knew what the smell was. Dragons' blood! It surprised him, because this was the most dangerous and powerful ingredient of magic. He put the next bundle on the carriage much more carefully and as he gingerly picked up the next one, knowing some of the things it could do, he looked across at Tacroy to see if Tacroy knew what the bundles were. But Tacroy was leaning against the wall of the yard staring sadly up the hill. Tacroy said he never had much sense of smell when he was out of his body anyway.

As Christopher looked, Tacroy's eyes went wide and

he jumped away from the wall. "I say!" he said.

One of the women yelled and pointed away up the hill. Christopher turned to see what was the matter, and stared, and went on staring in amazement, standing where he was with the bundle in his hands. A very large creature was on its way down towards the farm. It was a kind of purplish black.

The moment Christopher first saw it, it was folding its great leathery wings and putting its clawed feet down to land, gliding down the hill so fast that he did not see at once how very large it was. While he was still thinking it was a house-sized animal half-way up the hill, it had landed just behind the farm, and he realised he could still see most of it towering up above the farmhouse.

"It's a dragon!" Tacroy shrieked. "Christopher, get *down*! Look *away*!"

Around Christopher, the women were running for the barns. One came running back, carrying a big heavy gun in both arms, which she tried frantically to wrestle up on to a tripod. She got it up and it fell down.

While she picked the gun up again, the dragon put its gigantic jagged black head down on the farm roof between the chimneys, crushing it in quite casually, and gazed at the farmyard with huge shining green eyes.

"It's huge!" Christopher said. He had never seen anything like it.

"*Down!*" Tacroy screamed at him.

The dragon's eyes met Christopher's, almost soulfully.

Among the ruins and rafters of the farm roof, it opened its huge mouth. It was rather as if a door had opened into the heart of a sun. A white-orange prominence spouted from the sun, one strong accurate shaft of it, straight at Christopher. WHOOF. He was in a furnace. He heard his skin fry. During an instant of utter agony, he had time to think, Oh bother! Another hundred lines!

Tacroy's panting was the first thing Christopher heard, some time after that. He found Tacroy struggling to heave him off the charred bed of the horseless carriage on to the path. The carriage and Tacroy were wobbling about just beside Christopher's pyjamas.

"It's all right," Christopher said, sitting up wincingly. His skin smarted all over. His clothes seemed to have been burnt off him. The parts of him he could see were a raw pink and smirched with charcoal from the half-burnt carriage. "Thanks," he gasped, because he could see that Tacroy had rescued him again.

"You're welcome," Tacroy panted. He was fading to a grey shadow of himself. But he put forth a great effort. His eyes closed and his mouth spread into a grin with it, all transparent, with the grass of the valley shining through his face. Then, for a second, he became clear and solid. He bent over Christopher. "This is *it*!" he said. "You're not going on these jaunts ever again. You drop it, see? You stop. You come out here again and I won't be here." By this time he was fading to grey, and then to milkiness beyond the grey. "I'll square your uncle," his voice whispered. Christopher had to guess that the last word was "uncle". Tacroy had faded out by then.

Christopher flopped off the carriage and that disappeared too, leaving nothing but the empty, peaceful valley and a strong smell of burning.

"But I don't *want* to drop it!" Christopher said. His voice sounded so dry and cracked that he could hardly hear it above the brawling of the stream in the valley. A couple of tears made smarting tracks down his face while he collected his pyjamas and crawled back through the split in the spells.

CHAPTER FOURTEEN

✳

Again there was nothing wrong with Christopher when he woke up. He listened to Flavian that morning with a polite, vague look on his face while he marvelled about the dragon. His marvelling kept being interrupted by gusts of misery that he would never see Tacroy again, and he had to work quite hard to think of the dragon. It was awesome. It was almost worth losing a life to have seen a sight like that. He wondered how long it would be before someone in the Castle noticed he had lost another life. And a small anxious part of him kept saying, But have I lost it – yet?

"I've ordered us a packed lunch," Flavian said cheerfully, "and the housekeeper's dug out an oilskin that should fit you. We'll be off on our hike just as soon as you've finished that French."

It was raining quite heavily. Christopher took his time over the French, hoping that Flavian would decide that it was too wet for walking. But when Christopher could not think of any further ways to spin out the history of the pen of his aunt, Flavian said, "A little soaking never did anyone any harm," and they set out into a strong drizzle a little after midday.

Flavian was very cheerful. Tramping in the wet, with thick socks and a knapsack, was obviously his idea of heaven. Christopher licked up the water that kept running off his nose from his hair and thought that at least he was out of the Castle. But if he had to be out in wind and wet, he would have preferred to be in The Place Between. That brought him back to Tacroy, and he had to struggle with gusts of misery again. He tried to think of the dragon, but it was too wet. While they tramped across several miles of heath, all Christopher could think of was how much he was going to miss Tacroy, and how the soaking gorse bushes looked just as desolate as he felt. He hoped they would stop for lunch soon so that he could think about something else.

They came to the edge of the heath. Flavian pointed in a breezy, open-air way to a hill that was grey with distance. "That's where we'll stop for lunch. In those woods on that hill there."

"It's miles away!" Christopher said, appalled.

"Only about five miles. We'll just drop down into the

valley between and them climb up again," Flavian said, striding cheerfully down the hill.

Long before they reached that hill, Christopher had stopped thinking of Tacroy and could only think how cold and wet and tired and hungry he was. It seemed to him to be nearer tea-time than lunch-time when he finally struggled after Flavian into a clearing in that far-distant wood.

"Now," said Flavian, tossing off the knapsack and rubbing his hands together. "We'll have some really practical magic. You're going to collect sticks and make a good pile of them. Then you can try your hand at conjuring fire. When you've got a good fire going, we can fry sausages on sticks and have lunch."

Christopher looked up at the boughs overhead, hung with huge transparent blobs of rain. He looked around at the soaking grass. He looked at Flavian to see if he was really meaning to be fiendish. No. Flavian just thought this way was fun. "The sticks will be wet," Christopher said. "The whole wood's dripping."

"Makes it more of a challenge," Flavian said.

Christopher saw there was no point in telling Flavian he was weak with hunger. He grimly collected sticks. He piled them in a soggy heap, which collapsed, so he built the heap again, and then knelt with cold rain soaking into his knees and trickling under his collar, to conjure fire. Ridiculous. He conjured a thin yellow spire of smoke. It lasted about a second. The sticks were not even warm from it.

"Plenty of will as you raise your hands," Flavian said.

"I *know*!" Christopher said and willed savagely. Fire! *Fire*! FIRE!!

The pile of sticks went up with a roar in a sheet of flame ten feet high. Christopher once more heard his skin fry, and his wet oilskin crackled and burst into flame too. He was part of a bonfire almost instantly. *This* is the life the dragon burnt! he thought amid the agony.

When his fifth life took over, which seemed to be about ten minutes later, he heard Flavian saying hysterically, "Yes, I *know*, but it ought to have been perfectly *safe*! The wood is sopping wet. That's why I told him to try."

"Dr Pawson rather suggested that very little is safe once Christopher gets going," a dry voice observed from further away.

Christopher rolled over. He was covered with Flavian's oilskin and, under it, his skin felt very new and soft. The ground in front of him was burnt black, wet and smelly with rain. Overhead, the wet leaves on the trees were brown and curled. Gabriel de Witt was sitting on a folding stool some yards away, under a large black umbrella, looking annoyed and very much out of place. As Christopher saw him, the smoking grass beside the stool burst into little orange flames. Gabriel frowned at the flames. They shrank down into smoke again.

"Ah, you appear to have taken up the threads of life again," he said. "Kindly douse this forest fire of yours. It is uncommonly persistent and I do not wish to leave the countryside burning."

"Can I have something to eat first?" said Christopher "I'm starving."

"Give him a sandwich," Gabriel said to Flavian. "I recall that when I lost my life, the new life required a great deal of energy as it took over." He waited until Flavian had passed Christopher a packet of egg sandwiches. While Christopher was wolfing them down, he said: "Flavian says he takes full responsibility for this latest stupidity. You may thank him that I am lenient with you. I will simply point out that you have caused me to be called away at the moment when we were about to lay hands on a member of the Wraith gang I told you of. If he slips through our fingers, it will be your fault, Christopher. Now please get up and extinguish the fire."

Christopher stood up in some relief. He had been afraid that Gabriel was going to forbid him to work the scoreboard for the cricket match tomorrow. "Dousing a fire is like conjuring in reverse," Flavian told him. So Christopher did that. It was easy, except that his relief about the cricket caused little spurts of flame to keep breaking out all round the clearing.

When even the smoke was gone, Gabriel said, "Now I warn you, Christopher – if you have one more accident, fatal or not, I shall take very severe steps indeed." Having said this, Gabriel stood up and folded his stool with a snap. With the stool tucked under his arm, he reached into the umbrella and started to take it down. As the umbrella folded, Christopher found himself, with Flavian beside him, in the middle of the pentacle in the Castle hall. Miss Rosalie was standing on the stairs.

"He got away, Gabriel," she said. "But at least we know how they're doing it now."

Gabriel turned and looked at Christopher, witheringly. "Take him to his room, Flavian," he said, "and then come back for a conference." He called out to Miss Rosalie, "Tell Frederick to prepare for a trance at once. I want the World Edge patrolled constantly from now on."

Christopher pattered off beside Flavian, shivering under the oilskin. Even his shoes had been burnt. "You were a crisp!" Flavian told him. "I was terrified!" Christopher believed him. That dragon had crisped him thoroughly. He was absolutely sure now that if he lost a life in an Anywhere, it somehow did not count, and he had to lose that life properly in his own world, in a way that was as like the death in the Anywhere as possible. Moral, he thought: be careful in the Anywheres in future. And while he was putting on more clothes he skipped about with relief that Gabriel had not forbidden him to go to the cricket match. But he was afraid the rain would stop the game anyway. It was still pouring.

The rain stopped in the night, though the weather was still grey and chilly. Christopher went down to the village green with the Castle team, which was a motley mixture of Castle sorcerers, a footman, a gardener, a stable lad, Dr Simonson, Flavian, a young wizard who had come down from Oxford specially and, to Christopher's great surprise, Miss Rosalie. Miss Rosalie looked pink and almost fetching in a white dress and white mittens. She tripped along in little white shoes, loudly bewailing the fact that the trap to catch the Wraith had gone wrong. "I told Gabriel all along that we'd have to patrol the World Edge," she said. "By the time they get the stuff to London there are too many places for them to hide."

Gabriel himself met them on the village green, carrying his folding stool in one hand and a telegram in the other. He was dressed for the occasion in a striped blazer that looked about a hundred years old and a wide Panama hat. "Bad news," he said. "Mordecai Roberts has dislocated his shoulder and is not coming."

"Oh no!" everyone exclaimed in the greatest dismay.

"And how typical!" Miss Rosalie added. She pounced round on Christopher. "Can you bat, dear? Enough to come in at the end if necessary?"

Christopher tried to keep a cool look on his face, but it was impossible. "I should hope so," he said.

The afternoon was pure bliss. One of the stable lads lent Christopher some rather large whites, which a sorcerer obligingly conjured down from the Castle for him, and he was sent to field on the boundary. The village batted first – and they made rather a lot of runs, because the missing Mordecai Roberts had been the Castle's best bowler. Christopher got very cold in the chilly wind, but like a dream come true, he took a catch out there to dismiss the blacksmith. All the rest of the Castle people, standing round the green in warm clothes, clapped furiously.

When the Castle began their innings, Christopher sat with the rest of the team waiting his turn – or rather, hoping that he would get a turn – and was fascinated to discover that Miss Rosalie was a fine and dashing batswoman. She hit balls all round the field in the way Christopher had always wanted to do. Unfortunately, the blacksmith turned out to be a demonically cunning spin bowler. He had all the tricks that Tacroy had so often described to Christopher. He got Dr Simonson out for one run and the Oxford wizard out for two. After that the Castle team collapsed round Miss Rosalie. But Miss Rosalie kept at it, with her hair coming down on one shoulder and her face glowing with effort. She did so well that, when Flavian went out to bat at number ten, the Castle only needed two runs to win. Christopher buckled on his borrowed pads, fairly sure he would never get a chance to bat.

"You never know," said the Castle boot-boy, who was working the scoreboard instead of Christopher. "Look at him. He's hopeless!"

Flavian *was* hopeless. Christopher had never seen anyone so bad. His bat either groped about like a blind man's stick or made wild swings in the wrong place. It was obvious he was going to be out any second. Christopher picked up his borrowed bat hopefully. And Miss Rosalie was out instead. The blacksmith clean bowled her. The village people packed round the green roared, knowing they had won. Amid the roars, Christopher stood up.

"Good luck!" said all the Castle people round him. The

boot-boy was the only one who said it as if he thought Christopher had a chance.

Christopher waded out to the middle of the green – the borrowed pads were two sizes too large – to the sound of shouts and catcalls. "Do your best, dear," Miss Rosalie said rather hopelessly as she passed him coming in. Christopher waded on, surprised to find that he was not in the least nervous.

As he took his guard, the village team licked its lips. They crowded in close round Christopher, crouching expectantly. Wherever he looked there were large horny hands spread out and brown faces wearing jeering grins.

"Oh I say!" Flavian said at the other end. "He's only a boy!"

"We know," said the village captain, grinning even wider.

The blacksmith, equally contemptuous, bowled Christopher a slow, loopy ball. While Christopher was watching it arc up, he had time to remember every word of Tacroy's coaching. And since the entire village team was crowded round him in a ring, he knew he only had to get the ball past that ring to score runs. He watched the ball all the way on to the bat with perfect self-possession. It turned a little, but not much. He cracked it firmly away into the covers.

"Two!" he called crisply to Flavian.

Flavian gave him a startled look and ran. Christopher ran, with the borrowed pads going flurp, flurp, flurp at every stride. The village team turned and chased the ball frantically, but Flavian and Christopher had plenty of time to make two runs. They had time to have run three, even with the borrowed pads. The Castle had won. Christopher went warm with pride and joy.

The Castle watchers cheered. Gabriel congratulated him. The boot-boy shook his hand. Miss Rosalie, with her hair still trailing, banged him on the back. Everyone crowded round Christopher saying that they did not need Mordecai Roberts after all, and the sun came out behind the church tower for the first time that day. For that short time, Christopher felt that living in the Castle was not so bad after all.

But by Sunday lunch-time it was back to the usual ways. The talk at lunch was all about anxious schemes to catch the Wraith gang, except that Mr Wilkinson, the elderly sorcerer who looked after the Castle library, kept saying, "Those three rare books are still missing. I cannot imagine who would wish to make away with three girl's books from World B, but I cannot detect them anywhere in the Castle."

Since they were girl's books, Mr Wilkinson obviously did not suspect Christopher. In fact, neither he nor anyone else remembered Christopher was there unless they wanted him to pass the salt.

On Monday, Christopher said acidly to Flavian, "Doesn't it occur to anyone that I could help catch the Wraith?" This was the nearest he had ever come to mentioning the Anywheres to Flavian. Sunday had driven him to it.

"For heaven's sake! People who can cut up mermaids would soon make short work of *you*!" Flavian said.

Christopher sighed. "Mermaids don't come to life again. I do," he pointed out.

"The whole Wraith thing makes me sick," Flavian said and changed the subject.

Christopher felt, more than ever, that he was in a tunnel with no way out. He was worse off than the Goddess, too, because she could stop being the Living Asheth when she grew up, while he had to go on and turn into someone like Gabriel de Witt. His feelings were not improved when, later that week, he had a letter from Papa. This one had been opened and sealed up also, but unlike the letter from Mama, it had the most interesting stamps. Papa was in Japan.

My son,

My spells assure me that a time of utmost danger is coming for you. I implore you to be careful and not to endanger your future.

Your loving
Papa

From the date on the letter, it had been written a month ago. "Bother my future!" Christopher said. "His spells probably mean the lives I've just lost." And the worst of it, he thought, going back to his misery, was that he could not look forward to seeing Tacroy any more.

All the same, that Thursday night, Christopher went out through the split in the spell, hoping Tacroy would be there. But the valley was empty. He stood there for a moment feeling blank. Then he went back into his room, put on his clothes and set off through The Place Between to visit the Goddess again. She was the only other person he knew who did not try to make use of him.

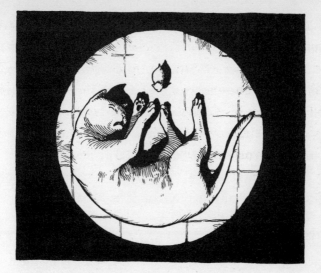

Chapter Fifteen

✳

*T*he Goddess was in her bedroom-place, sitting cross-legged on the white cushions with her chin on her fists, evidently brooding. Though she did not look ill any more, there was a new feeling about her, like thunder in the air, which Christopher rather wondered about as he came in.

The Goddess's jewellery went tunk as she looked up and saw him. "Oh good," she said. "I'd been hoping you'd come back soon. I've *got* to talk to you – you're the only person I know who'll understand."

"The same goes for me," Christopher said, and he sat down on the tiles with his back against the wall. "There's you shut up here with your Priestesses, and me shut up in

207

the Castle with Gabriel's people. Both of us are in this tunnel—"

"But that's just my trouble," the Goddess interrupted. "I'm not sure there is a tunnel for me. Tunnels have ends, after all." Her voice filled with the new thunderous feeling as she said this. The white cat knew at once. It got up from among the cushions and climbed heavily into her lap.

"What do you mean?" Christopher asked, thinking once more that girls really were a Complete Mystery.

"Poor Bethi," the Goddess said, stroking the white cat with a rhythmic tink-tink of bracelets. "She's going to have kittens *again*. I wish she wouldn't keep *on* having them – it wears her out. What I meant is that I've been thinking of all sorts of things since I was ill. I've been thinking of you and wondering how you manage to keep coming here from another world. Isn't it difficult?"

"No, it's easy," said Christopher. "Or it is for me. I think it's because I've got several lives. What I think I do is leave one of them behind in bed and set the other ones loose to wander."

"The luck of it!" the Goddess said. "But I mean what do you do to get to this world?"

Christopher told her about the valley and The Place Between and how he always had to find a corner in the bedroom to go round.

The Goddess's eyes travelled reflectively round the dim archways of her room. "I wish *I* had more than one life," she said. "But with me – you remember how you said when you were here last that I'd stop being the Living Asheth when I grew up?"

"*You* told me that when I first came here," Christopher reminded her. "You said, 'The Living Asheth is always a little girl.' Don't you remember?"

"Yes, but nobody said it the way round that you did," the Goddess said. "It made me think. What happens to the Living Asheth when she *isn't* a little girl any longer? I'm not little now. I'm nearly the age when other people are officially women."

That must happen remarkably early in Series Ten, Christopher thought. He wished he was anything like officially a man. "Don't you get made into a Priestess?"

"No," said the Goddess. "I've listened and I've asked and read all their records – and *none* of the Priestesses were ever the Goddess." She began sticking the white cat's fur up in ridges between fingers that trembled slightly. "When I asked," she said, "Mother Proudfoot said I wasn't to bother my head because Asheth takes care of all that. What do you think that means?"

She seemed to Christopher to be getting all emotional again. "I think you just get shoved out of the Temple and go home," he said soothingly. The idea made him feel envious. "But you've got all your Asheth gifts. You must be able to use those to find out for certain."

"What do you think I've been *trying* to do?" the Goddess all but screamed. Her bracelets chanked as she tossed the unfortunate Bethi aside and bounded to her feet, glaring at

209

Christopher. "You stupid boy! I've thought and *thought*, all this week, until my head *buzzes*!"

Christopher hurriedly got to his feet and pressed his back to the wall, ready to go through it at once if the Goddess went for him. But all she did was to jump up and down in front of him, screaming.

"Think of a way I can find out, if you're so clever! *Think of a WAY*!"

As always when the Goddess screamed, feet flapped in the rooms beyond and a breathless voice called, "I'm coming, Goddess! What is it?"

Christopher backed away into the wall, swiftly and gently. The Goddess flung him a brief look that seemed to be of triumph and went rushing into the arms of the skinny old woman who appeared in the archway. "Oh, Mother Proudfoot! I had *such* an awful dream again!"

Christopher, to his horror, found that he was stuck in the wall. He could not come out forwards and he could not push through backwards. The only thing he could seem to do was use what Flavian had taught him to make himself invisible. He did that at once. He had been moving with his face forward and his rear out, so that most of his head was outside the wall. Invisible or not, he felt like one of the stuffed animal heads on the walls of the Castle dining room.

At least he could see and hear and breathe, he thought in a stunned way. He was confounded at the treachery of the Goddess.

She was led away into the further rooms, with soothing

murmurs. After about ten minutes, by which time Christopher had a cricked neck and cramp in one leg, she came back again, looking perfectly calm.

"There's no point in looking invisible," she said. "Everyone here has witch-sight, even if you don't. Look, I'm sorry about this, but I do terribly need help and I promise I'll let you go when you've helped me."

Christopher did not make himself visible again. He felt safer like that. "You don't need help – you need hitting over the head," he said angrily. "How can I help anyone like this? I'm dying of discomfort."

"Then get comfortable and then help me," the Goddess said.

Christopher found he could move a little. The wall round him seemed to turn jelly-like, so that he could straighten up and move his arms a little and get his legs into a proper standing position. He tried doing some rapid squirming, in hopes that the jelly would give enough to let him out, but it would not. He could tell that what was holding him there was the same thing that the Goddess had used to fasten his feet to the floor when he first met her, and that was still just as mysterious to him as it had been then. "How do you want me to help?" he asked resignedly.

"By taking me with you to your world," the Goddess said eagerly, "so that I can go to a school like the one in the *Millie* books. I thought you could hide me somewhere in your Castle while I looked round for a school."

Christopher thought of Gabriel de Witt discovering the

Goddess hiding in an attic. "No," he said. "I can't. I absolutely can't. And what's more I won't. Now let me out of here!"

"You took Throgmorten," said the Goddess. "You can take me."

"Throgmorten's a cat," said Christopher. "He has nine lives like me. I *told* you I could only get here by leaving one of my lives behind. You've only got one life, so it stands to reason that I can't get you to my world because you'd be dead if I did!"

"That's just the *point*!" the Goddess whispered at him ferociously. He could tell she was trying very hard not to scream again. Tears rolled down her face. "I *know* I've only got one life and I don't want to lose it. Take me with you."

"Just so that you can go to a school out of a book!" Christopher snarled back, feeling more than ever like an animal head on a wall. "Stop being so stupid!"

"Then you can just stay in that wall until you change your mind!" the Goddess said, and flounced away with a chank and a jingle.

Christopher stood, sagging into the jelly of the wall, and cursed the day he had brought the Goddess those *Millie* books. Then he cursed himself for thinking the Goddess was sympathetic. She was just as selfish and ruthless as everyone else he knew. He squirmed and struggled and heaved to get out of the wall, but since he had not the first idea what had gone into the spell, it held him as fast as ever.

The worst of it was that now the Temple had woken up from its midday sleep, it was a decidedly busy place. Behind him, through the wall, Christopher could hear a crowd of people in the hot yard counting the cats and feeding them. Mixed with those sounds was a female voice barking orders, and the sound of armour clashing and spear butts thumping on the ground. Christopher began to be terribly afraid that his invisible backside was sticking out of the wall into that yard. He kept imagining a spear plunging into him there, and he squirmed and squidged and pulled himself in to make sure that it was not. He was not sure which he dreaded most: the feeling of a spear driving into him, or what Gabriel would do if he lost another life.

From in front of him, beyond the archway, he could hear the Goddess talking with at least three Priestesses and then all their voices muttering prayers. Why hadn't Flavian taught him any useful magic? There were probably six hundred quiet ways of breaking this spell and sliding invisibly out of the wall, and Christopher did not know one. He wondered if he could do it by blasting loose in a combined levitation, whirlwind and fire-conjuring. Maybe – although it would be terribly hard without his hands free – and people would still come running after him with spears. He decided he would try argument and cunning first.

Before long, the Goddess came in to see if he had changed his mind.

"I'll fetch it, dear," said one of the Priestesses beyond the archway.

"No, I want to have another look at Bethi, too," the Goddess said over her shoulder. For honesty's sake, she went over to look at the white cat, which was lying on her bed cushions panting and looking sorry for itself. The Goddess stroked it before she came over and put her face close to Christopher's.

"Well? Are you going to help me?"

"What happens," asked Christopher, "if one of them comes in and notices my face sticking out of the wall?"

"You'd better agree to help before they do. They'd kill you," the Goddess whispered back.

"But I wouldn't be any use to you dead," Christopher pointed out. "Let me go or I'll start yelling."

"You dare!" said the Goddess, and flounced out.

The trouble was Christopher did not dare. That line of argument only seemed to end in deadlock. Next time she came in, he tried a different line. "Look," he said, "I really am being awfully considerate. I could easily blast a huge hole in the Temple and get away this minute, but I'm not doing it because I don't want to give you away. Asheth and your Priestesses are not going to be pleased if they find out you're trying to go to another world, are they?"

Tears flooded the Goddess's eyes. "I'm not asking very much," she said, twisting a bangle miserably. "I thought you were kind."

This argument seemed to be making an impression. "I'm going to have to blow this Temple up before long, if you don't let me go," Christopher said. "If I'm not back before

214

morning, someone in the Castle is going to come in and find only one life of me lying in bed. Then they'll tell Gabriel de Witt and we'll both be in trouble. I told you he knows how to get to other worlds. If he comes here, you won't like it."

"You're selfish!" the Goddess said. "You aren't sympathetic at all – you're just scared."

At this Christopher lost his temper. "Let me go," he said, "or I'll blow the whole place sky high!"

The Goddess simply ran from the room, mopping at her face with a piece of her robe.

"Is something wrong, dear?" asked a Priestess outside.

"No, no," Christopher heard the Goddess say. "Bethi isn't very well, that's all."

She was gone for quite a long time after that. Probably she had to distract the Priestesses from coming and looking at the white cat. But soon after that, smells of spicy food began to fill the air. Christopher grew seriously alarmed. Time was getting on and it really would be morning at the Castle soon. Then he would be in real trouble. More time passed. He could hear people in the yard behind counting the cats and feeding them again. "Bethi's missing," someone said.

"She's with the Living One still," someone else answered. "Her kittens are due soon."

Still more time passed. By the time the Goddess reappeared, desperation had forced Christopher's mind into quite a new tack. He saw that he would have to give her some kind of help, even if it was not what she wanted,

215

or he would never get away before morning.

The Goddess in her ruthless way was obviously meaning to be kind-hearted. When she came in this time, she was carrying a spicy pancake thing wrapped round hot meat and vegetables. She tore bits off it and popped them into Christopher's mouth. There was some searing kind of pepper in it. His eyes watered. "Listen," he choked. "What's *really* the matter with you? What made you suddenly decide to make me help you?"

"I told you!" the Goddess said impatiently. "It was what you said when I was ill – that I wasn't going to be the Living Asheth when I grow up. After that I couldn't think of anything else but what was going to happen to me then."

"So you want to know for certain?" Christopher said.

"More than anything else in this world!" the Goddess said.

"Then will you let me go if I help you find out what's really going to happen to you?" Christopher bargained. "I can't take you to my world – you know I can't – but I can help you this way."

The Goddess stood twisting the last piece of pancake about in her fingers. "Yes," she said. "All right. But I can't see how you can find out any better than I can."

"I can," said Christopher. "What you have to do is go and stand in front of that golden statue of Asheth you showed me and ask it what's going to happen to you when you stop being the Living Asheth. If it doesn't say anything, you'll

216

know nothing much is going to happen and you'll be able to leave this Temple and go to school." This struck him as pretty cunning, since there was no way that he could see that a golden statue could talk.

"Now why didn't I think of that!" the Goddess exclaimed. "That's clever! But—" She twisted the piece of pancake about again. "But Asheth doesn't talk, you know, not exactly. She does everything by signs. Portents and omens and things. And she doesn't always give one when people ask."

This was annoying. "But she'll give *you* one," Christopher said persuasively. "You're supposed to *be* her, after all, so it only amounts to asking her to remind you of something both of you know already. Go and tell her to do you a portent – only make her put a time-limit on it, so that if there isn't one, you'll know that there isn't."

"I will," said the Goddess decisively. She stuffed the piece of pancake into Christopher's mouth and dusted her hands with a determined jangle. "I'll go and ask her this minute!" And she strode out of the room, chank-chink, chank-chink, sounding rather like the soldiers at that moment marching round the yard behind Christopher's back.

He spat the pancake out, shut his eyes to squeeze the water out, and wished he was able to cross his fingers.

Five minutes later, the Goddess strode back looking much more cheerful. "Done it!" she said. "She didn't want to tell me. I had to bully her. But I told her to take her Very Stupid face off and stop trying to fool me, and she gave in."

217

She looked at Christopher rather wonderingly. "I've never got the upper hand of her before!"

"Yes, but what did she *say*?" Christopher asked. He would have danced with impatience if the wall had not stopped him.

"Oh, nothing yet," said the Goddess. "But I promise faithfully I'll let you go when she does. She said she couldn't manage it at once. She wanted to wait till tomorrow, but I said that was far too long. So she said that the very earliest she could manage a portent was midnight tonight—"

"*Midnight*!" Christopher exclaimed.

"That's only three hours away now," the Goddess told him soothingly. "And I said she had to make it on the dot, or I'd be really angry. You must understand her point of view – she has to pull the strings of Fate and that does take time."

With his heart sinking, Christopher tried to calculate what time that would make it back at the Castle. The very earliest he could get it to was ten o'clock in the morning. But perhaps the maid who came to wake him would simply think he was tired. It would take her an hour or so to get worried enough to tell Flavian or someone, and by that time he would be back with any luck. "Midnight then," he said, sighing a bit. "And you're to let me go then, or I'll summon a whirlwind, set everything on fire and take the roof off the Temple."

During those three hours, he kept wondering why he did not do that at once. It was only partly that he did not want to lose another life. He felt a sort of duty to wait and set the Goddess's mind at rest. He had started her worrying by making that remark, and before that he had made her discontented by bringing her those school stories.

He had a lot of fellow-feeling for her in her strange lonely life. And of course Papa had told him that you did not use magic against a lady. Somehow all these things combined to keep Christopher sagging in a half-sitting way in the wall, patiently waiting for midnight.

Some of the time the Goddess sat on her cushions, tensely stroking the white cat, as if she expected the portent any moment. Much of the time she was busy. She was called away to lessons, and then to prayers, and finally to have a bath. While she was away, Christopher had the rather desperate idea that he might be able to get in touch with the life he knew must be lying in bed at the Castle. He thought he might be able to get it to get up and do lessons for him. But though he had a sort of feeling of a separate piece of him quite clearly, he did not seem to be in touch with it – or if he was, he had no means of knowing. Do lessons! he thought. Get out of bed and behave like me! And he wondered for the hundredth time why he did not simply blow up the Temple and leave.

Finally the Goddess came back in a long white night-gown and only two bracelets. She kissed Mother Proudfoot goodnight in the archway and got among her white cushions with her arms lovingly round her white cat.

"It won't be long now," she told Christopher.

"It had better not be!" he said. "Honestly, I can't think why you grumble about your life. I'd swop your Mother Proudfoot for Flavian and Gabriel any day!"

"Yes, maybe I am being silly," the Goddess agreed, rather drowsily. "On the other hand, I can tell you don't believe in Asheth and that makes you see it quite differently from me."

Christopher could tell by her breathing that she dropped off to sleep then. He must have dozed himself in the end. The jelly-like wall was not really uncomfortable.

He was roused by a strange high cheeping noise. It was an oddly desperate sound, a little like the noise baby birds make calling and calling to be fed. Christopher jumped awake to find a big bar of white moonlight falling across the tiles on the floor.

"Oh look!" said the Goddess. "It's the portent." Her pointing arm came into the moonlight, with a bracelet dangling from it. She was pointing at Bethi the white cat. Bethi was lying stiffly stretched out in the bar of moonlight. Something tiny and very, very white was crawling and scrambling all over Bethi, filling the air with desperate high crying.

The Goddess surged off her cushions and on to her knees and picked the tiny thing up. "It's frozen," she said. "Bethi's had a kitten and—" There was a long pause. "Christopher," said the Goddess, obviously trying to sound calm, "Bethi's dead. That means I'm going to die when they get a new Living Asheth."

Kneeling by the dead cat, she screamed and screamed and screamed.

Lights went on. Feet flapped on the tiles, running. Christopher struggled to get himself as far back in the wall as he could. He knew how the Goddess felt. He had felt the same when he woke up in the mortuary. But he wished she would stop screaming. As skinny Mother Proudfoot rushed into the room followed by two other Priestesses, he did his best to begin a levitation spell.

But the Goddess kept her promise. Still screaming, she backed away from Bethi's pathetic corpse as if it horrified her, and flung out one arm dramatically, so that her dangling bracelet flipped Christopher's invisible nose. Luckily the bracelet was silver.

Christopher landed back in his own bed in the Castle with the crash he was now used to. He was solid and visible and in his pyjamas, and, by the light, it was nearly midday. He sat up hastily. Gabriel de Witt was sitting in the wooden chair across the room, staring at him even more grimly than usual.

CHAPTER SIXTEEN

✳

Gabriel had his elbows on the arms of the chair and his long knob-knuckled hands together in a point under his eagle nose. Over them, his eyes seemed as hard to look away from as the dragon's.

"So you have been spirit travelling," he said. "I suspect you do so habitually. That would explain a great deal. Will you kindly inform me just where you have been and why it took you so long to come back."

There was nothing Christopher could do but explain. He rather wished he could have died instead. Losing a life was nothing compared with the way Gabriel looked at him.

"The Temple of Asheth!" Gabriel said. "You foolish boy!

Asheth is one of the most vicious and vengeful goddesses in the Related Worlds. Her military Arm has been known to pursue people across worlds and over many years, on far slighter grounds than *you* have given her. Thank goodness you refrained from blowing a hole in her Temple. And I am relieved that you at least had the sense to leave the Living Asheth to her fate."

"Her fate? They weren't really going to kill her off, were they?" Christopher asked.

"Of course they will," Gabriel said in his calmest and driest way. "That was the meaning of the portent: the older Goddess dies when the new Living Asheth is chosen. The theory, I believe, is that the older one will enrich the power of the deity. This one must be particularly valuable to them, as she seems to be quite an enchantress in her own right."

Christopher was horrified. He saw suddenly that the Goddess had known, or at least suspected, what was going to happen to her. That was why she had tried to get him to help her. "How can you be so calm about it?" he said. "She's only got one life. Can't you do something to help her?"

"My good Christopher," said Gabriel, "there are, over all the Series of all the Related Worlds, more than a hundred worlds, and in more than half of them there are practices which horrify any civilised person. If I were to expend my time and sympathy on these, I would have none left over to do what I am paid to do – which is to prevent the misuse of magic *here*. This is why I must take action over you. Do you deny that you have been misusing magic?"

"I—" said Christopher.

"You most certainly have," said Gabriel. "You must have lost at least three of your lives in some other world – and you may, for all I know, have lost all six while you were spirit travelling. But since the outer life, the life you *should* have lost, was lying here apparently asleep, natural laws have been forced to bend in order to enable you to lose it in the proper way. Much more of this, and you will set up a serious singularity throughout Series Twelve."

"I didn't lose one this time," Christopher said defensively.

"Then you must have lost it last time you went spirit travelling," Gabriel said. "You are definitely one short again. And this is not going to occur any more, Christopher. Oblige me by getting dressed at once and coming with me to my office."

"Er—" Christopher said. "I haven't had breakfast yet. Can I—?"

"No," said Gabriel.

By this Christopher knew that things were very bad indeed. He found he was shaking as he got up and went to the washroom. The door of the washroom would not shut. Christopher could tell Gabriel was holding it open with a strong spell to make sure he did not try to get away. Under Gabriel's eyes, he washed and dressed quicker than he had ever done in his life.

"Christopher," Gabriel said, while he was hurriedly brushing his hair, "you must realise that I am deeply concerned about you. Nobody should lose lives at the rate that you do. What is wrong?"

"I don't do it just to annoy you," Christopher said bitterly, "if that's what you think."

Gabriel sighed. "I may be a poor guardian, but I know my duty," he said. "Come along."

He stalked silently through the corridors with Christopher half running to keep up. What *had* become of his sixth life? Christopher wondered, with the bit of his mind that was not taken up with terror. He was inclined to think that Gabriel had miscounted.

Inside the twilight office, Miss Rosalie and Dr Simonson were waiting with one of the younger men on the Castle staff. All of them were swathed in a shimmering transparent spell.

Christopher's eyes flicked anxiously from them to the leather couch in the middle of the dark floor. It reminded him of a dentist's chair. Beyond it was a stand holding two bell jars. The one on the left had a large bobbin hanging from nothing inside it, while the one on the right seemed to be empty except for a curtain ring or something lying at the bottom.

"What are you going to do?" Christopher said, and his voice came out more than a little squeaky.

Miss Rosalie stepped up to Gabriel and handed him some gloves on a glass tray. As Gabriel worked his fingers into the gloves, he said, "This is the severe step I warned you of after your fire. I intend to remove your ninth life from you without harming either it or you. Afterwards I shall put it in the Castle safe, under nine charms that only I can unlock. Since you will then only be able to have that life by coming to me and asking me to unlock those nine charms, this might induce you to be more careful with the two lives you will have left."

Miss Rosalie and Dr Simonson began wrapping Gabriel in a sheeny spell like their own. "Taking a life out intact is something only Gabriel knows how to do," Miss Rosalie said proudly.

Dr Simonson, to Christopher's surprise, seemed to be trying to be kind. He said, "These spells are only for hygiene. Don't look so alarmed. Lie down on this couch now. I promise you it won't hurt a bit."

Just what the dentist said! Christopher thought as he quakingly lay down.

Gabriel turned this way and that to let the spell settle round him. "The reason Frederick Parkinson is here," he said, "and not patrolling the World Edge as he should be, is to make sure that you do no spirit travelling while your life is being detached. That would put you in extreme peril, Christopher, so please try to remain in this world while we work."

Someone cast a very strong sleep spell then. Christopher went out like a light. Dr Simonson turned out to have told the truth. He felt nothing at all for several hours. When he woke up, ravenously hungry and slightly itchy deep inside somewhere, he simply felt rather cheated. If he did have to have a life taken away, he would have liked to have watched how it was done.

Gabriel and the others were leaning against the black desk, drinking tea and looking exhausted. Frederick Parkinson said, "You *kept* trying to spirit travel. I had my work cut out to stop you."

Miss Rosalie hurried to bring Christopher a cup of tea too.

"We kept you asleep until your life was all on the bobbin," she said. "It's just winding down into the gold ring now – look." She pointed to the two bell jars. The bobbin inside the left hand jar was almost full of shiny pinkish thread, and it was rotating in a slow stately way in the air. In the right hand jar, the ring was up in the air now too, spinning fast and jerkily. "How are you now, dear?" Miss Rosalie asked.

"Can you feel anything? Are you quite well?" Gabriel asked. He sounded quite anxious.

Dr Simonson seemed quite as concerned. He took Christopher's pulse and then tested his mind by asking him to do sums. "He does seem to be fine," he told the others.

"Thank goodness!" Gabriel said, rubbing his face with his hands. "Tell Flavian – no he's out on the World Edge, isn't he? Frederick, would you put Christopher to bed and tell the housekeeper that he's ready for that nourishing meal now?"

Everyone was so nervous and concerned about him that Christopher realised that no one had ever tried to take someone's spare life away before. He was not sure what he felt about that. What would they have done if it hadn't worked? he wondered, while he was sitting in bed eating almost more chicken and cream puffs than he could hold. Frederick Parkinson sat by him while he ate, and went on sitting by him all evening. Christopher did not know which irritated him most: Frederick or the itch deep down inside him. He went to sleep early in order to get rid of both.

He woke up in the middle of the night to find himself alone in the room with the gaslight still burning. He got out of bed at once and went to see if the slit in the Castle spells had been mended. To his surprise, it was still there. It looked as if nobody had realised how he went to the Anywheres. He was just about to go through the slit, when he happened to look back at his bed. The boy lying there among the rumpled covers had a vague unreal look, like Tacroy before he was firmed up. The sight gave Christopher a most unpleasant jolt. He really did have only two lives left now. The last life was locked away in the Castle safe and there was no way he could use it without Gabriel's permission. Hating Gabriel more than ever, he went back to bed.

Flavian brought Christopher his breakfast in the morning. "Are you all right for lessons today?" he asked anxiously. "I thought we could take it easy – I had a fairly heavy day yesterday, in and out of the World Edge to absolutely no effect, so I could do with a quiet morning too.

I thought we'd go down to the library and look at some of the standard reference books – *Moore's Almanac, Prynne's List* and so forth."

The itch inside Christopher had gone. He felt fine, probably better than Flavian, who looked pale and tired. He was irritated at the way everyone was keeping watch on him, but he knew there was no point in complaining, so he ate his breakfast and got dressed and went along the corridors with Flavian to the pink marble staircase.

They were half-way down the stairs when the five-pointed star in the hall filled with sudden action. Frederick Parkinson sprang into being first. He waved at Flavian. "We've got some of them at last!" His jubilant shout was still ringing round the hall when Miss Rosalie appeared, struggling to keep hold of an angry old woman who was trying to hit her over the head with a violin. Two policemen materialised behind her. They were carrying someone between them, one at the man's head and one at his legs. They staggered round Miss Rosalie and the fighting old woman and laid the man carefully on the tiles, where he stayed, spread out a bit as if he was asleep, with his curly head turned peacefully towards the stairs.

Christopher found himself staring down at Tacroy.

At the same moment, Flavian said, "My God! It's Mordecai Roberts!"

"I'm afraid so," Frederick Parkinson called up to him. "He's one of the Wraith gang all right. I followed him all the way into Series Seven before I went back to trace his body.

He was one of their couriers. There was quite a lot of loot with him." More policemen were appearing behind him, carrying boxes and the kind of waterproof bundles Christopher knew rather well.

Gabriel de Witt hurried past Christopher and Flavian and stood at the foot of the stairs looking down at Tacroy like a black, brooding bird. "So Roberts was their carrier, was he?" he said. "No wonder we were making no headway." By then the hall was filled with people: more policemen, the rest of the Castle staff, footmen, the butler, and a crowd of interested housemaids. "Take him to the trance room," Gabriel told Dr Simonson, "but don't let him suspect anything. I want whatever he was fetching if possible." He turned to look up at Flavian and Christopher. "Christopher, you had better be present at the questioning when Roberts returns to his body," he said. "It will be valuable experience for you."

Christopher threaded his way across the hall beside Flavian, feeling rather as if he was out of his body too. He was empty with horror. So this was what Uncle Ralph's 'experiments' really were! Oh no! he thought. Let it all be a mistake!

He found it quite impossible to concentrate in the library. He kept hearing Miss Rosalie's voice saying, "But Gabriel, they had actually butchered a whole tribe of mermaids!" and his mind kept going to those fishy bundles he had loaded on the horseless carriage in Series Five, and then to the silly ladies who had thought he was something called a clistoffer.

He told himself that those fishy bundles had *not* been bundles of mermaid. It *was* all some terrible mistake. But then he thought of the way Tacroy had tried to warn him off, not only the time the dragon came, but several times before that, and he knew it was no mistake. He felt sick.

Flavian was almost as bad. "Fancy it being *Mordecai*!" he kept saying. "He's been on the Castle staff for years. I used to *like* him!"

Both of them jumped up with a sort of relief when a footman came to fetch them to the Middle Drawing Room. At least, Christopher thought, as he followed Flavian across the hall, when everything came out nobody would expect him to be the next Chrestomanci any longer. Somehow the thought was not as comforting as he had hoped.

In the enormous drawing room, Gabriel was sitting at the centre of a half-circle of gilded armchairs, like an old black and grey king on his throne. To one side of him sat serious and important-looking policemen with notebooks and three men carrying briefcases who all wore whiskers more imposing than Papa's. Flavian whispered that these were men from the Government. Miss Rosalie and the rest of Gabriel's staff sat on the other side of the semicircle. Christopher was beckoned to a chair about halfway along. He had an excellent view when two sturdy warlock footmen brought Tacroy in and sat him in a chair facing the others.

"Mordecai Roberts," one of the policemen said, "you are under arrest and I must warn you that anything you say will be taken down and may be used in evidence later. Do you wish to have a lawyer present with you?"

"Not particularly," said Tacroy. In his body, he was not quite the Tacroy Christopher knew. Instead of the old green suit, he was wearing a much smarter brown one, with a blue silk cravat and a handkerchief that matched it in his top pocket. His boots were handmade calf. Though his curls were exactly the same, there were lines on his face that never appeared on the face of his spirit, laugh-lines set in a rather insolent and bitter pattern. He was pretending to lounge in his chair with one handmade boot swinging in a carefree way, but Christopher could tell he was not carefree at all.

"No point in a lawyer," he said. "You caught me in the act after all. I've been a double agent for years now. There's no way I could deny it."

"What made you *do* it?" Miss Rosalie cried out.

"Money," Tacroy said carelessly.

"Would you care to expand on that?" Gabriel said. "When you left the Castle in order to infiltrate the Wraith organisation, the Government agreed to pay you a good salary and to provide comfortable lodgings in Baker Street. You still have both."

So much for the garret in Covent Garden! Christopher thought bitterly.

"Ah, but that was in the early days," said Tacroy, "when the Wraith only operated in Series Twelve. He couldn't offer me enough to tempt me then. As soon as he expanded into the rest of the Related Worlds, he offered me anything I cared to ask." He took the silk handkerchief out of his pocket and carefully flicked imaginary dust off his good boots. "I didn't take the offer straightaway, you know," he said. "I got deeper in by degrees. Extravagance gets a hold on you."

"Who *is* the Wraith?" Gabriel asked. "You owe the Government that information at least."

Tacroy's foot swung. He folded the handkerchief neatly and his eyes went carelessly round the half-circle of people facing him. Christopher kept the vaguest look on his face that he could manage, but Tacroy's eyes passed over him just as they passed over everyone else, as if Tacroy had never seen him before. "There I can't help you," he said. "The man guards his identity very carefully. I only had dealings with his underlings."

"Such as the woman Effisia Bell who owns the house in Kensington where your body was seized?" one of the policemen asked.

Tacroy shrugged. "She was one of them. Yes."

Miss Bell, the Last Governess, Christopher thought. She had to be one of them. He kept his face so vague that it felt as stiff as the golden statue of Asheth.

"Who else can you name?" someone else asked.

"Nobody much, I'm afraid," Tacroy said.

Several other people asked him the same question in different ways, but Tacroy simply swung his foot and said he couldn't remember. At length Gabriel leaned forward. "We have taken a brief look at that horseless carriage on which your spirit smuggled the plunder," he said. "It's an ingenious object, Roberts."

"Yes, isn't it?" Tacroy agreed. "It must have taken quite a while to perfect. You can see it had to be fluid enough to cross the World Edge, but solid enough so that the people in the other Series could load it when I got it there. I got the impression that the Wraith had to wait until he'd got the carriage right before he could expand into the Related Worlds."

That's not true! Christopher thought. And *I* used to load it! He's lying about everything!

"Several wizards must have worked on that thing, Mordecai," Miss Rosalie said. "Who were they?"

"Heaven knows," said Tacroy. "No – wait a minute. Effie Bell dropped a name. Phelps, was it? Felper? Felperin?"

Gabriel and the policemen exchanged glances. Flavian murmured, "The Felperin brothers! We've suspected they were crooked for years."

"Another curious thing, Roberts," Gabriel said. "Our brief inspection of the carriage shows that it seems at one time to have been almost destroyed by fire."

Christopher found that he had stopped breathing.

"Accident in the workshop, I suppose," Tacroy said.

"*Dragon* fire, Mordecai," said Dr Simonson. "I recognised it at once."

Tacroy let his bitter, anxious, laughing eyes travel round everyone's faces. Christopher still could not breathe. But once again Tacroy's eyes passed over Christopher as if he had never seen him before.

He laughed. "I was joking. The sight of you all sitting round in judgement brings out the worst in me. Yes, it was burnt by a dragon objecting to a load of dragons' blood I was collecting in Series Eight. It happened about a year ago." Christopher began breathing at that. "I lost the whole load," Tacroy said, "and was nearly too scalded to get back into my body. We had to suspend operations most of last autumn until the carriage was repaired. If you remember, I reported to you that the Wraith seemed to have stopped importing then."

Christopher drew in some long relieved breaths and tried not to make them too obvious. Then one of the whiskered Government men spoke up. "Did you always go out alone?" he asked, and Christopher almost stopped breathing again.

"Of course I was alone," said Tacroy. "What use would another traveller be? Mind you, I have absolutely no way of knowing how many other carriages the Wraith was sending out. He could have hundreds."

And that's nonsense! Christopher thought. Ours was the only one, or they wouldn't have had to stop last autumn when I went to school and forgot. If he had not realised by then that Tacroy was protecting him, he would have known by the end of the morning. The questions went on and on. Tacroy's eyes slid across Christopher over and over again, without a trace of recognition. And every time Tacroy's answer should have incriminated Christopher, Tacroy lied, and followed the lie up with a smokescreen of other confessions to take people's minds off the question.

Christopher's face went stiff from keeping the vague look on it. He stared at Tacroy's bitter face and felt worse and worse. At least twice, he nearly jumped up and confessed. But that seemed such a waste of all Tacroy's trouble.

The questions did not stop for lunch. The butler wheeled in a trolley of sandwiches, which everyone ate over pages of notes, while they asked more questions. Christopher was glad to see one of the footmen taking Tacroy some sandwiches too. Tacroy was pale as the milkiest coffee by then and his swinging boot was shaking. He bit into the sandwiches as if he was starving and answered the next questions with his mouth full.

Christopher bit into his own sandwich. It was salmon. He thought of mermaids and was nearly sick.

"What's the matter?" whispered Flavian.

"Nothing. I just don't like salmon," Christopher whispered back. It would be stupid to give himself away now after Tacroy had worked so hard to keep him out of it. He put the sandwich to his mouth, but he just could not bring himself to take another bite.

"It could be the effect of that life-removal," Flavian murmured anxiously.

"Yes, I expect that's it," Christopher said. He laid the sandwich down again, wondering how Tacroy could bear to eat his so ravenously.

The questions were still going on when the butler wheeled the trolley away. He came back again almost at once and whispered discreetly to Gabriel de Witt. Gabriel thought, decided something, and nodded. Then, to Christopher's surprise, the butler came and leaned over him.

"Your mother is here, Master Christopher, waiting in the Small Saloon. If you will follow me."

Christopher looked at Gabriel, but Gabriel was leaning forward to ask Tacroy who collected the packages when they arrived in London. Christopher got up to follow the butler. Tacroy's eyes flickered after him. "Sorry," Christopher heard him say. "My mind's getting like a sieve. You'll have to ask me that again."

Mermaids, Christopher thought, as he crossed the hall after the butler. Fishy packages. Bundles of dragon's blood. I knew it was dragon's blood in Series Eight, but I didn't know the dragon was objecting. What's going to happen to Tacroy now? When the butler opened the door of the Small Saloon and ushered him in, he could hardly focus his mind on the large elegant room or the two ladies sitting in it.

Two ladies?

Christopher blinked at two wide silk skirts. The pink and lavender one belonged to Mama, who looked pale and upset. The brown and gold skirt that was quite as elegant belonged to the Last Governess. Christopher's mind snapped away from mermaids and dragon's blood and he stopped short half-way across the oriental carpet.

Mama held out a lavender glove to him. "Darling boy!" she said shakily. "How *tall* you are! You remember dear Miss Bell, don't you, Christopher? She's my companion these days. Your uncle has found us a nice house in Kensington."

"Walls have ears," remarked Miss Bell in her dullest voice. Christopher remembered how her hidden prettiness never did come out in front of Mama. He felt sorry for Mama.

"Christopher can deal with that, can't you, dear?" said Mama.

Christopher pulled himself together. He had no doubt that the Saloon was hung with listening spells, probably one to each gold-framed picture. I ought to tell the police the Last Governess is here, he thought. But if the Last Governess was living with Mama, that would get Mama into trouble too. And he knew that if he gave the Last Governess away, she would tell about him and waste all Tacroy's trouble.

"How did you get in?" he said. "There's a spell round the grounds."

"Your mama cried her eyes out at the lodge gates," the Last Governess said, and gestured meaningly round the room to tell Christopher to do something about the listening spells.

Christopher would have liked to pretend not to understand, but he knew he dared not offend the Last Governess. A blanketing spell was enchanter's magic and easy enough. He summoned one with an angry blink and, as usual, he overdid it. He thought he had gone deaf. Then he saw that Mama was tapping the side of her face with a

238

puzzled expression and the Last Governess was shaking her head, trying to clear her ears. Hastily he scraped out the middle of the spell so that they could all hear one another inside the deafness.

"Darling," Mama said tearfully, "we've come to take you away from all this. There's a cab from the station waiting outside, and you're coming back to Kensington to live with me. Your uncle wants me to be happy and he says he knows I can't be happy until I've got you. He's quite right of course."

Only this morning, Christopher thought angrily, he would have danced with joy to hear Mama say this. Now he knew it was just another way to waste Tacroy's trouble. And another plot of Uncle Ralph's of course. Uncle Wraith! he thought. He looked at Mama and Mama looked appealingly back. He could see she meant what she said, even though she had let Uncle Ralph rule her mind completely. Christopher could hardly blame her for that. After all, he had let Uncle Ralph fascinate him, that time when Uncle Ralph tipped him sixpence years ago.

He looked at the Last Governess. "Your mama is quite well off now," she told him in her smooth, composed way. "Your uncle has already restored nearly half your mama's fortune."

Nearly half! Christopher thought. Then what has he done with the rest of the money I earned him for nothing? He must be a millionaire several times over by now!

"And with you to help," said the Last Governess, "in

the way you always used to, you can restore the rest of your mama's money in no time."

In the way I always used to! Christopher thought. He remembered the smooth way the Last Governess had worked on him, first to find out about the Anywheres and then to get him to do exactly what Uncle Ralph wanted. He could not forgive her for that, though she was even more devoted to Uncle Ralph than Mama was. And remembering that, he looked at Mama again. Mama's love for Christopher might be perfectly real, but she had left him to nursery maids and Governesses and she would leave him to the Last Governess as soon as they got to Kensington.

"We're relying on you, darling," said Mama. "Why are you looking so vague? All you have to do is climb out of this window and hide in the cab, and we'll drive away without anyone being the wiser."

I see, Christopher thought. Uncle Ralph knew Tacroy had been caught. So now he wanted Christopher to go on with the smuggling. He had sent Mama to fetch Christopher and the Last Governess to see that they did as Uncle Ralph wanted. Perhaps he was afraid Tacroy would give Christopher away. Well, if Tacroy could lie, so could Christopher.

"I wish I could," he said, in a sad, hesitating way, although underneath he was suddenly as smooth and composed as the Last Governess. "I'd love to get out of here – but I can't. When the dragon burnt me in Series

Eight, that was my last life but one. Gabriel de Witt was so angry that he took my lives and hid them. If I go outside the Castle now I'll die."

Mama burst into tears. "That horrid old man! How awkward for everyone!"

"I think," said the Last Governess, standing up, "that in that case there's nothing to detain us here."

"You're right, dear," Mama sobbed. She dried her eyes and gave Christopher a scented kiss.

"How terrible not to be able to call one's lives one's own!" she said. "Perhaps your uncle can think of something."

Christopher watched the two of them hurry away, rustling expensively over the carpet as soon as they came out from the silence spell. He cancelled the spell with a dejected wave. Though he knew what both of them were like, he still felt hurt and disillusioned as he watched them through the window climbing into the cab that was waiting under the cedar trees of the drive. The only person he knew who had not tried to use him was Tacroy. And Tacroy was a criminal and a double crosser.

And so am I! Christopher thought. Now he had finally admitted this to himself, he found he could not bear to go back to the Middle Drawing Room to listen to people asking Tacroy questions. He trudged miserably up to his room instead. He opened the door. He stared.

A small girl in a dripping wet brown robe was sitting shivering on the edge of his bed. Her hair hung in damp tails round her pale round face. In one hand she seemed to be gripping a handful of soaking white fur. Her other hand was clutching a large waxed-paper parcel of what looked like books.

This was all I needed! Christopher thought. The Goddess had somehow got here and she had clearly brought her possessions with her.

CHAPTER SEVENTEEN

✳

"**H**ow did you get here?" Christopher said. The Goddess shook with shivers. She had left all her jewellery behind, which made her look very odd and plain. "B-by remembering what you said," she answered through chattering teeth, "about having to leave a l-life b-behind. And of course there are t-two of me if you count the g-golden statue as one. B-but it wasn't easy. I w-walked into the w-wall s-six times round the corner of m-my r-room b-before I g-got it right. Y-you m-must be b-brave to keep g-going through th-that awful P-place B-between. It was h-horrible – I n-nearly d-dropped P-proudfoot t-twice."

"Proudfoot?" said Christopher.

The Goddess opened her hand with the white fur in it. The white fur squeaked in protest and began shivering too. "My kitten," the Goddess explained. Christopher remembered how hot it was in Series Ten. Some time ago someone had put the scarf old Mrs Pawson had knitted him neatly away in his chest of drawers. He began searching for it. "I c-couldn't leave her," the Goddess said pleadingly. "I brought her feeding bottle with m-me. And I *had* to g-get away as soon as they l-left me alone after the p-portent. They know I know. I heard M-mother P-proudfoot saying they were going to have to l-look for a new L-living One at once."

And clothes for the Goddess too, Christopher realised, hearing the way her teeth chattered. He tossed her the scarf. "Wrap the kitten in that. It was knitted by a witch so it'll probably keep her safe. How on earth did you find the Castle?"

"B-by looking into every v-valley I c-came to," said the Goddess. "I c-can't *think* why you s-said you didn't have w-witch-sight. I n-nearly m-missed the s-slit in the s-spell. It's really f-faint!"

"Is *that* witch-sight?" Christopher said distractedly. He dumped an armful of his warmest clothes on the bed beside her. "Go in the washroom and get those on before you freeze."

The Goddess put the kitten down carefully wrapped in a nest of scarf. It was still so young that it looked like a white rat. Christopher wondered how it had survived at all. "B-boy's clothes?" the Goddess said.

"They're all I've got," he said. "And be quick. Maids come in and out of here all the time. You've got to hide. Gabriel de Witt told me not to have anything to do with Asheth. I don't know what he'd do if he found you here!"

At this, the Goddess jumped off the bed and snatched up the clothes. Christopher was glad to see that she looked truly alarmed. He dashed for the door. "I'll go and get a hiding place ready," he said. "Wait here."

Off he went at a run to the larger of the two old tower rooms, the one that had once been a wizard's workshop. A runaway Goddess just about put the lid on his troubles, he thought. Still it was probably very lucky that everyone was taken up with poor Tacroy. With a bit of cunning, he ought to be able to keep the Goddess hidden here while he wrote to Dr Pawson to ask what on earth to do with her permanently.

He dashed up the spiral stair and looked round the dusty room. One way and another, he had not made much progress furnishing it as a den. It was empty apart from an old stool, worm-eaten workbenches and a rusty iron brazier. Hopeless for the Goddess! Christopher began conjuring desperately. He fetched all the cushions from the Small Saloon. Then on second thoughts he knew someone would notice.

He sent most of them back and conjured cushions from the Large Drawing Room, the Large Saloon, the Middle

Saloon, the Small Drawing Room and anywhere else where he thought there would be nobody to see. Charcoal from the gardeners' shed next to fill the brazier. Christopher summoned fire for it, almost in too much of a hurry to notice he had got it right for once. He remembered a saucepan and an old kettle by the stables and fetched those. A bucket of water he brought from the pump by the kitchen door.

What else? Milk for the kitten. It came in a whole churn and he had to tip some out into the saucepan and then send the churn back – the trouble was that he had no idea where things were kept in the Castle. Teapot, tea – he had no idea where those came from, and did the Goddess drink tea? She would have to. What then? Oh, cup, saucer, plates. He fetched the ones out of the grand cabinet in the dining room. They were quite pretty. She would like those. Then spoon, knife, fork. Of course none of the silver ones would respond. Christopher fetched what must have been the whole kitchen cutlery drawer with a crash, sorted hastily through it and sent it back like the churn. And she would need food. What was in the pantry?

The salmon sandwiches arrived, neatly wrapped in a white napkin. Christopher gagged. Mermaids. But he arranged them with the other things on the bench before taking a hasty look round. The charcoal had began to glow red in the brazier, but it needed something else to make it look homely. Yes, a carpet. The nice round one from the library would do. When the carpet came, it turned out twice as big as he had thought. He had to move the brazier to make room. There. Perfect.

He dashed back to his room. He arrived at the exact moment when Flavian opened its door and started to walk in.

Christopher hastily cast the fiercest invisibility spell he could. Flavian opened the door on utter blankness. To Christopher's relief, he stood and stared at it.

"Er-hem!" Christopher said behind him. Flavian whirled round as if Christopher had stabbed him. Christopher said airily, and as loudly as he could, "Just practising my practical magic, Flavian." The stumbling sounds he could hear from inside the blankness stopped. The Goddess knew Flavian was there. But he had to get her out of there.

"Oh. Were you? Good," Flavian said. "Then I'm sorry to interrupt, but Gabriel says I'm to give you a lesson now because I won't be here tomorrow. He wants a full muster of Castle staff to go after the Wraith."

While Flavian was speaking, Christopher felt inside the invisibility in his room – using a magical sixth sense which up to then he did not know he had – and located first the Goddess standing by his bed, then the kitten nestled in the scarf on the bed, and sent them both fiercely to the tower room. At least, he hoped he had. He had never transported living things before and he had no idea if it was the same. He heard a heavy *whoosh* of displaced air from among the invisibility, which was the same kind of noise the milk churn had made, and he knew the Goddess had gone somewhere.

He just had to hope she would understand. She had after all shown she could look after herself.

He cancelled the invisibility. The room seemed to be empty. "I like to practise in private," he told Flavian.

Flavian shot him a look. "Come to the schoolroom."

As they walked along the corridor, Christopher caught up with what Flavian had been saying. "You're going after the Wraith tomorrow?"

"If we can get him," Flavian said. "After you left, Mordecai cracked open enough to give us a few names and addresses. We think he was telling the truth." He sighed. "I'd look forward to catching them, except that I can't get over *Mordecai* being one of them!"

What about Mama? Christopher wondered anxiously. He wished he could think of a way to warn her, but he had no idea where in Kensington she was living.

They reached the schoolroom. The moment they got there, Christopher realised that he had only cancelled the invisibility on his room, not on the Goddess or the kitten. He fumbled around with his mind, trying to find her in the tower room – or wherever – and get her visible again. But wherever he had sent her, she seemed too far away for him to find. The result was that he did not hear anything Flavian said for at least twenty minutes.

"I said," Flavian said heavily, "that you seem a bit vague."

He had said it several times, Christopher could tell. He said hastily, "I was wondering what was going to happen to Ta— Mordecai Roberts now."

"Prison, I suppose," Flavian answered sadly. "He'll be in clink for years."

"But they'll have to put a special clink round his spirit to stop that getting away, won't they?" Christopher said.

To his surprise, Flavian exploded. "That's just the kind of damn-fool, frivolous, unfeeling remark you *would* make!" he cried out. "Of all the hard-hearted, toffee-nosed, superior little beggars I've ever met, you're the worst! Sometimes I don't think you have a soul – just a bundle of worthless lives instead!"

Christopher stared at Flavian's usually pale face all pink with passion, and tried to protest that he had not meant to be unfeeling. He had only meant that it must be quite hard to keep a spirit traveller in prison. But Flavian, now he had started, seemed quite unable to stop.

"You seem to think," he shouted, "that those nine lives give you the right to behave like the Lord of Creation! That, or there's a stone wall round you. If anyone so much as tries to be friendly, all they get is haughty stares, vague looks, or pure damn rudeness! Goodness knows, *I've* tried. Gabriel's tried. Rosalie's tried. So have all the maids, and *they* say you don't even notice *them*! And now you make jokes about poor Mordecai! I've had enough! I'm sick of you!"

Christopher had no idea that people saw him like this. He was astounded. What's gone wrong with me? he thought. I'm nice really! When he went to the Anywheres as a small boy, everyone had liked him. Everybody had smiled. Total strangers had given him things. Christopher saw that he had gone on thinking that people only had to see him to like him, and it was only too clear that nobody did.

He looked at Flavian, breathing hard and glaring at him. He seemed to have hurt Flavian's feelings badly. He had not thought Flavian had feelings to hurt. And it made it worse somehow that he had *not* meant to make a joke about Tacroy – not when Tacroy had just spent the whole day lying on his behalf. He *liked* Tacroy. The trouble was, he did not dare tell Flavian he did. Nor did he dare say that his mind had mostly been on the Goddess. So what *could* he say?

"I'm sorry," he said. "Truly sorry." His voice came out wobbly with shock. "I didn't mean to hurt your feelings – not this time anyway – really."

"Well!" said Flavian. The pink in his face died away. He leaned back in his chair, staring. "That's the first time I've ever heard you say sorry – meaning it, that is. I suppose it's some kind of breakthrough." He clapped his chair back to the floor and stood up. "Sorry I lost my temper. But I don't think I can go on with this lesson today. I feel too emotional. Run away, and I'll make up for it after tomorrow."

Christopher found himself free – and with mixed feelings about it – to go and look for the Goddess. He hurried to the tower room.

To his great relief she was there, in a strong smell of boiled-over milk, sitting on the many-coloured silk cushions, feeding the kitten out of a tiny dolls' feeding bottle. With the charcoal warming the air and the carpet –

which now had a singed patch beside the brazier – covering stone floor, the room seemed suddenly homely.

The Goddess greeted him with a most unGoddesslike giggle. "You forgot to make me visible again! I've never done invisibility – it took me ages to find how to cancel it, and I had to stand still the whole time in case I trod on Proudfoot. Thanks for doing this room. Those cups are really pretty."

Christopher giggled too at the sight of the Goddess in his Norfolk jacket and knee-breeches. If you looked just at the clothes, she was a plump boy, rather like Oneir, but if you looked at her grubby bare feet and her long hair, you hardly knew what she was. "You don't look much like the Living Asheth—" he began.

"Don't!" The Goddess sprang to her knees, carefully bringing the kitten and its bottle with her. "Don't say that name! Don't even think it! She's me, you know, as much as I'm *her*, and if anyone reminds her, she'll notice where I am and send the Arm of Asheth!"

Christopher realised that this must be true or the Goddess could not have got to his world alive. "Then what am I supposed to call you?"

"Millie," said the Goddess firmly, "like the girl in the school books."

He had known she would get round to school before long. He tried to keep her off the subject by asking, "Why do you call the kitten Proudfoot? Isn't that dangerous too?"

"A bit," the Goddess agreed. "But I had to put Mother Proudfoot off the scent – she was ever so flattered – I felt mean deceiving her. Luckily there was an even better reason to call her that. Look."

She laid the dolls' bottle down and gently spread one of the kitten's tiny front paws out over the top of her finger. Its claws were pink. The paw looked like a very small daisy, Christopher thought, kneeling down to look. Then he realised that there were an awful lot of pink claws – at least seven of them in fact. "She has a holy foot," the Goddess said solemnly. "That means she carries the luck of a certain golden deity. When I saw it, I knew it meant I should get here and go to school."

They were back on the Goddess's favourite subject again. Fortunately, at that moment a powerful contralto voice spoke outside the door. "Wong," it said.

"Throgmorten!" Christopher said. He jumped up in great relief and went to open the door. "He won't hurt the kitten, will he?"

"He'd better *not*!" said the Goddess.

But Throgmorten was entirely glad to see all of them. He ran to the Goddess with his tail up and the Goddess, despite greeting him, "Hallo, you vile cat!" rubbed Throgmorten's ears and was obviously delighted to see him. Throgmorten gave the kitten an owner-like sniff and then settled down between Christopher and the fire, purring like a rusty clock.

In spite of this interruption, it was only a matter of time before the Goddess got round to school again. "You got into trouble – didn't you? – when I kept you in the wall," she said, thoughtfully eating a salmon sandwich. Christopher had to look away. "I know you did, or you'd have said. What are these funny fishy things?"

"Salmon sandwiches," Christopher said with a shudder, and he told her about the way Gabriel had put his ninth life in a gold ring, in order to take his mind off mermaids.

"Without even asking you first?" the Goddess said indignantly. "Now you're the one who's worst off. Just let me get settled in at school and I'll think of a way to get that life back for you."

Christopher realised that the time had come to explain the realities of life in Series Twelve to the Goddess. "Look," he said, as kindly as he could, "I don't think you *can* go to school – or not to a boarding school like the one in your books. They cost no end of money. Even the uniforms are expensive. And you haven't even brought your jewellery to sell."

To his surprise, the Goddess was quite unconcerned. "My jewellery was nearly all silver. I couldn't bring it without harming you," she pointed out. "I came prepared to earn the money." Christopher wondered how. By showing her four arms in a freak show? "I know I will," the Goddess said confidently. "I have Proudfoot's holy foot as an omen."

She really did seem to believe this. "My idea was to write to Dr Pawson," Christopher said.

"That might help," the Goddess agreed. "When Millie's friend Cora Hope-fforbes's father broke his neck hunting, she had to borrow her school fees. I *do* know all about these things, you see."

Christopher sighed and conjured some paper and a pen from the schoolroom to write to Dr Pawson with. This intrigued the Goddess mightily.

"How did you do that? Can I learn to do it too?" she wanted to know.

"Why not?" said Christopher. "Gabriel said you were obviously an enchantress. The main rule is to visualise the thing you want to bring on its *own*. When Flavian started me conjuring, I kept fetching bits of wall and table too."

They spent the next hour or so conjuring things the Goddess needed: more charcoal, a dirt-tray for the kitten, socks for the Goddess, a blanket and several scent-sprays to counteract the strong odour of Throgmorten. In between, they considered what to write to Dr Pawson and the Goddess made notes about it in slanting foreign-looking handwriting. They had not made much progress with the letter when the gong sounded distantly for supper. Then Christopher had to agree that the Goddess could conjure his supper tray to the tower. "But I have to go to the schoolroom first," he warned her, "or the maid that brings it will guess. Give me five minutes."

He arrived at the schoolroom at the same time as the maid. Remembering Flavian's outburst, Christopher looked at the maid carefully and then smiled at her – at least, it was partly to keep her from suspecting about the Goddess, but he smiled at her anyway.

The maid was obviously delighted to be noticed. She leant on the table beside the tray and started to talk. "The police carried off that old woman," she said, "about an hour ago. Kicking and shouting, she was. Sally and I sneaked into the hall to watch. It was as good as a play!"

"What about Ta— Mordecai Roberts?" Christopher asked.

"Held for further questioning," said the maid, "with spells all over him. Poor Mr Roberts – Sally said he looked tired to death when she took him in his supper. He's in that little room next to the library. I know he's done wrong, but I keep trying to make an excuse to go in and have a chat to him – cheer him up a bit. Bertha's been in. She got to make up the bed there, lucky thing!"

Christopher was interested, in spite of wishing the maid would go. "You know Mordecai Roberts then?"

"Know him!" said the maid. "When he was working at the Castle, I reckon we were all a bit sweet on him." Here Christopher noticed that his supper tray was beginning to jiggle. He slammed his hand down on it. "You must admit," the maid said, luckily not looking at the tray, "Mr Roberts is that good-looking – and so pleasant with it. I'll name no names, but there were quite a few girls who went out of their way to bump into Mr Roberts in corridors. Silly things! Everyone knew he only had eyes for Miss Rosalie."

"Miss Rosalie!" Christopher exclaimed, more interested than ever, and he held the tray down with all his strength. The Goddess clearly thought she had got something wrong and was summoning it mightily.

"Oh yes. It was Mr Roberts taught Miss Rosalie to play

cricket," said the maid. "But somehow they never could agree. It was said that it was because of her that Mr Roberts got himself sent off on that job in London. She did him a bad turn, did Miss Rosalie." Then, to Christopher's relief, she added, "But I ought to get along and let you eat your supper before it's cold."

"Yes," Christopher said thankfully, leaning on the tray for all he was worth and desperately trying not to seem rude at the same time. "Er – if you do get to see Tac— Mr Roberts, give him my regards. I met him in London once."

"Will do," the maid said cheerfully and left at last. Christopher's arms were weak by then. The tray exploded out from under his hands and vanished. A good deal of the table vanished with it. Christopher pelted back to the tower.

"You silly *fool*!" he began as he opened the door.

The Goddess just pointed to two-thirds of the schoolroom table perched on a workbench. Both of them screamed with laughter.

This was wonderfully jolly, Christopher thought, when he had recovered enough to share his supper with the Goddess and Throgmorten. It was thoroughly companionable knowing a person who had the same sort of magic. He had a feeling that this was the real reason why he had kept visiting the Temple of Asheth. All the same, now that the maid had put Tacroy into his head again, Christopher could not get him out of it. While he talked and laughed with the Goddess, he could actually *feel* Tacroy, downstairs somewhere, at the other end of the Castle, and the spells which held him, which were obviously uncomfortable. He could feel that Tacroy had no hope at all.

"Would you help me do something?" he asked the Goddess. "I know I didn't help you—"

"But you did!" said the Goddess. "You're helping me now, without even grumbling about the nuisance."

"There's a friend of mine who's a prisoner downstairs," Christopher said. "I think it's going to take two of us to break the spells and get him away safely."

"Of course," said the Goddess. She said it so readily that Christopher realised he would have to tell her why Tacroy was there. If he let her help without telling her what she was in for, he would be as bad as Uncle Ralph.

"Wait," he said. "I'm as bad as he is." And he told her about the Wraith and Uncle Ralph's experiments and even about the mermaids – all of it.

"Gosh!" said the Goddess. It was a word she must have picked up from her *Millie* books. "You *are* in a mess! Did Throgmorten really scratch your uncle? Good *cat*!"

She was all for going to rescue Tacroy at once. Christopher had to hang on to the back of the Norfolk jacket to stop her. "No, listen!" he said. "They're all going to round up the rest of the Wraith gang tomorrow. We can set Tacroy free while they're gone. And if they catch my uncle, Gabriel might be so pleased that he won't mind finding Tacroy gone."

The Goddess consented to wait till morning. Christopher conjured her a pair of his pyjamas and left her finishing the salmon sandwiches as a bedtime snack. But, remembering her treachery over the portent, he took care to seal the door behind him with the strongest spell he knew.

He was woken up next morning by a churn of milk landing beside his bed. This was followed by the remains of the schoolroom table. Christopher sent both back to the right places and rushed to the tower, dressing as he went. It looked as if the Goddess was getting impatient.

He found her standing helplessly over a hamper of loaves and a huge ham. "I've forgotten the right way to send things back," she confessed. "And I boiled that packet of tea in the kettle, but it doesn't taste nice. What did I do wrong?"

Christopher sorted her out as well as he could and chased off to the schoolroom for his own breakfast. The maid was already there, holding the tray, looking quizzical. Christopher smiled at her nervously. She grinned and nodded towards the table. It had all four legs at one end, two of them sticking up into the air.

"Oh," he said. "I – er—"

"Come clean," she said. "It was you disappeared the antique cups in the dining room, wasn't it? I told the butler I'd tax you with it."

"Well, yes," said Christopher, knowing the Goddess was drinking freshly made tea out of one at the moment. "I'll put them back. They're not broken."

"They'd better not be," said the maid. "They're worth a fortune, those cups. Now do you mind putting this table to rights so that I can put this tray down before I drop it?"

While Christopher was turning the table to its proper shape, she remarked, "Feeling your gifts all of a sudden, aren't you? Things keep popping in and out all over the Castle this morning. If you'll take my advice, you'll have everything back in its proper place before ten o'clock. After Monsignor de Witt and the others leave to catch those thieves, the butler's going to go round checking the whole Castle."

She stayed and ate some of his toast and marmalade. As she remarked, she had had her breakfast two hours ago. Her name turned out to be Erica and she was a valuable source of information as well as being nice. But Christopher knew he should not have taught the Goddess to conjure. He would never keep her a secret at this rate. Then, when Erica had gone and he was free to consider his problems, it dawned on Christopher that he could solve two of them at one go. All he had to do was to ask Tacroy to take the Goddess with him when he escaped. That made it more urgent than ever to get Tacroy free.

CHAPTER EIGHTEEN

✳

Gabriel de Witt and his assistants left promptly at ten.
Everyone gathered in the hall round the five-pointed
star, some of them carrying leather cases, some simply in
outdoor clothes. Most of the footmen and two of the stable-
hands were going too. Everyone looked sober and
determined and Flavian, for one, looked outright nervous.
He kept running his finger round his high starched collar.
Christopher could see him sweating even from the top of the
stairs.

Christopher and the Goddess watched from behind the
marble balustrade near the black door of Gabriel's study.
They were inside a very carefully constructed cloud of

invisibility, which blotted out the two of them completely but not Throgmorten trotting at their heels. Throgmorten had refused to come near enough to be blotted out too, but nothing would stop him following them.

"Leave him," the Goddess said. "He knows what I'd do to him if he gives us away."

As the silver-voiced clock over the library struck ten, Gabriel came out of his study and stalked down the staircase, wearing a hat even taller and shinier than Papa's. Throgmorten, to Christopher's relief, ignored him. But he felt a strong wrench of worry about Mama. She was certainly going to be arrested, and all she had done was to believe the lies Uncle Ralph had told her.

Gabriel reached the hall and took a look round to see that all his troops were ready. When he saw they were, he pulled on a pair of black gloves and paced into the centre of the five-pointed star, where he went on pacing, growing smaller and smaller and further away as he walked. Miss Rosalie and Dr Simonson followed and began to diminish too. The others went after them two by two. When there was only a tiny, distant black line of them, Christopher said. "I think we can go now."

They began to creep downstairs, still in the cloud of invisibility. The distant line of Gabriel's troops disappeared before they were three stairs down. They went faster. But they were still only half-way down when things began to go wrong.

Flames burst out all over the surface of the star. They

were malignant-looking green-purple flames that filled the hall with vile-smelling green smoke. "What is it?" the Goddess coughed.

"They're using dragons' blood," Christopher said. He meant to sound soothing, but he found he was staring uneasily at those flames.

All at once, the pentacle thundered up into a tall five-pointed fire, ten feet, twenty feet high. The Goddess's invisible hair frizzled. Before they could back up the stairs out of range, the flames had parted, leaning majestically to left and right. Out of the gap Miss Rosalie stumbled, pulling Flavian by one arm. Following them came Dr Simonson dragging a screaming Castle sorceress – Beryl, Christopher thought her name was. By this time, he was standing stock still, staring at the utter rout of Gabriel's troops. Singed and wretched and staggering, all the people who had just set off came pouring back through the gap in the flames and backed away to the sides of the hall with their arms up in front of their faces, coughing in the green smoke.

Christopher looked and looked, but he could not see Gabriel de Witt anywhere among them.

As soon as Frederick Parkinson and the last footman had staggered out into the hall, the flames dipped and died, leaving the pink marble and the dome stained green. The pentagram shimmered into little blades of fire burning over blackness. Uncle Ralph came carefully stepping out among the flames. He had a long gun under one arm and what seemed to be a bag in his hand. Christopher was reminded of nothing so much as one of his Chant uncles going shooting over a stubble field. Probably it was Uncle Ralph's freckled tweeds which put that into his mind. Rather sadly, he wished he had known more about people when he first met Uncle Ralph. He had a foxy, shoddy look. Christopher knew he would never admire someone like Uncle Ralph now.

"Would you like me to throw a marble washstand at him?" whispered the Goddess.

"Wait – I think he's an enchanter too," Christopher whispered back.

"CHRISTOPHER!" shouted Uncle Ralph. The greened dome rang with it. "Christopher, where are you hiding? I can feel you near. Come out, or you'll regret it!"

Reluctantly, Christopher parted the invisibility round himself and stepped to the middle of the staircase. "What happened to Gabriel de Witt?" he said.

Uncle Ralph laughed. "This." He threw the bag he was carrying so that it spread and skidded to a stop at the foot of the stairs. Christopher stared down – rather as he had stared down at Tacroy – at a long, limp, transparent shape that was unquestionably Gabriel de Witt's. "That's his eighth life there," said Uncle Ralph. "I did that with those weapons you brought me from Series One, Christopher. This one works a treat." He patted the gun under his arm.

"I spread the rest of his lives out all over the Related Worlds. He won't trouble us again. And the other weapons you brought me work even better." He gave his moustache a sly tweak and grinned up at Christopher. "I had the weapons all set up to meet de Witt's folk and took the magic out of them in a twinkling. None of them can cast a spell to save their lives now. So there's nothing to stop us working together just like the old days. You *are* still working for me, aren't you, Christopher?"

"No," said Christopher, and stood there expecting to have his remaining lives blasted in all directions the next second.

Uncle Ralph only laughed. "Yes, you are, stupid boy. You're unmasked. All these people standing here *know* you were my main carrier now. You have to work with me or go to prison – and I'm moving into this Castle with you to make sure of you."

There was a long, warbling cry from behind Christopher. A ginger streak shot downstairs past him. Uncle Ralph stared, saw his danger, and made to raise his gun. But Throgmorten was almost on him by then. Uncle Ralph realised he had no time to shoot and prudently vanished instead, in a spiral of green steam. All Throgmorten got of him was a three-cornered piece of tweed with some blood on it. He stood in a frustrated arch on the blackened pentacle, spitting his rage.

Christopher raced down the stairs. "Shut all the doors!" he shouted to the stunned, staring Castle people. "Don't let Throgmorten out of the hall! I want him on guard to stop Uncle Ralph coming back."

"Don't be stupid!" the Goddess shouted, galloping after

him, visible to everyone. "Throgmorten's a Temple cat – he understands speech. Just *ask* him."

Christopher wished he had known that before. Since it was too late to do anything much about anything else, he knelt on the greenishly charred floor and spoke to Throgmorten. "Can you guard this pentacle, please, and make sure Uncle Ralph doesn't come back? You know Uncle Ralph wanted to cut you to pieces? Well, you can cut *him* to pieces if he shows up again."

"Wong!" Throgmorten agreed with his tail lashing enthusiastically. He sat himself down at one point of the star and stared fixedly at it, as still as if he were watching a giant mousehole. Malice oozed out of every hair of him.

It was clear Uncle Ralph would not get past Throgmorten in a hurry. Christopher stood up to find himself and the Goddess inside a ring of Gabriel's dejected helpers. Most of them were staring at the Goddess.

"This is my friend the G— Millie," he said.

"Pleased to meet you," Flavian said wanly.

Dr Simonson swept Flavian aside. "Well what are we going to do now?" he said. "Gabriel's gone and we're left with this brat – who turns out to be the little crook I always suspected he was – and not a spell to rub together between us! What I say—"

"We must inform the Minister," said Mr Wilkinson the librarian.

"Now wait a moment," said Miss Rosalie. "The Minister's only a minor warlock, and Christopher said he wasn't working for the Wraith any more."

"That child would say anything," said Dr Simonson.

In their usual way, they were behaving as if Christopher were not there. He beckoned to the Goddess and backed out from among them, leaving them crowded round Miss Rosalie arguing.

"What are we doing?" the Goddess asked.

"Getting Tacroy out before they think of stopping us," said Christopher. "After that, I want to make sure Throgmorten catches Uncle Ralph, even if it's the last thing I do."

They found Tacroy sitting dejectedly by the table in an empty little room. From the tumbled look of the camp bed in the corner, Tacroy had not managed to get much sleep that night. The door of the room was half open and at first sight there seemed no reason why Tacroy did not simply walk out. But now the Goddess had made it clear to Christopher what witch-sight was, all he had to do was look at the room the way he looked at The Place Between to understand why Tacroy stayed where he was. There were strands of spell across the doorway. The floor was knee-deep in more, crisscrossed all over. Tacroy himself was inside a perfect mass of other spells, intricately knotted over him, particularly round his head.

"You were right about it needing two of us," the Goddess said. "You do him, and I'll go and look for a broom and do the rest."

Christopher pushed through the spells over the door and

266

waded through the others until he reached Tacroy. Tacroy did not look up. Perhaps he could not even see Christopher or hear him. Christopher began gently picking the spells undone, rather in the way you untie a mass of tight knots round a parcel, and because it was so boring and fiddly, he talked to Tacroy while he worked. He talked all the time the Goddess was gone. Naturally, most of what he told him was about that cricket match. "You missed that deliberately, didn't you?" he said. "Were you afraid I'd give you away?"

Tacroy gave no sign of having heard, but as Christopher went on to tell him the way Miss Rosalie batted and how bad Flavian was, the hard tired lines of his face gradually smoothed out behind the strands of spell, and he grew more like the Tacroy Christopher knew from The Place Between.

"So, thanks to you teaching me, we won by two runs," Christopher was saying, when the Goddess reappeared with the broom Miss Rosalie used to chase Throgmorten and started sweeping the room-spells into heaps as if they were cobwebs.

Tacroy almost smiled. Christopher told him who the Goddess was and then explained what had just happened in the hall. The smile clouded away from Tacroy's face. He said, a little thickly, "Then I rather wasted my time trying to keep you out of it, didn't I?"

"Not really," said Christopher, wrestling with a spell-knot above Tacroy's left ear.

The bitter lines came back to Tacroy's face. "Don't run

away with the idea that I'm a knight in shining armour," he said. "I knew what was in most of those parcels."

"The mermaids?" Christopher asked. It was the most important question he had ever asked.

"Not till afterwards," Tacroy admitted. "But you notice I didn't stop when I knew. When I first met you, I would have reported you quite cheerfully to Gabriel de Witt if you hadn't been that small. And I knew Gabriel had some kind of a trap set up in Series Ten that time you lost a life. I just hadn't expected it would be that lethal. And—"

"Stow it, Tacroy," said Christopher.

"Tacroy?" said Tacroy. "Is that my spirit name?" When Christopher nodded, concentrating on the knot, Tacroy muttered, "Well, that's one less hold they have." Then as the Goddess, having dealt with the room-spells, came and leant on her broom, watching his face as Christopher worked, he said, "You'll know me again, young lady."

The Goddess nodded. "You're like Christopher and me, aren't you? There's a part of you that's somewhere else."

Tacroy's face flushed a sudden red. Christopher could feel sweat on it under his fingers. Very surprised, he asked, "Where is the rest of you?"

He saw Tacroy's eyes swivel towards his, imploringly. "Series Eleven – don't ask any more! Don't *ask* me!" he said. "Under these spells I'd have to tell you and then we'd *all* catch it!"

He sounded so desperate that Christopher considerately

did not ask any more – though he could not resist exchanging a look with the Goddess – and worked until he got that knot undone at last. It proved to be the key knot. The rest of the spell at once fell away in dissolving strands round Tacroy's handmade boots. Tacroy stood up stiffly and stretched.

"Thanks," he said. "What a relief! You can't imagine how vile it feels having a net bag round your spirit. What now?"

"Start running," said Christopher. "Do you want me to break the spells round the grounds for you?"

Tacroy's arms stopped in the middle of a stretch. "Now *you* stow it!" he said. "From what you said, there's no one apart from you two youngsters and me in this Castle with any magic worth speaking of, and your uncle could come back any minute. And you expect me just to walk out?"

"Well—"

But at that moment, Miss Rosalie came in with Dr Simonson and most of the rest of Gabriel's staff crowding behind her. "Why, Mordecai!" she said brightly. "Do I actually hear you uttering a noble sentiment?"

Tacroy took his arms down and folded them. "Strictly practical," he said. "You know me, Rosalie. Have you come to lock me up again? I can't see you doing it without your magic, but you're welcome to try."

Miss Rosalie drew herself up to a majestic five feet. "I wasn't coming to see you at all," she said. "We were looking for Christopher. Christopher, we're going to have to ask you to take over as the next Chrestomanci, at least for the moment. The Government will probably appoint some other enchanter in the end, but this is *such* a crisis. Do you think you can do it, dear?"

They were all staring at Christopher appealingly, even Dr Simonson. Christopher wanted to laugh. "You knew I'd have to," he said, "and I will on two conditions. I want Mordecai Roberts set free and not arrested again afterwards. And I want the G— Millie as my chief helper and she's to be paid by being sent to a boarding school."

"Anything you want, dear," Miss Rosalie said hastily.

"Good," said Christopher. "Then let's go back to the hall."

In the hall, people were gathering dejectedly under the green-stained dome. The butler was there and two men in cook's hats, and the housekeeper with most of the maids and footmen. "Tell them to get the gardeners and the stable people too," Christopher said, and went to look at the five-pointed star where Throgmorten sat watching. By screwing up his eyes and forcing his witch-sight to its utmost, he could see a tiny round space in the middle of the star – a sort of ghostly mousehole – which Throgmorten never took his eyes off. Throgmorten had quite impressive magic. On the other hand, Throgmorten would be only too pleased if Uncle Ralph came back. "How do we stop someone coming through?" Christopher asked.

Tacroy ran to a cupboard under the staircase and came back with an armful of queer candles in star-shaped holders. He showed Christopher and the Goddess where to put them and what words to say. Then he had Christopher stand back and conjure all the candles to flame. Tacroy was, Christopher realised, among other things, a fully-trained magician. As the candles flared up, Throgmorten's tail twitched scornfully.

"The cat's right," Tacroy said. "This would stop most people, but with the amount of dragon's blood your uncle has stored away, he could break through any time he wants."

"Then we'll catch him when he does," Christopher said. He knew what he would do himself, if he knew Throgmorten was lying in wait, and he was fairly sure Uncle Ralph would do the same. He suspected their minds worked the same way. If he was right, it would take Uncle Ralph a little time to get ready.

By this time, quite a crowd of people had come into the hall through the big front door, where they were standing clutching their caps and awkwardly brushing earth off their boots. Christopher went to stand a little way up the staircase, looking down on the long, limp remains of Gabriel de Witt and everyone's faces, anxious and depressed, lit half by the flames of the strange candles. He knew just what needed saying. And he was surprised to find he was enjoying himself hugely.

He shouted, "Hands up everyone who can do magic."

Most of the gardeners' hands went up and so did a couple of the stable lads'. When he looked at the indoor people, he saw the butler's hand was up and one of the cooks'. There was the boot-boy who had worked the scoreboard and three

271

of the maids, one of whom was Erica. Tacroy's hand was up and so was the Goddess's. Everyone else was looking at the floor, dismally.

Christopher shouted, "Now hands up anyone who can do woodwork or metalwork."

Quite a number of the dismal people put their hands up, looking surprised. Dr Simonson was one, Flavian was another. All the stable people had their hands up, and the gardeners too. Good. Now all they needed was encouragement.

"Right," said Christopher. "We've got two things to do. We've got to keep my uncle out of here until we're ready to catch him. And we've got to get Gabriel de Witt back."

The second thing made everyone murmur with surprise, and then with hope. Christopher knew he had been right to say it, even though he was not sure it could be done – and as far as his own feelings went, Gabriel could stay in eight limp pieces for the rest of both their lives. He found he was enjoying himself more than ever.

"That's what I said," he said. "My uncle didn't kill Gabriel. He just scattered all his lives. We'll have to find them and put them together. But first—" he looked at the greened glass of the dome and the chandelier that hung from it on its long chain "—I want a birdcage-thing made, big enough to cover the pentacle, and hung from there, so that it can be triggered by a spell to come down over anything that tries to get through." He pointed to Dr Simonson. "You're in charge of making it. Collect everyone who can do woodwork and metalwork, but make sure some of them can do magic too. I want it reinforced with spells to stop anyone breaking out of it."

Dr Simonson's beard began to jut in a proud, responsible way. He gave a slightly mocking bow. "It shall be done."

Christopher supposed he deserved that. The way he was behaving would have had the Last Governess accusing him of having a swelled head. But then he was beginning to suspect that he worked best when he was feeling bumptious. He was annoyed with the Last Governess for stopping him realising this before.

"But before anyone starts on the birdcage," he said, "the spells round the ground need reinforcing, or my uncle will try to bring the Wraith organisation in that way. I want everyone except T— Mordecai and the G— Millie to go all round the fences and walls and hedges casting every spell they can think of that will keep people out."

That made a mixed murmur. Gardeners and housemaids looked at one another doubtfully. One of the gardeners' hands went up. "Mr McLintock, Head Gardener," he announced himself. "I'm not questioning your wisdom, lad – just wishing to explain that our speciality is growing things, green fingers, and the like, and not any too much to do with defence."

"But you can grow cactuses and bushes with long spines and ten-foot nettles and so on, can't you?" Christopher said.

Mr McLintock nodded, with a pawky sort of grin. "Aye. Thistles too and poison ivy."

This emboldened the cook to put his hand up. "*Je suis chef de cuisine*," he said. "A cook only. My magic is with the good food."

"I bet you can reverse it," said Christopher. "Go and poison the walls. Or if you can't, hang rotten steaks and mouldy soufflées on them."

"Not since my student days have I—" the cook began indignantly. But this seemed to bring back memories to him. A wistful look came over his face, which was followed by a gleeful grin. "I will try," he said.

Now Erica's hand was up. "If you please," she said, "me and Sally and Bertha can only really do *little* things – charms and sendings and the like."

"Well go and do them – as many as you can," Christopher said. "A wall is built brick by brick after all." That expression pleased him. He caught the Goddess's eye. "If you can't think what charms to work, consult my assistant, Millie. She's full of ideas."

The Goddess grinned. So did the boot-boy. From the look on his face, he was full of appalling notions which he could hardly wait to try. Christopher watched the boot-boy troop out with the gardeners, the cook and the maids, and rather envied him.

He beckoned Flavian over. "Flavian, there's still loads of magic I don't know. Would you mind standing by to teach me things as they come up?"

"Well, I—" Flavian gave an embarrassed sideways look at Tacroy leaning on the banisters below Christopher.

"Mordecai could do that just as well."

"Yes, but I'm going to need him to go into trances and look for Gabriel's lives," said Christopher.

"Are you indeed?" said Tacroy. "And Gabriel's going to burst into tears of joy when he sees me, isn't he?"

"I'll go with you," said Christopher.

"Quite like old times," said Tacroy. "Gabriel's going to burst into tears when he sees you too. What it is to be loved!" His eyes flickered over at Miss Rosalie. "If only I had my young lady who plays the harp now—"

"Don't be absurd, Mordecai," said Miss Rosalie. "You shall have everything you need. What do you want the rest of us to do, Christopher? Mr Wilkinson and I are no good at woodwork, and nor are Beryl and Yolande."

"You can act as advisers," said Christopher.

CHAPTER NINETEEN

✷

*T*he next twenty-four hours were the busiest Christopher had ever spent. They held a council-of-war in Gabriel's twilight office, where Christopher discovered that some of the dark panels rolled back to connect it with the rooms on either side. Christopher had the desks and the typewriting machines shoved to the walls and turned the whole space into one big operations room. It was much lighter like that, and became more and more crowded and busy as the various plans were set up.

There were, everyone told Christopher, many different ways of divining whether a living person was present in a world. Mr Wilkinson had whole lists of methods. It was agreed that they try to use these to narrow down Tacroy's search for Gabriel. One of every kind was set up, but since nobody was sure if Gabriel's separated lives quite counted as alive, they all had to be set to maximum strength, and it turned out that, apart from Christopher, only the Goddess had strong enough magic to activate them and tune them from Series to Series. But anyone could watch them. The room was soon full of tense helpers staring into globes, mirrors, pools of mercury or ink, and spare sheets coated with liquid crystal, while the Goddess was kept busy adjusting the various spells and making a chart, in her foreign writing, of the readings from all the devices.

Miss Rosalie insisted that the council-of-war should also decide how to tell the Ministry what was going on, but that never did get decided, because Christopher kept getting called away. First Dr Simonson called him down to the hall to explain how they planned to make the birdcage. Dr Simonson was taking it much more seriously than Christopher expected. "It's highly unorthodox," he said, "but who cares so long as it catches our man?"

Christopher was half-way upstairs again when the butler came to tell Christopher that they had done all they could think of to defend the grounds, and would Master Christopher come and see? So Christopher went – and marvelled. The main gates, and the other smaller ones, were hung with curses and dripping poison. Brambles with six-inch thorns had been grown along the walls, while the hedges put Christopher in mind of Sleeping

Beauty's castle, so high and thick with thorns, nettles and poison weeds were they. Ten-foot thistles and giant cactus guarded the fences, and every single weak place had been booby-trapped by the boot-boy.

He demonstrated, using his pet ferret, how anything that stepped here would become a caterpillar; or here would sink into bottomless sewage; or here would be seized by giant lobster-claws; or here – anyway, he had made nineteen, each one nastier than the last. Christopher ran back to the Castle thinking that if they did manage to get Gabriel back, he would have to ask him to promote the boot-boy. He was too good to waste on boots.

Back in the operations room, he had a set of magic mirrors set up, each focused on a different part of the defences, so that they would know at once if anyone tried to attack. Flavian was just showing him how to activate the spells painted on the backs of the mirrors, when it was the housekeeper's turn to interrupt. "Master Christopher, this Castle isn't supplied to stand a siege. How am I to get the butcher and the baker and the milk through? There's a lot of mouths to feed here."

Christopher had to make a list of when the deliveries arrived, so that he and the Goddess could conjure them through at the right moment. The Goddess pinned it up beside the mirror-watch rota, the divining charts, the duty rota, the patrol rota – the wall was getting covered with lists.

In the midst of all this, two ladies called Yolande and Beryl (whom Christopher still could not tell apart) sat themselves down at the typewriters and started to clatter away. "We may not be sorceresses any longer," said Beryl (unless she was Yolande), "but that doesn't stop us trying to keep the usual business running. We can deal with urgent enquiries or advice at least."

Shortly they were calling Christopher away too. "The trouble is," Yolande (unless her name was Beryl) confessed, "Gabriel usually signs all the letters. We don't think you should forge his signature, but we wondered if you simply wrote Chrestomanci—?"

"Before you conjure the mailbag down to the Post Office for us," Beryl (or maybe Yolande) added.

They showed Christopher how to set the sign of a nine-lifed enchanter on the word *Chrestomanci*, to protect it from being used against him in witchcraft. Christopher had great fun developing a dashing style of signature, sizzling with the enchanter's mark that kept it safe even from Uncle Ralph. It occurred to him then that he was enjoying himself more than he had ever done in his life. Papa had been right. He really was cut out to be the next Chrestomanci. But suppose he hadn't been? Christopher thought, making another sizzling signature. It was simply luck that he was. Well then, he thought, something could have been done about it. There had been no need at all to feel trapped.

Someone called him from the other end of the room then. "I think I've got the most restful job," Tacroy laughed up at him from the couch in the middle, where he was preparing to go into his first trance. They had agreed that Tacroy should try a whole lot of short trances, to cover as many worlds as possible. And Miss Rosalie had agreed to play the harp for him, despite not having any magic. She was sitting on the end of the couch. As Christopher passed, Tacroy shut his eyes and Miss Rosalie struck a sweet rippling chord. Tacroy's eyes shot open. "For crying out loud, woman! Are you trying to clog my spirit in toffee or something? Don't you know any *reasonable* music?"

"As I remember, you always object to anything I play!" Miss Rosalie retorted. "So I shall play something *I* like, regardless!"

"I hate your taste in music!" Tacroy snarled.

"Calm down, or you won't go into a trance. I don't want to have sore fingers for nothing!" Miss Rosalie snapped.

They reminded Christopher of something – of someone. He looked back on his way over to the pool of ink where Flavian was beckoning. Tacroy and Miss Rosalie were staring at each other, both making sure the other knew their feelings were deeply hurt. Who have I seen look like that before? Christopher wondered. Underneath, he could tell, Tacroy and Miss Rosalie were longing to stop being rude to one another, but both too proud to make the first move. Who was that like?

As Christopher bent over the pool of ink, he got it. Papa and Mama! They had been exactly the same!

When the pool of ink was showing World C in Series Eight, Christopher went back past Miss Rosalie staring stormily ahead and playing a jig, to where Yolande and Beryl were typing. "Can I send someone an official letter of my own?" he asked.

"Just dictate," Yolande (or possibly Beryl) said, with her fingers on the keys.

Christopher gave her Dr Pawson's address. "Dear Sir," he said, in the way all the letters he had signed went. "This office would be obliged if you would divine the whereabouts of Mr Cosimo Chant, last heard of in Japan, and forward his address to Mrs Miranda Chant, last heard of living in Kensington." Blushing a bit, he asked, "Will that do?"

"For Dr Pawson," Beryl (or perhaps Yolande) said, "you have to add, 'The customary fee will be forwarded.' Dr Pawson never works without a fee. I'll put the request through Accounts for you. Mr Wilkinson needs you at the quicksilver bowl now."

While Christopher rushed back across the room, the Goddess remembered that Proudfoot the kitten would be starving by then. She conjured her from the tower room, scarf, bottle and all. One of the helpers ran for milk. It took a while. Proudfoot, impatient with the delay, opened eyes like two chips of sapphire and glared blearily around. "Mi-i-i-i-ilk!" she demanded from an astonishingly wide pink mouth.

Even when an ordinary kitten opens its eyes for the first time, it is a remarkable moment. Since Proudfoot was an Asheth Temple cat, the effect was startling. She suddenly had a personality at least as strong as Throgmorten's, except that it seemed to be just the opposite. She was passed from hand to hand for people to take turns at cooing over her and feeding her. Flavian was so besotted with her that he would not let go of her until Tacroy came out of his trance, very dejected because he had not been able to sense Gabriel in any of the three worlds he had visited. Flavian gave him Proudfoot to cheer him up. Tacroy put her under his chin and purred at her, but Miss Rosalie took her away in order to give Tacroy a strong cup of tea instead, and then spent the next half hour doting on Proudfoot herself.

All this devotion seemed to Christopher to be unfair on Throgmorten. He went out on the stairs to see if Throgmorten was all right, where he paused for a moment, struck with how different it all was. The green from the dragon's blood was fading, but there was still quite a greenish tinge in the light from the dome. Under it, Dr Simonson, Frederick Parkinson and a crowd of helpers were sawing, hammering and welding in their shirt-sleeves. The hall was littered with timber, tools and metal rods, and more helpers were constantly bringing further wood and tools in through the open front door. Various people sat on the stairs drinking cups of tea while they waited to take a turn in front of the divining spells. If someone had told Christopher a week ago that Chrestomanci Castle would look like a rather disorderly workshop, he would never have believed them, he thought.

The candles were still burning, flaring sideways in the draught from the front door, and there in the blackened pentacle Throgmorten sat like a statue, staring fiercely at his

Uncle Ralph mousehole. Christopher was glad to see that he was surrounded by all that a cat could desire. An earth-tray, a bowl of milk, saucers of fish, a plate of meat and a chicken wing had been carefully pushed between the candle-holders to the edges of the star. But Throgmorten was ignoring it all.

It was clear no one had liked to disturb Gabriel's life. It was still lying on the floor where Uncle Ralph had thrown it, limp and transparent. Someone had carefully fenced it off with black rope tied round four chairs from the library. Christopher stared down at it. No wonder Tacroy couldn't find anything and none of the divining spells showed anything, if all the lives were like this, he was thinking, when one of the gardeners ran in through the front door and waved at him urgently.

"Can you come and look?" he panted. "We don't know if it's the Wraith or not. There's hundreds of them, all round the grounds in fancy-dress-like!"

"I'll look in the mirrors," Christopher called back. He raced back into the operations room to the magic mirrors. The one trained on the main gate was giving a perfect view of the peculiar soldiers staring through the bars. They wore short tunics and silver masks and they were all carrying spears. Christopher's stomach jumped nastily at the sight. He turned round and looked at the Goddess. She was white.

"It's the Arm of Asheth," she whispered, "They've found me."

"I'll go and make sure they can't get in," Christopher said. He ran back down the stairs and through the hall and then out into the grounds with the gardener. On the lawn, Mr McLintock was lining up all the rest of the outside workers and making sure each of them had a billhook or a sharp hoe.

"I'm not letting any of those heathen bodies into *my* gardens," he said.

"Yes, but those spears are deadly. You'll have to keep everyone out of throwing-range," Christopher said. He felt a sharp stabbing pain in his chest just at the thought.

He went round the gardens with Mr McLintock, as near as they dared to the fences and walls. The soldiers of the Arm of Asheth were just standing outside, as if the spells were keeping them out, but to be on the safe side, Christopher doubled the strength of each one as he came to it. The distant glimpses he got of silver masks and spear points made him feel ill.

As he turned and hurried back to the Castle, he realised that he was not enjoying himself any longer. He felt weak and young and anxious. Uncle Ralph was one thing, but he knew he just did not know how to deal with the Arm of Asheth. If only Gabriel was here! he found himself thinking. Gabriel knew all about the Temple of Asheth. Probably he could have sent the soldiers away with one cool, dry word. And then, Christopher thought, he'd punish me for hiding the Goddess here when he told me not to, but even that would be worth it.

He went back through the hall, where the birdcage was only a pile of sawn wood and three bent rods. He knew it would be nothing like ready by the night, and Uncle Ralph was bound to try to come back tonight. Past Gabriel's limp fenced-off life, he went, and up the stairs into the operations room, to find Tacroy coming out of another trance shaking his head dismally. The Goddess was white and trembling and everyone else was exasperated because none of the various shadows and flickers in the divining spells seemed to be anything to do with Gabriel.

"I think I'd better conjure out a telegram to the Ministry to send in the army," Christopher said dejectedly.

"You'll do no such thing!" snapped Miss Rosalie. She made Christopher and the Goddess sit beside Tacroy on the couch and made them all drink the hot, sweet tea that Erica had just brought in. "Now listen, Christopher," she said. "If you let the Ministry know what's happened to Gabriel, they'll insist on sending some adult enchanter to take over, and he won't be the slightest good because his magic won't be as strong as yours. You're the only nine-lifed enchanter left. We need you to put Gabriel back together when we find him. You're the only one who can. And it's not as if the Arm of Asheth can get into the grounds, is it?"

"No – I doubled the spells," Christopher said.

"Good," said Miss Rosalie. "Then we're no worse off than we were. I didn't argue all this through with Dr Simonson just to have *you* let me down, Christopher! We'll find Gabriel before long and then everything will be all right, you'll see."

"Mother Proudfoot always says the darkest hour is before the dawn," the Goddess put in. But she did not say it as if she believed it.

As if to prove Mother Proudfoot right, Christopher was just finishing his tea when Flavian cried out, "Oh, I understand now!" Flavian was sitting at the big dark desk trying to make sense of all the shadows and flickers showing up on the divining spells. All the people sitting slumped around the operations room sat up and looked at him hopefully.

"It's taking Gabriel's lives a long time to settle," Flavian said. "There are clear signs of one drifting about Series Nine, and another in Series Two, but neither of them have come down into a world yet. I think we may find the rest of them are still floating about the World Edge if we retune all the spells."

Tacroy jumped up and came to look over Flavian's shoulder. "You may be right at that!" he said. "The one time I thought I caught a whiff of Gabriel was on the World Edge near Series One. Does anything show up there?"

The World Edge means The Place Between, Christopher thought, as he hurried with the Goddess to adjust all the divining apparatus. "I can go and climb about there and bring them in," he said.

There was an instant outcry against him. "No," said Flavian. "I'm still your tutor and I forbid it."

"We need you here to deal with your uncle," Tacroy said.

"You can't leave me here with the Arm of Asheth!" said

286

the Goddess. "Besides, what happens if you lose another life?"

"Exactly," said Miss Rosalie. "Your last life is shut in the safe under charms only Gabriel can break. You daren't risk losing another one. We'll just have to wait until the lives settle. Then we can set up a properly guarded Gate and send you through to collect them."

With even the Goddess against him, Christopher gave in for the moment. He knew he could always sneak off to The Place Between if he needed to. Just now, Uncle Ralph was more important than Gabriel and probably more of a danger even than the Arm of Asheth.

He arranged watches and patrols for the night with Tacroy and Mr McLintock. They had supper camped about the hall and up the stairs, under the ladders and planks Dr Simonson was using to lower the chandelier. At this stage, the birdcage was still only a collection of metal hoops and wooden rods. The cooks carried cauldrons and casseroles to Dr Simonson's team as they worked, so that they could carry on until the daylight failed, but Christopher knew they were not going to get it finished that day. Throgmorten came off duty long enough to eat a plate of caviar to strengthen him for the night's work. Proudfoot was taken to the kitchen for safety, to be doted on there, and everyone settled down tensely for the night.

Christopher had arranged the watches so that there was always a mixture of able-bodied people with ones that still had magic. He took the first watch himself. The Goddess took the next one. Christopher was asleep in the library next to Frederick Parkinson when something happened in the middle of the Goddess's watch. The Goddess was panting and flustered and said she was sure Uncle Ralph had tried to come through the pentacle. "I conjured him away," she kept saying. There was certainly a wild hullaballoo from Throgmorten. But by the time Christopher got there all he saw was a wisp of steam rising from the invisible mousehole and Throgmorten pacing round it like a frustrated tiger.

Oddly enough, there was no smell of dragons' blood. It looked as if Uncle Ralph had either been testing their defences or trying to deceive them about his plans. The real attack came just before dawn, when Tacroy and the boot-boy were on watch. And it came from outside the Castle grounds. Bells rang all over the Castle, showing that the spells had been breached. As Christopher pelted across the dewy lawn, he thought that the screams, yells and clangs coming from the walls would have woken everyone even if the bells had not rung. Again he got there too late. He arrived to find Tacroy and the boot-boy furiously chanting spells to fill two gaps in Mr McLintock's vast spiny hedge. He could dimly see a few figures in silver armour milling about beyond the gaps. Christopher hastily reinforced the spells for all he was worth.

"What happened?" he panted.

"The Wraith seems to have walked into the Arm of Asheth," Tacroy said, shivering in the early mist. "It's an ill wind." While the gardeners hurried up with cactuses to fill the gaps and the boot-boy booby-trapped them, he said he thought that a small army of the Wraith's men had tried to break into the grounds. But the Arm of Asheth must have thought the Wraith was attacking *them* and accidentally defended the Castle. At all events, the attackers had run for their lives.

Christopher sniffed the reek of dragons' blood in the mist and thought Tacroy was certainly right.

By the time he got back to the Castle, it was light enough for Dr Simonson and his helpers to be hard at work again. Flavian was stumbling about the operations room, pale and yawning from having been up all night. "I was right about Gabriel's lives!" he said jubilantly. "They're all settling down into the Related Worlds. I've got six of them more or less pin-pointed now – though I can't spot the seventh at all yet. I suggest you go and collect those six anyway as soon as they've finished that lobster pot of yours."

The Lobster Pot, as everyone came to call it, was hoisted triumphantly up into the air above the pentacle soon after breakfast. Christopher jumped into the star himself to test it. The spell tripped, just as it was supposed to, and the cage came crashing down around him. Throgmorten looked up irritably. Christopher grinned and tried to conjure the thing away. It would not budge. He rattled the flimsy bars with his hands and tried to heave up one edge, but he could not budge it that way either. In something of a panic, he realised that the thing was impossible to get out of, even though he had set most of the spells on it himself.

"Your face was rather a study," the Goddess said, with a weak chuckle. "You should have seen the relief on it when they hauled it up again!" The Goddess was not at all happy. She was pale and nervous in spite of trying to joke.

She has only one life, Christopher reminded himself, and the Arm of Asheth is waiting outside for her. "Why don't you come with me to collect Gabriel's lives?" he said. "It will puzzle the Arm of Asheth no end if you start hopping from world to world."

"Oh *may* I?" the Goddess said gladly. "I feel so responsible."

There had been much discussion, some of it very learned, among Flavian, Beryl, Yolande and Mr Wilkinson about how to collect Gabriel's lives. Christopher had no idea there were so many ways to send people to different worlds. Miss Rosalie settled it by saying briskly, "We set up a Gate here in this room and send Mordecai into a trance with a spirit-trace so that we can focus the Gate on him as soon as he finds a Gabriel. Then Christopher and Millie go through and persuade the Gabriel that he's needed at the Castle. What could be simpler?"

Many things could have been simpler, Christopher thought, as he and the Goddess worked on the complex magics of the Gate to Flavian's endless, patient instructions. He felt slow and reluctant anyway. Even though only Gabriel could give him his ninth life back, even though Gabriel was desperately needed, Christopher did not want him back. All the fun would end then. Everything in the

Castle would go quiet and respectable and grown-up again. Only the fact that he always liked working on magic that really did something kept Christopher working properly on the Gate.

When it was finished, the Gate looked simple indeed. It was a tall square frame of metal, with two mirrors sloping together to make a triangle at the back of it. No one would know, to look at it, how difficult it had been to do.

Christopher left Tacroy lying on the couch with the little blue blob of the spirit-trace on his forehead and went, rather moodily, to conjure the baker's cart into the Castle grounds. This is the last time they'll let me do this, he thought, as the Arm of Asheth angrily shook their spears at the baker.

When he came back, Tacroy was pale and still, covered with blankets and Miss Rosalie was gently playing her harp.

"There he is in the Gate," Flavian said.

The two mirrors had become one slightly misty picture of somewhere in Series One. Christopher could see a line of the great pylons that carried the ring trains stretching away into the distance. Tacroy was standing under the nearest one, wearing the green suit Christopher knew so well. It must be what Tacroy's spirit always wore. The spirit had its hands spread out frustratedly.

"Something seems to be wrong," Flavian said.

Everyone jumped when the body lying on the couch spoke suddenly in a strange, husky voice. "I had him!"

Tacroy's body said. "He was watching the trains. He was just telling me he could invent a better train. Then he simply vanished! What do I do?"

"Go and try for the Gabriel in Series Two," Miss Rosalie said, plucking a rippling, soothing tune.

"It'll take a moment," Tacroy's body croaked.

The picture in the Gate vanished. Christopher imagined Tacroy scrambling and wafting through The Place Between. Everyone round him wondered anxiously what had gone wrong.

"Maybe Gabriel's lives just don't trust Mordecai," Flavian suggested.

The mirrors combined into a picture again. This time they all saw Gabriel's life. It was standing on a hump-backed bridge, gazing down into the river below. It was surprisingly frail and bent and old, so old that Christopher realised that the Gabriel he knew was nothing like as elderly as he had thought. Tacroy's spirit was there too, edging gently up the hump of the bridge towards Gabriel's life, for all the world like Throgmorten stalking a big black bird. Gabriel did not seem to see Tacroy. He did not look round. But his bent black figure was suddenly not there any more. There was only Tacroy on the bridge, staring at the place where Gabriel had been.

"That one went too," Tacroy's body uttered from the couch. "What *is* this?"

"Hold it!" Flavian whispered and ran to check the nearest divining spells.

"Stay there a moment, Mordecai," Miss Rosalie said gently.

In the mirrors, Tacroy's spirit leant its elbows on the bridge and tried to look patient.

"I don't *believe* this!" Flavian cried out. "Everyone check, quickly! All the lives seem to be disappearing! Better call Mordecai back, Rosalie, or he'll waste his strength for nothing."

There was a rush for the crystals, bowls, mirrors and scrying pools. Miss Rosalie swept both hands across her harp and, inside the Gate, Tacroy's spirit looked up, looked surprised and vanished as suddenly as Gabriel's life. Miss Rosalie leant over and watched anxiously as Tacroy's body stirred. Colour flooded back to his face. His eyes opened. "What's going on?" he said, pushing the blankets back.

"We've no idea," said Miss Rosalie. "All the Gabriels are disappearing—"

"No they're not!" Flavian called excitedly. "They're all collecting into a bunch, and they're coming this way, the lot of them!"

There was a tense half-hour, during which everyone's hopes and fears see-sawed. Since Christopher's hopes and fears on the whole went the opposite way to everyone else's, he thought he could not have borne it without Proudfoot the kitten. Erica brought Proudfoot with her when she hurried in with a tray of tea to restore Tacroy. Proudfoot became very busy taking her first long walk, all the way under Gabriel's black desk, with her string of a tail whipping about for balance. She was something much better to watch than the queer clots and whorls that Gabriel's lives made as they drifted steadily towards Series Twelve. Christopher was watching Proudfoot when Flavian said, "Oh dear!" and turned away from the scrying pool.

"What's the matter?" he asked.

Flavian's shoulders drooped. He tore off his tight, crumpled collar and threw it on the floor. "All the lives have stopped," he said. "They're faint but certain. They're in Series Eleven, I'm afraid. I think that was where the seventh life was all along. So much for our hopes!"

"Why?" said Christopher.

"Nobody can get there, dear," said Miss Rosalie. She looked as if she might cry. "At least, nobody ever comes back from there if they do."

Christopher looked at Tacroy. Tacroy had gone pale, paler even than he went in a trance. He was the colour of milk with a dash of coffee in it.

CHAPTER TWENTY

✳

*H*ere was the perfect excuse to stop looking for Gabriel. Christopher expected to have a short struggle with himself. He quite took himself by surprise when he stood up straight away. He did not even have to think that the Goddess had also heard Tacroy confess that part of himself was in Series Eleven. "Tacroy," he said. He knew it was important to call Tacroy by his spirit name. "Tacroy, come to that empty office for a moment. I have to talk to you."

Slowly and reluctantly Tacroy stood up. Miss Rosalie said sharply, "Mordecai, you look ill. Do you want me to come with you?"

"No!" Tacroy and Christopher said together.

Tacroy sat on the edge of a desk in the empty office and put his face in his hands. Christopher was sorry for him. He had to remind himself that he and Tacroy were the ones who had brought Uncle Ralph the weapon which had blown Gabriel's lives apart, before he could say, "I've got to ask you."

"I know that," Tacroy said.

"So what is it about Series Eleven?" said Christopher.

Tacroy raised his head. "Put the strongest spell of silence and privacy round us that you can," he said. Christopher did so, even more fiercely than he had done for Miss Bell and Mama. It was so extreme that he went numb and could hardly feel to scrape out the centre of the spell so that he and Tacroy could hear one another. When he had done it, he was fairly sure that even someone standing just beside them could not have overheard a word. But Tacroy shrugged. "They can probably hear anyway," he said. "Their magic's nothing like ours. And they have my soul, you see. They know most of what I do from that, and what they don't know I have to go and report to them in spirit. You saw me going there once – they summon me to a place near Covent Garden."

"Your soul?" said Christopher.

"Yes," Tacroy said bitterly. "The part that makes you the person you are. With you, it's the part that carries on from life to life. Mine was detached from me when I was born, as it is with all Eleven people. They kept it there when they sent me here to Twelve as a baby."

Christopher stared at Tacroy. He had always known that Tacroy did not look quite like other people, with his coffee-coloured skin and curly hair, but he had not thought about it before because he had met so many stranger people in the Anywheres. "Why did they send you?"

"To be their guinea pig," said Tacroy. "The Dright puts someone in another world from time to time when he wants to study it. This time he decided he wanted to study good and evil, so he ordered me to work for Gabriel first and then for the worst villain he could find – who happened to be your uncle. They don't go by right and wrong in Eleven. They don't consider themselves human – or no, I suppose they think they're the only real people, and they study the rest of you like something in a zoo when the Dright happens to feel interested."

Christopher could tell from Tacroy's voice that he hated the Eleven people very deeply. He well understood that. Tacroy was even worse off than the Goddess. "Who's the Dright?"

"King, priest, chief magician—" Tacroy shrugged. "No he's not quite any of those, quite. He's called High Father of the Sept and he's thousands of years old. He's lived that long because he eats someone's soul whenever his power fails – but he's quite within his rights, doing that. All the Eleven people and their souls belong to him by Eleven law. *I* belong to him."

"What's the law about him fetching himself all Gabriel's

lives?" Christopher asked. "That's what he's done, hasn't he?"

"I knew he had – as soon as Flavian said 'Series Eleven'," Tacroy said. "I know he's always wanted to study someone with nine lives. They can't get them in Eleven, because there's only one world there, not a Series. The Dright keeps it down to one world so he won't have any rivals. And you know how your nine lives came about – don't you? – because all the doubles you might have had in the other worlds in Twelve never got born for some reason."

"Yes, but what's Eleven law about pinching most of an enchanter?" Christopher insisted.

"I'm not sure," Tacroy confessed. "I'm not sure they *have* laws like we do. It's probably legal if the Dright can get away with it. They go by pride and appearance and what people *do* mostly."

Christopher at once resolved that the Dright should *not* get away with this if he could help it. "I suppose he just waited to see how many lives there were loose and then collected them," he said. "Tell me everything about Eleven that you can think of."

"Well," said Tacroy, "I've never been there, but I know they control everything with magic. They have the weather controlled, so that they can live out in the open forest and control what trees grow and where. Food comes when they call and they don't use fire to cook it. They don't use fire at all. They think you're all savages for using it, and they're just as scornful about the kind of magic all the other worlds use.

The only time they think any of you are any good is when one of you is absolutely loyal to a king or chief or someone. They admire people like that, particularly if they cheat and lie out of loyalty…"

Tacroy talked for the next half hour. He talked as if it was a relief for him to tell it at last, but Christopher could see it was a strain too. Halfway through, when the lines on Tacroy's face made him look haggard, Christopher told him to wait and slipped out of the secrecy spell to the door. As he had expected, Miss Rosalie was standing outside looking more than usually fierce.

"Mordecai's worked himself to the bone for you, one way and another!" she hissed at him. "What are you *doing* to him in there?"

"Nothing, but he needs something to keep him going," Christopher said. "Could you—?"

"What do you take me for?" snapped Miss Rosalie. Erica rushed up with a tray almost at once. As well as tea, and two plates piled high with cakes, there was a tiny bottle of brandy nestling in the corner of the tray. When Christopher carried the tray back inside the spell, Tacroy looked at the brandy, grinned and poured a good dollop of it into his cup of tea. It seemed to revive him as much as the cakes revived Christopher. While they polished off the trayful together, Tacroy thought of a whole new set of things to say.

One of the things he said was, "If you saw some Eleven people without being warned, you might take them for noble savages, but you'd be making a big mistake if you did.

They're very, very civilised. As for being noble—" Tacroy paused with a cake halfway to his mouth.

"Eat your elevenses," said Christopher.

Tacroy gave a brief grin at the joke. "Your worlds know about them a bit," he said. "They're the people who gave rise to all the stories about Elves. If you think about them like that – cold, unearthly people who go by quite different rules – that will give you some idea. I don't understand them really, even though I was born one of them."

By this time Christopher knew that getting Gabriel back was going to be the toughest thing he had ever done in his lives. If it was not impossible. "Can you bear to come to Eleven with me?" he asked Tacroy. "To stop me making mistakes."

"As soon as they realise I've told you, they'll haul me back there anyway," Tacroy said. He was very pale again. "And you're in danger for knowing."

"In that case," said Christopher, "we'll tell everyone in the Castle, and get Yolande and Beryl to type a report to the Government about it. The Dright can't kill everyone."

Tacroy did not look any too sure about this, but he went back with Christopher to the operations room to explain. Naturally, it caused another outcry. "*Eleven*!" everyone exclaimed. "You can't!" People crowded in from the rest of the Castle to tell Christopher he was being a fool and that getting Gabriel back was quite impossible. Dr Simonson left off making final adjustments to the Lobster Pot to march upstairs and forbid Christopher to go.

Christopher had expected this. "Fudge!" he said. "You can catch the Wraith without me now."

What he had not expected was that the Goddess would wait for the clamour to die down and then announce, "And I'm coming with you."

"Why?" said Christopher.

"Out of loyalty," the Goddess explained. "In the *Millie* books, Millie never let her chums down."

There was no accounting for the Goddess's obsession, Christopher thought. He suspected she was really afraid to stay where the Arm of Asheth could find her on her own, but he did not say so. And if she came along, she would almost double the amount of magic they had between them.

Then, on Tacroy's advice, he dressed for the journey. "Fur," Tacroy said. "The more you wear, the higher your rank." Christopher conjured the tigerskin rug from the Middle Saloon and the Goddess cut a hole in it for his head. Miss Rosalie found him a lordly belt with great brass studs in it to go round the middle, while the housekeeper produced a fox fur to wrap round his neck and a mink stole for the Goddess. "And it would help to have it hung all over with ornaments," said Tacroy.

"Not silver ones, remember," Christopher called as everyone rushed away to find things.

He ended up with three gold necklaces and a rope of pearls. Yolande's entire stock of earrings was pinned artfully here and there on the tigerskin, with Beryl's brooches in between. Round his head he had Miss

Rosalie's gold evening belt with Erica's mother's mourning brooch pinned to the front of it over his forehead. He tinked in a stately way when he moved, rather like the Goddess in the Temple. The Goddess herself merely had a cluster of ostrich feathers at the front of her head and somebody's gold bracelets round the bottom of her Norfolk breeches. They wanted to make it clear that Christopher was the most important one. Tacroy stayed just as he was.

"They know me," he said. "I have no rank in the Sept at all."

They shook hands with everyone in the operations room and turned to the Gate. It was now tuned to Eleven as far as Flavian and Tacroy knew, but Miss Rosalie warned Christopher that the spells round Eleven would probably take all their strength to break, and even that might not be enough. So Christopher paced tinking in the lead, pushing with all his might, and the Goddess walked after with her ghostly pair of arms spread under the real pair. Behind them, Tacroy muttered an incantation.

And it was easy. Suspiciously easy, they all felt at once. There was an instant of formlessness, like one short breath of The Place Between. Then they were in a forest and a man who looked like Tacroy was staring at them.

The forest was smoothly beautiful, with a green grassy floor and no bushes of any kind. There were simply tall slender trees that all seemed to be the same kind. Among the smooth and slightly shiny trunks, the man was poised on one foot, something like a startled deer, looking over his naked brown shoulder at them. He was like Tacroy in that he had the same sort of coffee-coloured skin and paler curly hair, but there the likeness ended. He was naked except for a short fur skirt, which made him look like a particularly stylish Greek statue, apart from his face. The expression on the man's face reminded Christopher of a camel. It was all haughty dislike and scorn.

"Call him. Remember what I told you," Tacroy whispered.

You had to be rude to Eleven people or they did not respect you. "Hey, you!" Christopher called out in the most lordly way he could. "You there! Take me to the Dright at once!"

The man behaved as if he had not heard. After staring a second longer, he took the step he had been in the middle of and walked away among the trees.

"Didn't he hear?" asked the Goddess.

"Probably," said Tacroy. "But he wanted to make it clear he was more important than you. He was obviously low in the Sept. Even the lowest ones like to think they're better than anyone else in the Related Worlds. Walk on, and we'll see if anything comes of it."

"Which way?" asked Christopher.

"Any way," said Tacroy, with a slight smile. "They control distance and direction here."

They walked forward the way they were facing. The trees were all so much the same and so evenly spaced that, after about twenty steps, Christopher wondered if they were moving at all. He looked round and was relieved to see the square frame of the Gate among the tree-trunks about the right distance behind. He wondered if the whole of Eleven was covered with trees. If it was, it was hardly surprising that its people did not use fire. They would risk burning the whole forest down. He looked to the front again and found that, without any change in the landscape, they were somehow walking towards a fence.

The fence stretched for as far as they could see into the trees on either side. It was made of stakes of wood, nicely varnished and wickedly pointed on top, driven into the turf about a foot apart. The points at the top only came to Tacroy's waist. It did not look much of a barrier. But when they turned sideways to get between the stakes, the stakes seemed much too close together to let them through. When Tacroy took his jacket off to cover the points on top so that they could climb over, his jacket would not go anywhere that was not their side of the fence. As Tacroy picked his jacket up for the sixth time, the Goddess looked to the left and Christopher looked to the right, and they discovered that the fence was now all round them. Behind them, there was no sign of the Gate among the trees – nothing but a row of stakes blocking the way back.

"He did hear," said the Goddess.

"I think they were expecting us," said Christopher.

Tacroy spread his jacket on the grass and sat on it. "We'll just have to wait and see," he said glumly. "No, not you," he said to Christopher as Christopher started to sit down too. "The important people always stand here. I was told that the Dright hasn't sat down for years."

The Goddess sank down beside Tacroy and rubbed her bare toes on the grass. "Then I'm not going to be important," she said. "I'm sick of being important anyway. I say! Was *he* here before?"

A nervous-looking boy with a scruffy piece of sheepskin wound round his hips like a towel was standing on the other side of Tacroy. "I *was* here," he said shyly. "You just didn't seem to see me. I've been inside this fence all morning."

The fence surrounded a small grassy space no bigger than the tower room where Christopher had hidden the Goddess. Christopher could not understand how they could have missed seeing the boy, but given the queerness of everything, perhaps they could. Judging by the boy's lank white body and straight fair hair, he was not one of the Eleven people.

"Did the Dright take you prisoner?" the Goddess asked.

The boy rubbed his funny little hooked nose in a puzzled way. "I'm not sure. I don't seem to remember coming here. What are you doing here?"

"Looking for someone," said Tacroy. "You don't happen to have seen a man – or several men, maybe – called Gabriel de Witt, do you?"

"Gabriel de Witt!" said the boy. "But that's *my* name!"

They stared at him. He was a timid, gangling boy with mild blue eyes. He was the kind of boy Christopher – and probably the Goddess too – would naturally have started to boss about in the next minute or so. They would have bossed him quite kindly though, because it was easy to see that it would not take much to upset him and make him sick with nerves, rather like Fenning at school. In fact, Christopher thought, this boy reminded him of a tall, thin Fenning more than anything else. But now he knew, he saw that the boy's face had the same pointed outline as Gabriel's.

"How many lives have you?" he asked disbelievingly.

The boy seemed to look within himself. "That's odd," he said. "Usually I have nine. But I can only seem to find seven."

"Then we've got all of him," said the Goddess.

"With complications," said Tacroy. "Does the title Chrestomanci mean anything to you?" he asked the boy.

"Isn't he some boring old enchanter?" asked the boy. "I think his real name's Benjamin Allworthy, isn't it?"

Gabriel had gone right back to being a boy. Benjamin Allworthy had been the last Chrestomanci but one. "Don't you remember Mordecai Roberts or me?" Christopher asked. "I'm Christopher Chant."

"Pleased to meet you," Gabriel de Witt said, with a polite, shy smile. Christopher stared at him, wondering how Gabriel had come to grow up so forbidding.

"It's no use," Tacroy said. "Neither of us was born when he was that age."

"More people," said the Goddess.

There were four of them, three men and a woman, a little way off among the trees. The men all wore fur tunics that only covered one shoulder and the woman had a longer one that was more like a dress. The four of them stood half turned away from the fence, chatting together. Occasionally one of them looked scornfully over a bare shoulder at the fence.

Tacroy sank down into himself. His face was full of misery. "Take no notice, Christopher, definitely," he whispered. "Those are the ones I usually had to report to. I think they're important."

Christopher stood and stared haughtily over everyone's heads. His feet began to ache.

"They keep turning up like that," Gabriel said. "Rude beasts! I asked them for something to eat and they pretended not to hear."

Five minutes passed. Christopher's feet felt wider and hotter and more over-used every second. He began to hate Eleven. There seemed to be no birds here, no animals, no wind. Just ranks of beautiful trees that all looked alike. The temperature never changed from just right. And the people were horrible.

"I hate this forest," Gabriel said. "It's so *samey*."

"That woman-one," said the Goddess, "reminds me of Mother Anstey. She's going to giggle about us behind her hand any moment, I know she is."

The woman put her hand up to her mouth and gave a scornful, tinkling laugh.

"What did I tell you?" the Goddess said. "And good riddance!"

The group of people was suddenly gone.

Christopher stood on one foot, then on the other. It made

no difference to the ache. "You were lucky, Tacroy," he said. "If they hadn't dumped you in our world, you'd have had to *live* here." Tacroy looked up with a crinkled, unhappy smile and shrugged.

A minute or so after that, the man they had seen first was back, strolling among the trees a little way off. Tacroy nodded at Christopher. Christopher called out loudly and angrily, "Hey, you! I told you to take us to the Dright! What do you mean by disobeying me like this?"

The man gave no sign that he had heard. He came and leaned on the fence and stared at them as if they were something in a zoo. In order to put his elbows on top of the sharp stakes, he had somehow made a wooden armrest appear. Christopher could not fathom the peculiar magic he used to do that. But the Goddess always seemed a little quicker on the uptake than Christopher. She frowned at the armrest and seemed to get the hang of it. The block of wood hurtled away into the trees sending the man's arms down on to the spikes, quite hard. Gabriel laughed, an ordinary, unforbidding gurgle. The man sprang upright indignantly, went to rub his arm and then remembered that he should not show pain before inferiors. He swung round and went marching away.

Christopher was annoyed, both with the man and with the Goddess for being so much quicker than he was. The two things together made him so angry that he raised his arms and tried to hurl the man upwards, the way he had levitated all the things in Dr Pawson's house. It was almost impossible to do. True, the man went up six feet or so. But he came down again gently and easily the next second, and looked jeeringly over his shoulder as he slipped earthwards.

This seemed to make the Goddess even angrier than Christopher. "*All* do it!" she said. "Come on, Gabriel!"

Gabriel shot her a mischievous grin and they all heaved together. Between them they only seemed to be able to raise the man three feet into the air, but they found they could keep him there. He pretended nothing was happening and kept walking as if he was still on the ground, which looked decidedly silly. "Take us to the Dright!" Christopher yelled.

"Now down," said the Goddess. And they bumped him to the ground again. He walked away, still pretending nothing was happening, which gave Gabriel a fit of the giggles.

"Did that do any good?" Christopher asked Tacroy.

"No way of knowing," said Tacroy. "They always like to keep you waiting until you're too tired and angry to think straight." He settled down in a miserable huddle, with his arms round his knees.

They waited. Christopher was wondering whether it was worth the enormous effort it would take to levitate himself in order to get the weight off his feet, when he noticed that the trees were sliding aside, to the right and left of the fence. Or perhaps the fenced enclosure was moving forward without any change to the smooth grass inside or out. It was hard to tell which. Either made Christopher feel queasy. He swallowed and kept his eyes haughtily on the trees ahead.

But in less than a second those trees had wheeled away to nowhere, leaving a widening green glade. A person was in sight at the distant end of the glade, a tall, bulky person, who was sauntering slowly towards them.

Tacroy gulped a little. "That's the Dright."

Christopher narrowed his eyes to get his witch-sight working and watched the trees sliding further and further apart. It reminded him of the way he had played at shunting the trees up the Trumpington Road. He could see the Dright doing it now. In order to work magic in this world, you seemed to have to work in a way that was tipped sideways from the way you did it on any other world, with a bend and a ripple to the magic, as if you were watching yourself work it in a wavy glass ball. Christopher was not sure he was going to be able to do it.

"I don't get the hang of this foreign magic," Gabriel sighed.

As the Dright sauntered slowly nearer, Christopher squeezed the corners of his mouth in, in order to stop a grin of delight at the thought that he was actually quicker at understanding it than Gabriel was. By now, the trees had sped away to leave a big circular meadow full of greenish sunlight. The Dright was near enough for them to see that he was dressed rather like Christopher in at least two lion skins hung all over with bright chinking ornaments. His curly hair and his crisp beard were white. There were rings on the toes of his smooth brown feet.

"He looks like one of those rather nasty gods – the ones

that eat their own children," Gabriel said in a clear and carrying voice.

Christopher had to bite his tongue or he would have laughed. He was beginning to like this version of Gabriel. By the time he had the laugh under control, he was standing facing the Dright some yards outside the fence. He looked back incredulously. The Goddess and Gabriel were standing behind the fence, still prisoners, looking a little stupefied. Tacroy was still sitting on the ground, doing his best not to be noticed.

Christopher lifted his chin and looked up at the Dright's face. The smooth brown features did not have any expression on them at all. But Christopher stared, trying to see the person behind the blankness. What feelings the Dright had were so different from his own, and so lofty, that for a moment he felt like an insect. Then he remembered that glacier, years ago in Series Seven, which Tacroy had said reminded him of two people. Christopher knew that one of the people was the Dright. Like the glacier, the Dright was cold and high and too crusted with ancient knowledge for ordinary people to understand.

On the other hand, the other person the glacier had reminded Tacroy of was Uncle Ralph. Christopher looked carefully for any signs that the Dright was like Uncle Ralph. There was not much of Uncle Ralph's shoddy look to the Dright's grand face, but his features did not seem sincere. Christopher could tell that the Dright would cheat and lie if it suited him, like Uncle Ralph, but he thought that the main way the two were alike was that they were both utterly selfish. Uncle Ralph used people. So did the Dright.

"What are you?" the Dright said. His voice was deep and scornful.

"I'm the Dright," said Christopher. "Dright for world Twelve A. The word for it there is Chrestomanci, but it amounts to the same thing." His legs were shaking at the sheer cheek of this. But Tacroy *had* said that the one thing the Dright respected was pride. He held his knees stiff and made his face haughty.

There was no way of telling whether the Dright believed Christopher or not. He did not answer and his face was blank. But Christopher could feel the Dright putting out small tendrils of sideways, rippled Eleven magic, testing him, feeling at him to see what his powers were and what were his weak points. To himself, Christopher felt he was all weak points. But it seemed to him that, since the magic here was so peculiar, he had no idea what his own powers were, and that meant the Dright probably had no idea either.

The meadow behind the Dright became full of people. They had not been there at first, but they were there now, a pale-headed, brown-skinned crowd, wearing all possible degrees of fur, from tiny loin-wraps to long bear-skin robes. It seemed that the Dright was saying, "Call yourself Dright if you like, but take a look at the power *I* have." Every one of the people was staring at Christopher with contempt and dislike. Christopher put his face into the same expression and stared back. And he realised that his face was rather used

312

to looking this way. He had worn this expression most of the time he had lived at the Castle. It gave him an unpleasant shock to find that he had been quite as horrible as these Eleven people.

"Why are you here?" said the Dright.

Christopher pushed aside his shock. If I get out of here, I'll try to be nicer, he thought, and then concentrated carefully on what Tacroy had told him might be the best thing to say. "I've come to fetch back something of my own," he said. "But first let me introduce you to my colleague the Living Asheth. Goddess, this is the Dright of Eleven." The ostrich feather fluttered on the Goddess's head as she stepped up to the sharp stakes and bowed graciously. There was the slightest twitch to the Dright's features that suggested he was impressed that Christopher had actually brought the Living Asheth, but the Goddess was still behind the fence in spite of that. "And of course you know my man Mordecai Roberts already," Christopher said grandly, trying to slip that point past as a piece of pride.

The Dright said nothing about that either. But behind him, the people were now all sitting down. It was as if they had never been any other way. By this, the Dright seemed to be saying, "Very well. You are my equal, but I'd like to point out that my followers outnumber yours by several thousand to one – and mine are obedient to my slightest whim."

Christopher was amazed that he had won even this much. He tried to squash down his amazement by watching the people. Some were talking and laughing together, though he could not hear them. Some of them were cooking food over little balls of bluish witch-fire, which they seemed to use instead of fire. There were very few children. The two or three Christopher could see were sitting sedately doing nothing. I'd hate to grow up on Eleven! he thought. It must be a hundred times more boring than the Castle.

"What thing of your own have you allowed to stray into my world?" the Dright said at length.

They were getting down to business at last, even though the Dright was trying to pretend that Christopher had been careless. Christopher smiled and shook his head, to show he thought that was a joke of the Dright's. "Two things," he said. "First, I have to thank you for retrieving the lives of Gabriel de Witt for me. It saved me a lot of trouble. But you seem to have put the lives together in the wrong way and made Gabriel into a boy."

"I put them into the form which is easiest to deal with," said the Dright. Like everything he said, this was full of other meanings.

"If you mean that boys are easy to deal with," Christopher said, "I'm afraid this is not the case. Not boys from Twelve A."

"And not girls either," the Goddess said loudly. "Not from anywhere."

"What is Gabriel de Witt to you?" the Dright asked.

"He is as father to son," said Christopher. Rather proud of the way he had carefully not said who was which, he glanced through the fence at Tacroy. Tacroy was still sitting wrapped into a ball, but Christopher thought his curly head nodded slightly.

"You have a claim to de Witt," the Dright said. "He can be yours, depending on what else you have to say." The fence round the other three slid and poured smoothly away sideways until it was out of sight, just as the trees had.

Gabriel looked puzzled. The Goddess stood where she was, clearly suspicious. Christopher looked warily at the Dright. This was too good to be true. "The other thing I have to say," he said, "is about this man of mine who is usually known as Mordecai Roberts. I believe he used to be yours, which means you still have his soul. Since he is my man now, perhaps you could let me have his soul?"

Tacroy's head came up and he stared at Christopher in horror and alarm. Christopher took no notice. He had known this would be pressing his luck, but he had always meant to try for Tacroy's soul. He planted his aching feet astride, folded his arms across his fur and jewellery, and tried to smile at the Dright as if what he was asking was the most ordinary and reasonable thing in any world.

The Dright gave no sign of anger or surprise. It was not simply self-control or pride. Christopher knew the Dright had been expecting him to ask and did not mind if Christopher knew. His mind began to work furiously. The Dright had made it easy for them to come to Eleven. He had pretended to accept Christopher as an equal, and he had told him he could have Gabriel's lives. That meant there was something the Dright expected to get out of this, something he must want very much indeed. But what?

"If my Septman claims to be your man, you should have his soulname," the Dright observed. "Has he given you that name?"

"Yes," said Christopher. "It's Tacroy."

The faces of all the people sitting in the meadow behind the Dright turned his way. Every one of them was outraged. But the Dright only said, "And what has Tacroy done to make himself yours?"

"He lied for me for a whole day," Christopher said. "And he was *believed*."

The first real sound in this place swept through the seated people. It was a long throaty murmur. Of awe? Approval? Whatever it was, Christopher knew he had said the right thing. As Tacroy had told him, these people naturally lied for their Dright. And to lie convincingly for a whole day showed the utmost loyalty.

"He could then be yours," the Dright admitted, "but on two conditions. I make two conditions because you have asked me for two things. The first one is of course that you show you know which the Septman's soul *is*." He made a small gesture with one powerful brown hand.

A movement in the trees to one side caught Christopher's eye. He looked and found the slender trunks pouring silently aside there. When they stopped, there was a grassy lane leading to the square framework of the Gate. It was about fifty feet away. The Dright was showing him that he *could* get home, provided he did what was wanted.

"There's a huge block of their magic in the way," the Goddess whispered.

Gabriel craned over his shoulder to look longingly at the Gate. "Yes, it's just a carrot in front of the donkey," he agreed.

Tacroy simply groaned, with his head on his knees.

In front of Christopher, people were bringing things and laying them out in a wide crescent-shape. Each man or woman brought two or three, and stared derisively at Christopher as he or she thunked the things down in the growing line. He looked at the things. Some were almost black, some yellowish, and others white or shiny. He was not sure if they were statuettes or blobs of stuff that had melted and hardened into peculiar shapes. A few of them looked vaguely human. Most were no shape that meant anything. But the stuff they were made of meant a great deal. Christopher's stomach twisted and he had a hard job to go on staring haughtily as he realised that all the things were made of silver.

When there were about a hundred of the objects sitting on the green turf, the Dright waved his hand again and the people stopped bringing them. "Pick out the soul of Tacroy from the souls of my people," he said.

Miserably, Christopher paced along the curving row with his hands clasped behind him to stop them trembling and Beryl's ornaments clinking. He felt like a general reviewing an army of metal goblins. He paced the entire line, from left to right, and none of the objects meant anything to him. Use witch-sight, he told himself, as he wheeled on the right wing and started back again. It might just work on the silver statues provided he did not touch them.

He forced himself to look in that special way at the statues. It was a real effort to do it through the wavy sideways magic of Eleven. And, as he had feared, the things looked just the same, just as grotesque, just as meaningless. His witch-sight was working, he knew. He could tell that a number of the people sitting in the meadow were not really there. They were in other parts of the forest busy with other schemes of the Dright's and projecting their images here in obedience to the Dright's command. But his witch-sight would not work on silver.

So how else could he tell? He paced along the line, thinking. The people watched him jeeringly and the Dright's head turned majestically to follow him as he passed. They were all so unpleasant, he thought, that it was no wonder their souls were like little silver monsters. Tacroy was the only nice one – Ah! *There* was Tacroy's soul! It was some way round to the left. It looked no more human than any of the others, but it looked *nice*, fifty times nicer than the rest.

Christopher tried to go on pacing towards it as if he had not seen it, wondering what would happen when he picked it up and lost every scrap of his magic. He would have to rely on the Goddess. He hoped she realised.

His face must have changed. The Dright knew he had found the right soul and instantly began to cheat – as Christopher had known he would. The line of twisty objects

318

was suddenly a good mile long, with Tacroy's soul away in the far distance. And all of them were changing shape, melting into new queer blobs and fresh formless forms.

Then, with a sort of wavy jolt, everything went back to the way it was at first. Thank goodness! Christopher thought. The Goddess! He had kept his eye on the soul and it was quite near. He dived forward and picked it up. As soon as he touched it, he was weak and heavy and tired. He felt like crying, but he stood up holding the soul. Sure enough, the Goddess was staring at the Dright with her arms spread. Christopher was surprised to find that, even without his magic, he could see her second pair of ghostly arms spread out underneath.

"My priestesses taught me that it was low to cheat," she said. "I'd have thought you were too proud to stoop to it."

The Dright looked down his nose at her. "I named no rules," he said. Being without magic was a little like another kind of witch-sight, Christopher thought. The Dright looked smaller to him now and not nearly so magnificent. There were clear signs of the shoddiness that he had seen in Uncle Ralph. Christopher was still scared stiff, but he felt much better about things now he had seen that.

While the Goddess and the Dright stared at one another, he lumbered weakly over to Tacroy. "Here you are," he said, thrusting the strange statue at him. Tacroy scrambled on to one knee, looking as if he could not believe it. His hands shook as they closed round the soul. As soon as he had hold of it, the thing melted into his hands. The fingernails and the veins turned silvery. An instant later, Tacroy's face flushed silvery too. Then the flush faded and Tacroy looked much as usual, except that there was a glow about him which made him much more like the Tacroy Christopher knew from The Place Between.

"Now I really am your man!" Tacroy said. He was laughing in a way that was rather like sobbing. "You can see I couldn't ask Rosalie – watch the Dright!"

Christopher spun round and found the Goddess on her knees, looking bewildered. It was not surprising. The Dright had thousands of years of experience. "Leave her alone!" he said.

The Dright looked at him and for a moment Christopher felt the strange distorted magic trying to force him to his knees too. Then it stopped. The Dright still had not got what he wanted from Christopher. "We now come to my second condition," the Dright said calmly. "I am moderate. You came here demanding seven lives and a soul. I give you them. All I ask in exchange is one life."

Gabriel laughed nervously. "I *have* got a few to spare," he said. "If it means getting out of here—"

This was what the Dright wanted, Christopher realised. He had been aiming for the life of a nine-lifed enchanter, freely handed over, all along. If Christopher had not dared to ask for Tacroy's soul, he would have asked for a life for setting Gabriel free. For just a second, Christopher thought they might as well let him have one of Gabriel's lives. He had seven, after all, and another lying on the floor back in the

320

Castle. Then he saw it would be the most dangerous thing he could do. It would give the Dright a hold over Gabriel – the same hold he had had over Tacroy – for as long as his other lives lasted. The Dright was aiming to control the Chrestomanci, just like Uncle Ralph was aiming to control Christopher. They did not dare give him one of Gabriel's lives.

"All right," Christopher said. For the first time, he was truly grateful to Gabriel that his ninth life was safely locked in the Castle safe. "As you see, I've still got two lives left. You can have *one* of them," he said, naming conditions very carefully, because he knew the Dright would cheat if he could, "because if you take more than one it would kill me and give my world the right to punish yours. Once you have the life in your hands, your conditions are fulfilled and you must let all four of us go through the Gate back to Twelve A."

"Agreed," said the Dright. He was keeping his face as expressionless as always, but underneath Christopher could tell he was hugging himself and chuckling. He stepped solemnly up to Christopher. Christopher braced himself and hoped it would not hurt much. In fact, it hurt so little that he was almost taken by surprise. The Dright stepped back a mere instant later with a floppy transparent shape dangling in his hands. The shape was wearing a ghostly tiger skin and it had a dim gold band fluttering from its transparent head.

Christopher conjured fire to that shape, hard and sideways and wavily, with all the power he had. Fire was the one thing the Dright was not used to. He knew it was the one thing that might cancel out those thousand years of experience. To his relief, the Goddess had made exactly the same calculations. He had a glimpse of her, with all four arms spread, conjuring fire down as he called it up.

His seventh life leapt into flame all over at once. The Dright hung on to its shoulders as it blazed, grimly trying to quench it, but Christopher had been right. Fire magic was the Dright's weak point. His attempt to reverse the spell was slow and hesitating. But he kept trying, and hung on to the life by its shoulders, until he had to let go or lose both hands. By that time the front of his lion skin was on fire too. Christopher glimpsed him trying to beat it out and coughing in the smoke, as he collapsed himself into a writhing heap on the turf. It was worse than being crisped by the dragon. He was in agony. He had not realised it would hurt at all, let alone this much.

Tacroy scooped him up, threw him over one shoulder in a fireman's hoist, and raced for the Gate. Every step bumped Christopher and every bump was torment. But his watering eyes caught sight of the Goddess seizing Gabriel's arm in at least three hands and dragging him to the Gate in a mixture of brute force and magic. They all reached it together and plunged through. Christopher kept just enough sense to cancel the spells and slam the Gate shut behind them.

CHAPTER TWENTY-ONE

✳

*T*he pain stopped the instant the Gate shut. Tacroy lowered Christopher gently to the floor, and looked at him to see if he was all right, and made for Miss Rosalie.

"Gosh – look!" said the Goddess, pointing at Gabriel.

Tacroy did not look. He was too busy hugging Miss Rosalie. Christopher sat on the floor and stared with the rest of the people in the operations room. As the Dright's magic left him, Gabriel was growing up in bursts. First he was a young man with a floral silk tie and a keen, wistful look; then he was an older keener man in a dingy suit. After that he was middle-aged and bleached and somehow hopeless and desperate, as if everything he hoped for was gone. The next instant, this man had pulled himself together into a brisk, silvery gentleman; and then the same gentleman, older and grimmer.

Christopher stared, awed and rather touched. He realised that Gabriel had hated being the Chrestomanci, and they were seeing the stages by which he had come to terms with it. I'm glad I'm going to find it easier than *that*! Christopher thought, as Gabriel finally became the grim old man that Christopher knew. At which point, Gabriel tottered to Tacroy's trance-couch and folded down on to it.

Beryl and Yolande rushed forward with cups of tea. Gabriel drank Beryl's (or Yolande's) at a gulp. Then he took Yolande's (or Beryl's) and sipped it slowly with his eyes almost shut. "My heartiest thanks, Christopher," he said. "I hope the pain has gone."

"Yes, thanks," Christopher said, taking the cup of tea Erica handed him.

Gabriel glanced to where Tacroy was still wrapped round Miss Rosalie. "By the look of him, Mordecai has even more to thank you for than I have."

"Don't let him get sent to prison," Christopher said. And there was the boot-boy to ask about too, he thought distractedly.

"I'll do what I can," Gabriel promised. "Now that I know the circumstances. That fearsome Dright has much to answer for – though I *may* be right in supposing that Mordecai went on working with you for your equally fearsome uncle, because he knew that any other spirit traveller your uncle chose would have turned you into a hardened criminal before long. Would you agree?"

"Well," said Christopher, trying to be honest, "I think some of it was because we were both so keen on cricket."

"Really?" Gabriel said politely. He turned to the Goddess. She had found Proudfoot and was holding her lovingly in both hands. Gabriel looked from the kitten to the Goddess's bare feet. "Young lady," he said. "You *are* a young lady, are you not? Pray show me the sole of your left foot."

A little defiantly, the Goddess turned round and tipped her foot up. Gabriel looked at the purple-blue mark. He looked at Christopher.

"Yes, I am really Asheth," said the Goddess, "but you're not to look at Christopher like that! I came here of my own accord. I did it quite capably."

Gabriel's eyes narrowed. "By using the Goddess Asheth as your second life?" Gabriel put down his empty cup and took the full one Flavian handed him. "My dear girl," he said as he sipped it, "what a very foolish thing to have done! You are clearly a powerful enchantress in your own right. You had no need to use Asheth. You have simply given her a hold over you. The Arm of Asheth is going to haunt you for the rest of your life."

"But I thought that the magic I can do *came* from Asheth!" the Goddess protested.

"Oh no," said Gabriel. "Asheth has powers, but she

never shares them. The ones you have are yours."

The Goddess's mouth dropped open. She looked as if she might cry.

Flavian said apologetically, "Gabriel, I'm afraid the Arm of Asheth is all round—"

There was a violent CRASH from below as the Lobster Pot came down.

Everyone raced for the stairs, except for Gabriel. He put his cup down slowly, obviously wondering what was happening. Christopher dashed to the stairs and then, for speed, did what he had always longed to do and slid down the rosy curve of marble bannister. The Goddess followed him. When they tumbled off at the bottom, Gabriel was already there, standing by the black rope gazing down at his limp transparent life. But no one else had eyes for that.

Uncle Ralph had come through the pentacle in a suit of armour, carrying a heavy mace. Christopher had thought he might. If he had brought any anti-cat spells, however, these obviously did not work on Temple cats. The Lobster Pot had come down precisely over the pentacle, trapping Throgmorten in with Uncle Ralph, and Throgmorten was doing his best to get Uncle Ralph.

Through the wreathing smoke of dragons' blood, Uncle Ralph could be seen tramping slowly round and round inside the cage, smashing cat-saucers under his metal feet and taking violent swings at Throgmorten with his mace. Throgmorten could move faster than Uncle Ralph, or his mace, and he could climb the walls of the Lobster Pot, but he could not get at Uncle Ralph through his armour. All he could do was make shrill metal scratches on it. It was a stand off.

Christopher looked round to find Gabriel beside him. Gabriel's face had a most unusual big wicked smile on it – no, not unusual, Christopher thought: it was the same smile Gabriel had worn when they levitated the man in Eleven.

"Shall we give the cat his chance?" Gabriel said. "For one minute?"

Christopher nodded.

Uncle Ralph's armour vanished, leaving him in his foxy tweed suit. Throgmorten instantly became a seven-legged, three-headed, razor-clawed, flying, spitting fury. He was up and down and all over Uncle Ralph several times in the first second. So much blood got shed that Christopher was quite sorry for Uncle Ralph after fifteen such seconds. After thirty seconds, he was quite glad when Throgmorten vanished with a snarl and a jerk.

Throgmorten reappeared kicking and struggling over the Goddess's arm. "*No*, Throgmorten," she said. "I told you before you're not to go for people's eyes. That's not nice."

"Nice or not," Gabriel said regretfully, "I was enjoying it." He was busy winding something unseen into a careful skein over one hand. "Simonson," he called. "Simonson, are you in charge of the cage? I got his magic off him while his mind was elsewhere. You can move the cage now and shut him up until the police can come for him."

This produced another stand off. Throgmorten leapt for the space under the cage as soon as it started to rise. Uncle Ralph screamed. In the end, one of the stable lads had to climb up and unhook the cage from the chandelier chain. Then the cage was shoved across the floor with Uncle Ralph stumbling inside it and Throgmorten prowling after, uttering low throbbing sounds.

As soon as the cage was off the pentacle, a silver pillar rose out of the blood-spattered floor. The pillar looked human, but it was impossibly tall for a human, a good foot taller than Gabriel. Up and up it rose, a woman robed in silver, wearing a silver mask and carrying a silver spear.

The Goddess wailed with terror and tried to hide behind Christopher. "Silver," he warned her. "I can't help against silver." His teeth chattered. For the first time, he realised how naked and soft it felt to have only one life.

The Goddess dashed behind Gabriel and clutched his black frock coat. "It's Asheth! Save me!"

"Madam," Gabriel said politely to the apparition, "to what do we owe the honour of this visitation?"

The apparition looked keenly through the slits in its mask, first at Gabriel and the Goddess crouching behind him, then at Christopher, then at the Lobster Pot and the general chaos in the hall. "I had hoped to find this a more respectable establishment," she said. The voice was deep and melodious. She pushed up her mask to the top of her head, revealing a severe narrow old face. It was the kind of face that at once made Christopher feel very silly to be dressed in a tiger rug and earrings.

"Mother Proudfoot!" exclaimed the Goddess.

"I've been trying to get through this pentacle ever since I traced you, child," Mother Proudfoot said testily. "I wish you had talked to me before you bolted like that. You surely knew I would have stretched the rules for you if I could." She turned commandingly to Gabriel. "You seem respectable enough. You're that Twelve A enchanter, de Witt, aren't you?"

"At your service, madam," said Gabriel. "Do forgive our present disorder. There have been problems. We are usually a highly respectable body of people."

"That was what I thought," Mother Proudfoot said. "Would you be able to take charge of this Asheth Daughter for me? It would suit me ideally if you could, since I have to report her dead."

"In what way – take charge?" Gabriel asked cautiously.

"See her educated at a good school and so forth – consider becoming her legal guardian," said Mother Proudfoot. She stepped majestically down from what seemed to be her pedestal. Now she was about the same height as Gabriel. They were quite alike in a gaunt, stern way. "This one was always my favourite Asheth," she explained. "I usually try to spare their lives anyway when they get too old, but most of them are such stupid little lumps that I don't bother to do much more. But as soon as I knew this one was different, I started saving from the

329

Temple funds. I think I have enough to pay her way."

She swept her trailing skirt aside. The pedestal turned out to be a small strong chest. Mother Proudfoot threw back the lid of it with a flourish. Inside, it seemed to be full of blurred glassy quartz in little pieces, like road gravel. But Gabriel's face was awestruck. Christopher caught sight of Tacroy and Flavian mouthing a word at one another with their eyes popping. The word seemed to be "Diamonds!"

"The diamonds are uncut, I'm afraid," said Mother Proudfoot. "Do you think there will be enough of them?"

"I think less than half that number would be more than adequate," Gabriel said.

"But I had in mind a Swiss finishing school too," Mother Proudfoot said sharply. "I've studied this world and I want no skimping. Will you do this for me? Naturally I shall make sure that followers of Asheth will do any favour you care to ask in return."

Gabriel looked from Mother Proudfoot to the Goddess. He hesitated. He looked at Christopher. "Very well," he said at last.

"Gosh, you *darling*!" said the Goddess. She scrambled to the front of Gabriel and hugged him. Then she hurled herself on Mother Proudfoot and hugged her mightily too. "I love you, Mother Proudfoot," she said, all mixed in silver drapery.

Mother Proudfoot sniffed a little as she hugged the Goddess in return. But she pulled herself together and looked sternly at Gabriel over the Goddess's head. "There is one tiresome detail," she said. "Asheth truly does require a life, you know, one for each living Asheth." Christopher sighed. Everyone in all the Anywheres seemed to want him to give them lives. Now he would be down to the one in the Castle safe.

Gabriel drew himself up, looking his most forbidding.

"Asheth isn't very discriminating," Mother Proudfoot said, before he could speak. "I usually strip a life off one of the Temple cats." She pointed with her silver spear to where Throgmorten was stalking round the Lobster Pot making noises like a kettle boiling. "That old ginger's still got three lives or so left. I'll take one of his."

The kettle noises stopped. Throgmorten showed what he thought of this proposal by becoming a ginger streak racing upstairs.

"No matter," Gabriel said. "Now I think of it, I have a spare life, as it happens." He stepped over to the black ropes and picked his limp transparent likeness out from among the library chairs. Courteously, he draped it over the end of Mother Proudfoot's spear. "There. Will this one serve?"

"Admirably," said Mother Proudfoot. "Thank you." She gave the Goddess a kiss and descended majestically into the ground beside the chest of diamonds.

The Goddess shut the chest and sat on it. "School!" she said, smiling blissfully. "Rice pudding, prefects, dormitories, midnight feasts, playing the game—" She stopped without changing the smile, although it was not a smile any more. "Honour," she said. "Owning up. Sir de Witt, I think I'd better stay in the Castle because of all the trouble I caused Christopher. He – er – he's lonely, you know."

"I would be a fool not to have realised that," Gabriel said. "I am in the middle of arranging with the Ministry to bring a number of young enchanters here to be trained. At the moment, you know, I am only able to employ them as domestics – like young Jason the boot-boy over there – but this will shortly change. There is no reason why you should not go to school—"

"But there *is*!" said the Goddess. Her face was very red and there were tears in her eyes. "I have to own up, like they do in the books. I don't *deserve* to go to school! I'm very wicked. I didn't use Asheth as my second life in order to come here. I used one of Christopher's. I didn't dare use Asheth in case she stopped me, so I took one of Christopher's lives when he was stuck in the wall and used that instead." Tears ran down her face.

"Where is it?" Christopher asked, very much astonished.

"Still in the wall," the Goddess sobbed. "I pushed it right in so that no one will find it, but I've felt bad ever since. I've tried to help and atone for it, but I haven't done much and I think I ought to be punished."

"There is absolutely no need," said Gabriel. "Now we know where the life is, we can send Mordecai Roberts to fetch it. Stop crying, young lady. You will have to go to school because I should be misusing your chest of diamonds if you do not. Regard that as your punishment. You may come and live in the Castle with the rest of the young enchanters during the holidays."

The Goddess's blissful smile came back and diverted the tears on her face round her ears and into her hair. "Hols," she corrected Gabriel. "The books always call them the hols."

That is really all, except for a letter that arrived for Christopher from Japan soon after New Year.

Darling Christopher,

Why did you not tell me that your dear papa was settled here in Japan? It is such an elegant country, once one is used to the customs, and your papa and I are both very happy here. Your papa's horoscopes have had the honour to interest some people who have the ear of the Emperor. We are already moving in the highest circles and hope to move higher still before long.

Your dear papa sends love and best wishes for your future as the next Chrestomanci. My love as well.

Mama

More than a Story

*

The DWJ Guide to Enchanters

The Girl Jones

If you like, you'll love

*

Enchanters are the strongest magic users there are. Not only is their magic at least twice as strong as that of, say, a witch or a wizard, but they do not need to mutter spells, perform a ritual or wave a wand. They can do it with their minds alone.

But enchanters vary in strength too. Quite a few of them have more than one life, and the more lives they have, the stronger they are. The very strongest are nine-lifed enchanters. All these extra lives arise when, for one reason or another, the double(s) they might have had in the other worlds along the Series of Related Worlds do not get born. (We all have doubles: the other worlds in a Series are closely parallel, so the people in them are too. Some of the strangest dreams you have may come from your making, just for a moment, a brief contact with some other you in one of the other worlds).

There are always nine separate worlds in a Series (except for Eleven, which is only one world because the Dright of Eleven keeps it that way) and everyone usually has a double in most of them. The different ways in which a double gets lost are:

(i)   His or her parents marry
      someone else.
(ii) Someone else gets born instead
      of him or her.
(iii) The person gets born but
      dies at birth.

Then, provided the person on another world is an enchanter anyway, they get the life from the other world.

On the very rare occasions when the person gets lives from all eight other worlds in the Series, he or she is a nine-lifed enchanter. Chrestomanci of course is one of these.

The Girl Jones

It was 1944. I was nine years old and fairly new to the village. They called me "The girl Jones". They called anyone "The girl this" or "The boy that" if they wanted to talk about them a lot. Neither of my sisters was ever called "The girl Jones". They were never notorious.

On this particular Saturday morning I was waiting in our yard with my sister Ursula because a girl called Jean had promised to come and play. My sister Isobel was also hanging around. She was not exactly with us, but I was the one she came to if anything went wrong and she liked to keep in touch. I had only met Jean at school before. I was thinking that she was going to be pretty fed up to find we were lumbered with two little ones.

When Jean turned up, rather late, she was accompanied by two little sisters, a five-year-old very like herself and a tiny three-year-old called Ellen. Ellen had white hair and a little brown stormy face with an expression on it that said she was going to bite anyone who gave her any trouble. She was alarming. All three girls were dressed in impeccable starched cotton frocks that made me feel rather shabby. I had dressed for the weekend. But then so had they, in a different way.

"Mum says I got to look after them," Jean told me dismally. "Can you have them for me for a bit while I do her shopping? Then we can play."

I looked at stormy Ellen with apprehension. "I'm not very good at looking after little ones," I said.

"Oh, go on!" Jean begged me. "I'll be much quicker without them. I'll be your friend if you do."

So far, Jean had shown a desire to play, but had never offered friendship. I gave in. Jean departed, merrily swinging her shopping bag.

Almost at once a girl called Eva turned up. She was an official friend. She wore special boots and one of her feet was just a sort of blob. Eva fascinated me, not because of the foot, but because she was so proud of it. She used to recite the list of all her other relatives who had queer feet, ending with, "And my uncle has only one toe." She too carried a shopping bag and had a small one in tow, a brother in her case, a wicked five-year-old called Terry. "Let me dump him on you while I do the shopping," Eva bargained, "and then we can play. I won't be long."

"I don't know about looking after boys," I protested. But Eva was a friend and I agreed. Terry was left standing beside stormy Ellen, and Eva went away.

A girl I did not know so well, called Sybil, arrived next. She wore a fine blue cotton dress with a white pattern and was hauling along two small sisters, equally finely dressed. "Have these for me while I do the shopping and I'll be your friend." She was followed by a rather older girl called Cathy, with a sister, and then a number of girls I only knew by sight. Each of them led a small sister or brother into our yard. News gets round in no time in a village. "What have you done with your sisters, Jean?" "Dumped them on the girl Jones." Some of these later arrivals were quite frank about it.

"I heard you're having children. Have these for me while I go down the rec."

"I'm not good at looking after children," I claimed each time before I gave in. I remember thinking this was rather odd of me. I had been in sole charge of Isobel for years. As soon as Ursula was four, she was in my charge too. I suppose I had by then realised I was being had for a sucker and this was my way of warning all these older sisters. But I believed what I said. I was not good at looking after little ones.

In less than twenty minutes I was standing in the yard surrounded by small children. I never counted, but there were certainly more than ten of them. None of them came above my waist. They were all beautifully dressed because they all came from what were called the "clean families". The "dirty families" were the ones where the boys wore big black boots with metal in the soles and the girls had grubby frocks that were too long for them. These kids had starched creases in their clothes and clean socks and shiny shoes. But they were, all the same, skinny, knowing, village children. They knew their sisters had shamelessly dumped them and they were disposed to riot.

"Stop all that damned *noise!*" bellowed my father. "Get these children out of here!" He was always angry. This sounded near to an explosion.

"We're going for a walk," I told the milling children. "Come along." And I said to Isobel, "Coming?"

She hovered away backwards. "No." Isobel had a perfect instinct for this kind of thing. Some of my earliest memories are of Isobel's sturdy brown legs flashing round and round as she rode her tricycle for dear life away from a situation I had got her into. These days she usually arranged things so that she had no need to run for her life. I was annoyed. I could have done with her help with all these kids. But not that annoyed. Her reaction told me that something interesting was going to happen.

"We're going to have an adventure," I told the children.

"There's no adventures nowadays," they told me. They were, as I said, knowing children, and no one, not even me, regarded the War that was at the time going on around us as any kind of adventure. This was a problem to me. I craved any kind of adventure, of the sort people had in books, but nothing that had ever happened to me seemed to qualify. No spies made themselves available to be unmasked by me, no gangsters ever had nefarious dealings where I could catch them for the police.

But one did what one could. I led the crowd of them out into the street, feeling a little like the Pied Piper – or no: they were so little and I was so big that I felt really old, twenty at least, and rather like a nursery school teacher. And it seemed to me that since I was landed in this position I might as well do something I wanted to do.

"Where are we going?" they clamoured at me.

"Down Water Lane," I said. Water Lane, being almost the only unpaved road in the area, fascinated me. It was like lanes in books. If anywhere led to adventure, it would be Water Lane. It was a moist, mild, grey day, not adventurous weather, but I knew from books that the most unlikely conditions sometimes led to great things.

But my charges were not happy about this. "It's wet there. We'll get all muddy. My mum told me to keep my clothes clean," they said from all around me.

"You won't get muddy with me," I told them firmly. "We're only going as far as the elephants." There was a man who built life-sized mechanical elephants in a shed in Water Lane. These fascinated everyone. The children gave up objecting at once. Ellen actually put her hand trustingly in mine and we crossed the main road like a great liner escorted by coracles.

Water Lane was indeed muddy. Wetness oozed up from its sandy surface and ran in dozens of streams across it. Mr Hinkston's herd of cows had added their contributions. The children minced and yelled. "Walk along the very edge," I commanded them. "Be adventurous. If we're lucky, we'll get inside the yard and look at the elephants in the sheds."

Most of them obeyed me except Ursula. But she was my sister and I had charge of her shoes along with the rest of her. Although I was determined from the outset to treat her exactly like the other children, as if this was truly a class from nursery school, or the Pied Piper leading the children of Hamlin Town, I decided to let her be. Ursula had times when she bit you if you crossed her. Besides, what were shoes? So, to cries of, "Ooh! Your sister's getting in all the pancakes!" we arrived outside the big black fence where the elephants were, to find it all locked and bolted. As this was a Saturday, the man who made the elephants had gone to make money with them at a fête or fair somewhere.

There were loud cries of disappointment and derision at this, particularly from Terry, who was a very outspoken child. I looked up at the tall fence – it had barbed wire along the top – and contemplated boosting them all over it for an adventure inside. But there were their clothes to consider, it would be hard work, and it was not really what I had come down Water Lane to do.

"This means we have to go on," I told them, "to the really adventurous thing. We are going to the very end of Water Lane to see what's at the end of it."

"That's ever so far!" one of them whined.

"No, it's not," I said, not having the least idea. I had never had time to go much beyond the river. "Or we'll get to the river and then walk along it to see where it goes to."

"Rivers don't go anywhere," someone pronounced.

"Yes they do," I asserted. "There's a bubbling fountain somewhere where it runs out of the ground. We're going to find it." I had been reading books about the source of the Nile, I think.

They liked the idea of the fountain. We went on. The cows had not been on this further part, but it was still wet. I encouraged them to step from sandy strip to sandy island and they liked that. They were all beginning to think of themselves as true adventurers. But Ursula, no doubt wanting to preserve her special status, walked straight through everything and got her shoes all wet and crusty. A number of children drew my attention to this.

"She's not good like you are," I said.

We went on in fine style for a good quarter of a mile until we came to the place where the river broke out of the hedge and swilled across the lane in a ford. Here the expedition broke down utterly.

"It's water! I'll get all wet! It's all muddy!"

"I'm *tired*!" said someone. Ellen stood by the river and grizzled, reflecting the general mood.

"This is where we can leave the lane and go up along the river," I said. But this found no favour. The banks would be muddy. We would have to get through the hedge. They would tear their clothes.

I was shocked and disgusted by their lack of spirit. The ford across the road had always struck me as the nearest and most romantic thing to a proper adventure. I loved the way the bright brown water ran so continuously there – in the mysterious way of rivers – in the shallow sandy dip.

"We're going on," I announced. "Take your shoes off and walk through in your bare feet."

This, for some reason, struck them all as highly adventurous. Shoes and socks were carefully removed. The quickest splashed into the water. "Ooh! Innit *cold*!"

"I'm paddling!" shouted Terry. "I'm going for a paddle." His feet, I was interested to see, were perfect. He must have felt rather left out in Eva's family.

I lost control of the expedition in this moment of inattention. Suddenly everyone was going in for a paddle. "All right," I said hastily. "We'll stay here and paddle."

Ursula, always fiercely loyal in her own way, walked out of the river and sat down to take her shoes off too. The rest splashed and screamed. Terry began throwing water about. Quite a number of them squatted down at the edge of the water and scooped up muddy sand. Brown stains began climbing up crisp cotton frocks, the seats of beautifully ironed shorts quickly acquired a black splotch. Even before this was pointed out to me, I saw this would not do. These were the "clean children". I made all the little girls come out of the water and spent some time trying to get the edges of their frocks tucked upwards into their knickers. "The boys can take their trousers off," I announced.

But this did no good. The frocks just came tumbling down again and the boys' little white pants were no longer really white. No one paid any attention to my suggestion that it was time to go home now. The urge to paddle was upon them all.

"All right," I said, yielding to the inevitable. "Then you all have to take your clothes off."

This caused a startled pause. "That ain't right," someone said uncertainly.

"Yes it is," I told them, somewhat pompously. "There is nothing whatsoever wrong with the sight of the naked human body." I had read that somewhere and found it quite convincing. "Besides," I added, more pragmatically, "you'll all get into trouble if you come home with dirty clothes."

That all but convinced them. The thought of what their mums would say was a powerful aid to nudity. "But won't we catch cold?" someone asked.

"Cavemen never wore clothes and they never caught cold," I informed them. "Besides, it's quite warm now." A mild and misty sunlight suddenly arrived and helped my cause. The brown river was flecked with sun and looked truly inviting. Without a word, everybody began undressing, even Ellen, who was quite good at it considering how young she was. Back to nursery teacher mode again, I made folded piles of every person's clothing, shoes underneath, and put them in a long row along the bank under the hedge. True to my earlier resolve, I made no exception for Ursula's clothes, although her dress was an awful one my mother had made out of old curtains, and thoroughly wet anyway.

There was a happy scramble into the water, mostly to the slightly deeper end by the hedge. Terry was throwing water instantly. But then there was another pause.

"*You* undress too." They were all saying it.

"I'm too big," I said.

"You *said* that didn't matter," Ursula pointed out. "You undress too, or it isn't *fair*."

"Yeah," the rest chorused. "It ain't *fair*!"

I prided myself on my fairness, and on my rational, intellectual approach to life, but...

"Or we'll all get dressed again," added Ursula.

The thought of all that trouble wasted was too much. "All right," I said. I went over to the hedge and took off my battered grey shorts and my old, pulled jersey and put them in a heap at the end of the row. I knew as I did so why the rest had been so doubtful. I had never been naked out of doors before. In those days, nobody ever was. I felt shamed and rather wicked. And I was so big, compared with the others. The fact that we all now had no clothes on seemed to make my size much more obvious. I felt like one of the man's mechanical elephants, and sinful with it. But I told myself sternly that we were having a rational adventurous experience and joined the rest in the river.

The water was cold, but not too cold, and the sun was just strong enough. Just.

Ellen, for some reason, would not join the others over by the hedge. She sat on the other side of the road, on the opposite bank of the river where it sloped up to the road again, and diligently scraped river mud up into a long mountain between her legs. When the mountain was made, she smacked it heavily. It sounded like a wet child being hit.

She made me nervous. I decided to keep an eye on her and sat facing her, squatting in the water, scooping up piles of mud to form islands. From there, I could look across the road and make sure Terry did not get too wild. They were, I thought, somewhat artificially, a most romantic and angelic sight, a picture an artist might paint if he wanted to depict young angels (except Terry was not being angelic and I told him to *stop throwing mud*). They were all tubular and white and in energetic attitudes, and the only one not quite right for the picture was Ursula with her chalk white skin and wild black hair. The others all had smooth fair heads, ranging from neat white in the young ones, to honey in the older ones. My own hair had gone beyond the honey, since I was so much older, into dull brown.

Here I noticed how *big* I was again. My torso was thick, more like an oil drum than a tube, and my legs looked *fat* beside their skinny little limbs. I began to feel sinful again. I had to force myself to attend to the islands I was making. I gave them landscapes and invented people for them.

"What you doing?" asked Ellen.

"Making islands." I was feeling back-to-nature and at ease again.

"Stupid," she said.

More or less as she spoke, a tractor came up the lane behind her, going towards the village. The man driving it stopped it just in front of the water and stared. He had one of those oval narrow faces that always went with people who went to Chapel in the village. I know I thought he was Chapel. He was the sort of age you might expect someone to be who was a father of small children. He looked as if he had children. And he was deeply and utterly shocked. He looked at the brawling, naked little ones, he looked at Ellen and he looked at me. Then he leaned down and said, quite mildly, "You didn't ought to do that."

"Their clothes were getting wet, you see," I said.

He just gave me another mild, shocked look, started the tractor and went through the river, making it all muddy. I never, ever saw him again.

"Told you so," said Ellen.

That was the end of the adventure. I felt deeply sinful. The little ones were suddenly not having fun any more. Without making much fuss about it, we all quietly got our clothes and got dressed again. We retraced our steps to the village. It was just about lunchtime anyway.

As I said, word gets round in a village with amazing speed. "You know the girl Jones? She took thirty kids down Water Lane and encouraged them to do wrong there. They was all there, naked as the day they was born, sitting in the river there, and her along with them, as bold as brass. A big girl like the girl Jones did ought to know better! Whatever next!"

My parents interrogated me about it the next day. Isobel

was there, backward hovering, wanting to check that her instinct had been right, I think, and fearful of the outcome. She looked relieved when the questions were mild and puzzled. I thnk my mother did not believe I had done anything so bizarre.

"There is nothing shameful about the naked human body," I reiterated.

Since my mother had given me the book that said so, there was very little she could reply. She turned to Ursula. But Ursula was stoically and fiercely loyal. She said nothing at all.

The only result of this adventure was that nobody ever suggested I should look after any children except my own sisters (who were strange anyway). Jean kept her promise to be my friend. The next year, when the Americans came to England, Jean and I spent many happy hours sitting on the church wall and watching young GIs stagger out of the pub to be sick. But Jean never brought her sisters with her. I think her mother had forbidden it.

When I look back, I rather admire my nine-year-old self. I had been handed the baby several times over that morning. I took the most harmless possible way to disqualify myself as a child-minder. Everyone had fun. And I never had to do it again.

If you like, you'll love...

* If you like **Christopher Chant**, you'll love
  Conrad's Fate.

Conrad Grant is young and good at heart, yet
there seems to be nothing in his future but
terrible things. He goes in disguise to Stallery
Mansion, where he searches for the person who
is affecting his Fate so badly.

* If you like **cats**, you'll love *The Magicians
  of Caprona*.

Caprona is a place where music is enchantment
and spells are as slippery as spaghetti. The magical
business is run by two great spell-houses –owned
by the Montanas and the Petrocchis – and they
are deadly rivals. So when all the spells starts
going wrong, they naturally blame each other.

* If you like **travelling between worlds**, you'll
  love *The Homeward Bounders*.

When Jamie discovers the sinister, dark-cloaked
Them playing with human lives, he becomes part
of their game. If he can get Home, he is free…